Seneca Falls Library
47 Cayuga Street
Seneca Falls, NY 13148

CIRQUE

CIRQUE

MARY ELLEN DENNIS

FIVE STAR
A part of Gale, a Cengage Company

GALE
A Cengage Company

Farmington Hills, Mich • San Francisco • New York • Waterville, Maine
Meriden, Conn • Mason, Ohio • Chicago

LIBRARY OF CONGRESS CATALOGING-IN-PUBLICATION DATA

Names: Dennis, Mary Ellen, author.
Title: Cirque / Mary Ellen Dennis.
Description: First edition. | Waterville, Maine : Five Star Publishing, [2018]
Identifiers: LCCN 2017053606 (print) | LCCN 2017056165 (ebook) | ISBN 9781432845025 (ebook) | ISBN 9781432845018 (ebook) | ISBN 9781432845001 (hardback)
Subjects: LCSH: Frontier and pioneer life—Fiction. | BISAC: FICTION / Mystery & Detective / Historical. | FICTION / Mystery & Detective / General. | GSAFD: Western stories.
Classification: LCC PS3554.I368 (ebook) | LCC PS3554.I368 C57 2018 (print) | DDC 813/.54—dc23
LC record available at https://lccn.loc.gov/2017053606

First Edition. First Printing: May 2018
Find us on Facebook–https://www.facebook.com/FiveStarCengage
Visit our website–http://www.gale.cengage.com/fivestar/
Contact Five Star™ Publishing at FiveStar@cengage.com

Printed in the United States of America
1 2 3 4 5 6 7 22 21 20 19 18

For Gordon, who built me an office that lets my fingers type in comfort and my imagination soar.
And for the furry little humans who have crossed the Rainbow Bridge: Suzy Q, Chien, Peter, Sam, Shadow, Tumbleweeds, Butterscotch, Cherokee, Sydney, Pandora and Lady.

ACKNOWLEDGMENTS

A fervent thank you to Lillian Stewart Carl, my dear friend and first reader.

And to Alice Duncan, my diligent editor, and Cathy Kulka, Five Star's exceptional copy editor.

And to the Five Star crew, who give "author friendly" a rare and special meaning.

I would be remiss if I didn't mention my Rocky Mountain Fiction friends (you know who you are!), who, many years ago, took a fledgling author and taught her how to fly.

CIRQUE: a circus (archaic); a deep steep-walled basin on a mountain, usually forming the blunt end of a valley.—*Merriam Webster Dictionary*

"Every crowd has a silver lining."—P. T. Barnum

CHAPTER ONE:
BRIDGEPORT, CONNECTICUT
FEBRUARY, 1851

Police chief Malachi Daniel Connolly, known far and wide as Mad Dog Connolly, opened the massive wooden door and stepped into the stately home's Billiard Room. Reflexively, he held his thumb, index, and middle fingers together, tucked his other two fingers into the palm of his hand, and crossed himself. Then he said a word his native Ireland would have banned.

"Did you touch anything?" Mad Dog asked the butler, who had found his mistress—dead as a dodo—and summoned the police.

"No, sir. As you can see, the cats had a bit of a go at her," he said, backing out of the room as if the police chief were King George III . . . or Queen Victoria.

Dancing an awkward jig, Mad Dog fell arse over ears as seven cats clouted his ankles on their way to the open doorway. He hadn't known the cats were lurking behind the twelve-foot-long billiards table. However, he did know that his officers would have to round the kitties up and cage them before they evolved into feral rather than household killers. He also knew that he should give the order right away. But as he brushed off his trousers and shook his legs, unbroken, thanks be to God, his eyes were once again drawn to the elderly woman who lay on the floor.

Her body was straight as an arrow, one might even say straight as a *die*, her arms folded across her bosom, her hands forming a prayer wedge. If she had been felled by a heart attack or a brain

11

sickness, wouldn't her arms have flopped? On the floor, next to the top of the woman's forehead, was a small, stuffed canary, lying on its back. Had it been alive, its talons would have been pedaling the air.

Mad Dog tried to gulp down his disbelief but found he couldn't swallow anything at all. His throat had become clogged with question marks. Loosening his cravat, he thought of an Irish proverb his wife, Kate, oft stated: "No man ever wore a cravat as nice as his own child's arm around his neck." He wished he could wish himself home with Katie and his five children.

Because he was flummoxed, and he didn't like being flummoxed. Because this parlor scene was *much* too uncommon, not that murder-by-cats was exactly an everyday occurrence.

He tiptoed closer to the lifeless woman, thinking himself an *eejit* for pussyfooting. If he danced a céile reel to the loud wail of bagpipes, she couldn't hear him. He stared down at her hands and arms. They were as scratched and bloody as the rest of her, but they looked too submissive.

"Would she have used *prayer* as a weapon against a cat's sharp claws?" Mad Dog asked the stoical gents who occupied the framed portraits on the wall's velvety motif. "Would that not be like genuflecting in order to halt an angry swarm of wasps?"

Something didn't smell right, and it wasn't only the sardine oil emanating from the dead woman's body.

CHAPTER TWO:
MAD DOG EXAMINES THE
MURDER SCENE

"Dash my wig!" Mad Dog exclaimed. "The lady's mouth is open, as if gasping for air."

Cop on, he thought. *Don't be stupid. Many people die with their mouths unhinged. That's not anything out of the ordinary. Like, say, the fishy odor.*

While his fellow coppers herded cats and rounded up the servants, he surveyed the grandiose room, noting two stuffed armchairs, two molded footstools, a heavy credenza, a vase of waxed flowers, and a stuffed woodpecker, its *tap-tap-tap* forever silenced, its stiff tail feathers, red cockade and razor-sharp claws perpetually stranded underneath a glass dome. Next to the stuffed woodpecker was a much smaller dome—empty.

Obviously, the small, stuffed canary's previous "home."

Pewter oil lamps with tasseled brown shades squatted on top of spindle-legged tables. An ornately framed painting above a cold fireplace depicted a bounding ship that rode choppy, green-tinged waves. Mad Dog tore his gaze away from the painting before he succumbed to seasickness.

Atop a scarlet, tufted settee were two tasseled pillows. One had the embroidered words: "God stores up the punishment of the wicked for their children." The other read: "If I whet my glittering sword, and mine hand take hold on judgment; I will render vengeance to mine enemies, and will reward them that hate me."

Ironic, thought Mad Dog, since it looked as though someone, aside from the cats, might very well have rendered vengeance to Mrs. Bernadette Browning-Hale McCoy, the elderly lady who lay on the floor, her mouth open, her cat-scratched hands in a prayer wedge.

But who? And how? And did she treat her cats *so badly they wanted vengeance?*

The "punishment of the wicked" pillow was neatly placed against the scrolled arm of the red velvet settee while the "reward them that hate me" pillow looked as if it had been hastily tossed upon the ornate piece of furniture by someone in a great hurry.

Not the kitties, Mad Dog thought with a grin that swiftly turned into a grimace.

Up close, leaning over the sofa, he noted a couple of large, dirty handprints on the pillow. He retrieved the pillow by its tassels and, using both hands, clumsily turned it over.

The side that had no embroidered biblical verse was damp and somewhat sticky, as if someone—Mrs. Browning-Hale Mc-Coy, for example—had drooled on it. Mucus and a small amount of blood stained the cloth, as well. From Mrs. Browning-Hale McCoy's aristocratic nose?

Cop on, thought Mad Dog with a self-deprecating smile. *Unless there's a second, upright corpse leaning against the sheer curtains behind the floor-length, tied-back window drapery, Mrs. McCoy's life was snuffed out, like a candle, by a dastardly pillow.*

Then her body had been anointed with sardine oil so the imprisoned cats could have a go at her.

Jaysus, what a way to die! Mad Dog offered up a little prayer that she'd been good and dead, or at the very least good and unconscious, before the cats clawed her.

Death by cat, or in this case cats, had to be as rare as shit from a rocking horse, but Mad Dog resolved to let everybody believe that the cats' clapperclawing had, in the housekeeper's words, "done Mrs. McCoy in." Perhaps the killer would become complacent, thinking he or she couldn't be caught. Smug enough to stay put rather than beat a hasty retreat, because Mad Dog had a gut feeling one of the servants might have done the dirty deed. And his or her *dirty* hand would go a long way toward proving it. Mad Dog had asked the housekeeper for a list of servants. All of the females seemed to be named Mary.

The damp pillow meant the murder had to be less than six hours old. How long did it take for saliva to dry?

Mad Dog gingerly held the pillow by its tassels as he gazed down upon the body, already experiencing rigor mortis in the neck and jaw. "*Two* hours," he said, correcting himself aloud. If rigor mortis had just begun to set in, Mrs. Browning-Hale Mc-Coy had been killed within the last two hours.

He saw that she was clothed in a somewhat ill-fitting, frilly, pink and white dressing gown, at odds with her somber, horribly scratched face.

Somber in life, as well, Mad Dog recalled. He had met Mrs. McCoy and her husband, Alistaire Q. McCoy, during the Astor Place Opera House riots. Even though the riots had occurred a couple of years ago, Mad Dog remembered them as if they had happened yesterday, for the event had led to his position as chief of police.

The riots were prompted by William Charles Macready, a well-known, greatly respected British actor, and Edwin Forrest, a vastly popular American actor. On Macready's second visit to America, Forrest had pursued him around the country and appeared in the same plays. It was meant to be a challenge, and most newspapers supported Forrest, the "home-grown" star.

On Macready's third trip to America, somebody had tossed half the carcass of a dead sheep on the stage. That was, Mad Dog reasoned, the beginning of the end.

The home-grown Edwin Forrest catered to a working class

audience, drawn largely from the violent, immigrant-heavy Five Points neighborhood of lower Manhattan. William Charles Macready, much more subdued and genteel, drew a well-mannered audience.

To avoid mingling with the immigrants and the Five Points crowd, wealthy theatre goers had built the Astor Place Opera House on Lafayette Street, between Astor Place and East 8th. Street, where entertainment venues catered to the upper classes. The theatre was created for the comfort of the upper classes, with special box seats and upholstered orchestra seats. However, five hundred general admission patrons were relegated to the benches of a "cockloft" that could be reached by a narrow stairway.

The theatre enforced a dress code, which required freshly shaven faces, white vests and kid gloves, an insult to the lower classes for whom the theater was traditionally the gathering place for all classes.

On May seventh, despite the incident with the sheep carcass, William Charles Macready was scheduled to appear in *Macbeth* at the Opera House, while Edwin Forrest was to perform *Macbeth* only a few blocks away. The American actor's supporters had purchased hundreds of tickets to the Opera House's cockloft, and they brought Macready's performance to a grinding halt by throwing rotten eggs, potatoes, apples, lemons, shoes, and bottles of stinking liquid at the stage. The British performers managed to persist despite the cockloft audience's hissing and groaning and screaming, "Down with the codfish aristocracy!" But the actors were forced to perform in pantomime, unable to make themselves heard over the noise of the disorderly crowd.

Meanwhile, at Edwin Forrest's May seventh performance, the audience had leapt from their seats and cheered when Forrest spoke a Macbeth line about purging Englishmen.

After his disastrous performance, William Charles Macready announced he'd leave for England on the next boat, but he was persuaded to stay and perform again by a petition signed by wealthy New Yorkers, including well-known authors Herman Melville and Washington Irving, who told the actor that good sense and respect for order would surely prevail.

Good sense and respect for order? Mad Dog could have told them different. So could the pigeons that bombarded Reservoir Square with their bird guano.

On Thursday, May tenth, William Charles Macready was scheduled to, once again, take the stage as Macbeth. Fearful of a riot, the state's Seventh Regiment assembled in Washington Square Park, along with mounted troops, light artillery, and hussars—a total of three hundred-fifty men who would be added to the one-hundred policemen outside the theatre. Additional policemen were assigned to protect the homes in the area of the city's rich, elite "upper tens."

Mad Dog was one of the policemen assigned to protect the upper tens. He chafed at the task but had no choice. His brain—and his gut—told him that he should be on duty at the Opera House, especially since posters in saloons and restaurants across the city invited working men and *patriots* to show their feelings about the British by asking: SHALL AMERICANS OR ENGLISH RULE THIS CITY?

Free cockloft tickets were handed out to William Charles Macready's show. By the time the play opened at seven thirty, up to ten thousand people filled the streets around the theatre. They bombarded the theatre with stones and tried, but failed, to set fire to the building. Although the audience was in a state of siege, Macready finished the play and then slipped out in disguise.

The troops arrived at nine fifteen, only to be jostled, attacked, and injured.

At long last the soldiers lined up and, after unheard warnings, opened fire, first into the air and then several times at point blank range into the crowd. Many of those killed were innocent bystanders, and almost all of the casualties were from the working class. Dozens of injured and dead were laid out in nearby saloons and shops.

Mr. and Mrs. McCoy had attended Macready's performance, along with friends who lived in close proximity. Bernadette and Alistaire had made plans to stay overnight with their friends and leave for Connecticut the next morning. Accosted by angry ruffians as they neared the massive iron fence encircling their friends' house, a fearful Alistaire had tried to hide in the shadows, while a furious Bernadette attacked one of the ruffians with her handbag, her face as somber as the corpses in a nearby cemetery—a graveyard Mad Dog honestly believed was one of the more *cheerful* places in the upper ten district.

He had saved Bernadette Browning-Hale McCoy from certain death by inserting his body between her swinging handbag and the angry scoundrel who had taken to wielding a Bowie knife while shouting threats to sever Mrs. McCoy's solemn head from her ermine-clad torso.

In doing so, Mad Dog's arm had almost been severed from *his* torso.

His wound had been life-threatening, but, thanks be to God, it hadn't been fatal, and upon his recovery a grateful Alistaire McCoy had paved the way for Mad Dog to assume the exalted position he now occupied. McCoy was on the city council; otherwise, there'd have been no way in hell Mad Dog could have become chief of—

Jaysus! Mad Dog would have to inform his benefactor that his wife had given up the ghost, so to speak, and gone to meet her maker.

Could Alistaire have committed the unlawful act? Nine times

out of ten, the husband turned out to be the guilty party. Did he have a paramour hidden in the wings? Nine times out of ten, the husband had a young whore in his back pocket. Or had Mc-Coy's mistress—if he truly had a mistress—done the dirty deed and then clothed the dead woman in a dressing gown from her own whore's wardrobe?

Was it the hope that, with the wife dead, the mistress would become the next Mrs. Alistaire Q. McCoy?

A misbegotten, wretched hope, but hope springs eternal and all that rubbish.

What other clues did the room reveal? A shame the stodgy gents in the paintings couldn't speak. Didn't Mr. and Mrs. Mc-Coy have a niece in residence? Agnes? No. Angel? No, that didn't sound right, close but . . . *Angelique!* The niece's name was Angelique.

Where the bloody hell was the niece?

It would be just like a woman to set a horde of cats on a body, thinking no one would notice the dead woman's hands in a prayer wedge, not to mention the carelessly tossed pillow.

Squinting once again at the stiffening body, Mad Dog saw something he'd missed. He would bet his bottom dollar that before Mrs. Browning-Hale McCoy had been "laid to rest," she had fought her tormenter. Despite the bloody face-scratches, there appeared to be a bruise on her cheek, directly underneath her right eye.

Had the bruise been caused by a fist or by the sharp beak of the stuffed canary?

Or had the killer simply been baiting the cats by placing the yellow bird on top of Mrs. McCoy's head? Mad Dog thought he could see a few hairs in its talons.

If true, the cats hadn't taken the bait. He didn't know for sure, but he thought maybe cats didn't relish dead birds. Squirrels, yes. Dead birds, no. His cat, Glumdalclitch, went bonkers over squirrels, though she'd never gotten close enough to meet one face to face. Mad Dog figured Glum's enthusiasm was due to the squirrels' feather-duster tails . . . and why was he procrastinating?

Still clutching the tasseled pillow by its edging, he circled the corpse one last time. Someone else would have to summon the dead wagon that would transport Bernadette Browning-Hale McCoy to the morgue. Mad Dog needed to question the servants straight away. He had lots of questions, but first off he needed to find out if they could tell him the whereabouts of the missing niece.

His gut feeling, which had never failed him, was making his stomach roil. His list of suspects now included Alistaire McCoy, a minimum of one servant, and the missing niece.

Mad Dog smacked his forehead with the heel of his hand. He was an *eejit*! Why hadn't he assigned somebody to search every nook and cranny of the stately home—and the carriage house— just in case the niece . . .Angelique . . . had also met a sticky end?

CHAPTER THREE:
HORTENSE KELLEY IS STUFFED LIKE A SAUSAGE INSIDE A RED BOX

TEN MONTHS EARLIER
Paris, France
April, 1850

"The lady is about to fall, Mum," the little girl gasped, pigtails swaying, her chin tilted like the prow of a miniature ship. Had her face stopped moving, even momentarily, it would have looked like the miniature ship's figurehead.

Hortense Downing-Cox Kelley, a woman who falsely proclaimed she was twenty-and-nine, momentarily turned away from her daughter, Charlotte, and peered up at the jezebel who flaunted a pretty parasol as she pranced blithely across a thin rope.

"That's part of her performance, Charlotte dear," Hortense said, pasting a tired smile on her face. "She *pretends* she is going to fall. Sometimes it is all right to pretend."

Hortense heaved a deep sigh and slanted an angry glance toward her stepson, Sean. He was the reason she and five-year-old Charlotte were stuffed like sausages inside this small compartment, this ridiculous red box. He was the reason she was surrounded by other spectators, all of whom were shouting and applauding in *French*. He was the reason every time Hortense took a breath, she smelled sawdust and horse manure.

Sean had effectively beguiled little Charlotte with promises of "a spectacle fit for a king and queen," and, in doing so, had enticed Hortense as well. Consequently, *he* was the reason she

21

spent the afternoon at the circus when any sensible woman would be sipping tea in the comfort of her own parlour.

But then, any *sensible* woman wouldn't have married Sean's father, Timothy Kelley, a dustman who came periodically to collect her proper British family's ashes and refuse. As a rule, a lady situated atop the pinnacle of British hierarchy would not have given a thirty-nine-year-old dustman a second glance. However, Hortense, her heart palpitating like a hummingbird's wings, had given Timothy a somewhat reluctant second glance and then, eagerly, a third and fourth glance. No other man had expressed delight at her modest features. No other man had admired her reserved deportment. No other man had called her *mo shiorghrá*, which he said meant "my eternal love." And no other man had wooed her with Irish endearments that sounded like the light, clear ring of the bell she used to summon one of her proper British family's many servants.

Hortense had succumbed to Timothy's devilish charms, enhanced by the Irish brogue—and the warm Irish tongue—that tickled her ears. Thirty years old and, according to one of her mother's friends, "as plain as a pudding," she had disregarded every cautionary word of warning issued by her proper British father; had even ignored his threat to disinherit her.

Unsoiled before marriage, she would nevertheless swear on a stack of bibles that she had become impregnated the instant the officiating priest said, "I now pronounce you man and wife in the name of the Father, of the Son, and of the Holy Ghost."

Prudently, she hadn't told Timothy about her parents' caveat. Which, as it turned out, had been her biggest mistake.

With a baby on the way, an annulment was out of the question. Therefore, when Timothy discovered she was penniless, cut off from the family fortune *and* disinherited, he thrashed her with Gaelic profanity and then carted her across the sea to his widowed auntie, who owned a café and smelled of garlic and raw onions. Timothy had the decency to wait for the birth of his daughter before setting sail for America, but that had been four and a half years ago, and Hortense had not heard from him since.

Furthermore, if she had tricked him into marrying her by insinuating he'd be rich beyond his wildest dreams, his duplicity was far more profound. For he had neglected to tell her that he had narrowly escaped starvation in his native Ireland and then buried the first Mrs. Kelley in France, or that the issue from his previous marriage, a twenty-year-old son named Sean, lived above the widow's café.

Sean had been cordial during their introduction, but Hortense had been astute enough to read the unspoken words he directed toward his father: *Did ye wed yourself an elderly lass with an inheritance, Da?*

A pity Hortense had been too busy running toward the loo, or whatever the blasted French called it, to hear Timothy's response. Carrying a child was a bloody nuisance. Truth be told, Sean had been of more assistance than her slothful husband, who was, more often than not, rooted in a public house, downing pints of ale, playing games of chance, and selecting a *fille de joie* from a daily *menu de repas*. Hortense had no idea where he secured the funds for his ale, his gambling, and his whores, but she had a sneaking suspicion his pecuniary endeavors were not precisely aboveboard.

Or perhaps he simply had the luck of the Irish.

In any case, as her belly expanded into an unbelievable girth, reminiscent of an upright whale, it was Sean who helped her straddle a chamber pot when she became too fat to waddle to the water closet. Naturally, she received no help from Timothy or the onion woman. Sean also finished her chores, helped her rise from chairs, and fetched the midwife when her labor pains began. Despite his lowly birth, he was a true gentleman.

To the extent that Hortense could ascertain, the only advantage to birthing a child was that one's figure tended to change. Before Charlotte, she had been bony. In fact, she had overheard another friend of her mum's respond to the "plain as a pudding" description with, "And Hortense is significantly raw boned, too, poor thing."

Even as a child, Hortense's elbows had been sharp as a butcher knife. So had her knees.

Now her breasts were globes, her hips bounteous, her elbows and knees plump enough to flaunt dimples. Even her hair could be considered more mahogany than brown. A pity Timothy hadn't stayed long enough to savor his wife's new, enticingly abundant body.

Sean hadn't left with his father, and Hortense knew why. The lad, now twenty-five, had an Irishman's fondness for children. He adored Charlotte, and while one half of Hortense deplored what she considered a lamentable, if not downright disgraceful, weakness in a man, the other half was eternally grateful.

In Hortense's opinion, a baby was just as bothersome as a pregnancy. Especially since Charlotte was a stick of a child with a button nose, large puppy-dog eyes, and none of her father's robust qualities. Nor Sean's, for that matter.

Which was the bloody fly in the bloody ointment. Sean looked too much like Timothy. The same thick ebony hair, the same merry green eyes, the same broad shoulders, narrowed waist and muscular legs. In truth, Sean possessed every facial and physical quality that had attracted a cosseted London heiress to an Irish dustman. And if that wasn't enough, Hortense's stepson had inherited his father's charm. She had seen young ladies pretend to swoon so that Sean could catch them.

If honest, and Hortense was always honest with herself, she had seriously considered the same ploy. However, she feared rejection. Not because she was older than Sean, Timothy's wife, and, to all intents and purposes, Sean's stepmother, but because she knew full well he wanted to woo an heiress.

To that end, Hortense had re-established contact with her parents. It had taken five years, but her mum's desire to see her only grandchild had helped a great deal. Hortense had finally swallowed her pride, begged for mercy, vowed she'd never stray from the fold again, and was anxiously awaiting a reply.

She lied, of course. About straying.

Sean was *le boheme*, an artist who was somewhat lazy and undeniably careless about his future. He believed an artist should always have debts in order to be appreciated. When he needed money—and to Hortense's knowledge he'd never sold as much as a sketch—he joined the men building streets, earning a few francs a day. However, despite his scorn for what he called the *bourgeoisie*, he possessed one fatal flaw: his body, if not his soul, could be bought.

"Look, Mum! Look, Sean!"

Charlotte's strident voice pierced Hortense's haze, and she allowed her gaze to follow her daughter's small finger, gesturing toward the building's apogee.

The girl atop the rope, now minus her flimsy parasol, was taking dainty, tentative steps, as if she wanted to tease the prudent people who were safely rooted below. And what on earth was she wearing? From Hortense's standpoint, the brazen hussy appeared to be wearing nothing at all. Hortense darted another quick glance toward Sean. His mouth had become unhinged, his attention riveted on the rope. No. His entire focus was on the piece of baggage who had just finished performing a series of dazzling back-flip somersaults.

Hortense's heart sank to the very bottom of her silken boots. The young Cirque de Délices performer was no heiress, and yet Sean's expression clearly revealed that he didn't give two hoots in hell. Hortense's corset felt tighter than a gnat's chuff. The candied apple she'd eaten earlier rose in her throat, whole.

Even while she lost what remained of her breath, her mind raced. She wanted Sean to play the part of her devoted companion. An obstacle to that scheme danced above her head. Surely there was some clever way to get rid of that damned rope walker, that damned *Petite Ange*.

Along with the rest of the audience, Sean was applauding wildly and yelling, *"C'est magnifique!"*

The world whirled, and the applause dimmed, and Hortense keeled over.

CHAPTER FOUR:
SEAN KELLEY MULLS OVER *Petite Ange*

Sean Kelley wondered if his stepmother's convenient swoon yesterday had been a ruse to leave the Cirque de Délices. Reluctantly, he had carried her outside, Charlotte walking in his shadow. Once they had reached their hired carriage and drawn its curtains, he had loosened Hortense's corset stays. Whereupon, her eyes had fluttered open, and she whispered, *"Fais-moi l'amour,"* and God only knows what might have happened had Charlotte not been present.

Where had Hortense leaned the phrase *fais-moi l'amour?* From the patrons at the café?

"Make love to me" sounded so much prettier in French than in English, and Sean had no illusions. He had no guilt, either. He wasn't related by blood to Hortense, and his father had spent the last four and a half years in America. Furthermore, he guessed his stepmother was about to regain her inheritance, and he had no qualms about playing the part of her amorist.

That is, until he'd seen *Petite Ange.*

His first glimpse of the "Small Angel"—whom he now thought of as *his* small angel—had not been during her performance. On the rope she'd been too high up for anyone to appreciate her flashing gray-green eyes, too high up for anyone to admire the honey-colored hair that framed her blush-stained cheeks. Although they seemed in perfect proportion, her lower limbs and hips were small for her robustly developed breasts and shoulders.

She was, in a word, perfection. And it was this perfection that had brought him back to the Cirque's cellarage, despite Hortense's wrath, despite the fact that today's post had included a generous draft from her father.

Upon cashing the draft, her anger at Sean's fascination with *Petite Ange* had swiftly become a list of promises. Sean could have a dozen new suits, a new horse, an opulent townhouse in London or Paris.

Except that wasn't his dream. Nobody knew his dream.

He wanted to own a traveling circus, the finest in the world. He wanted to work for P. T. Barnum's Museum in New York City, America. Someday, when he had learned all he could about showmanship, he wanted to establish the Sean Kelley Circus.

And he wanted *Petite Ange* for his circus.

In truth, he wanted *Petite Ange* for his wife.

CHAPTER FIVE:
ANGELIQUE AUMONT MEETS SEAN KELLEY

The Cirque de Délices was housed in an octagonal building, with seats facing three sides of a single ring. Along the ring bank were plush red boxes. Behind the boxes were arena seats, then a gallery that extended to the roof. There was no menagerie or Congress of Freaks, but the audience could descend to the basement and inspect the horses. A forty-piece string and woodwind orchestra occupied a platform above the performers' entrance. The Cirque changed its bill monthly, holding over the most popular acts, and regardless of this afternoon's enthusiastic applause, Angelique Aumont feared she might not be held over.

"You silly peagoose." London-born Gertrude Starling, the Cirque's pretty trapeze artist, gave Angelique an elbow nudge. "Even if your rope act weren't spot-on, half the fellows would pay dear for your maidenhead."

Since Angelique usually thought in French, it took her a moment to translate Gertrude's remarks. Then, cheeks hot, she reached out to caress a dray horse's velvet muzzle.

"That cannot be true," she replied in her heavily-accented English.

"Wot cannot be true? That they'd pay dear or that you have a maidenhead?"

"Do hush, Gertie."

"God-a-mercy, *Petite Ange,* my brother Allen says he'll marry you!" Gertrude flung her callused, oversized hands frontward, palms up, as though offering Angelique a valuable gift.

"*Mon Dieu,* I shall never wed a *cirque* performer," Angelique exclaimed, then smiled to take the sting out of her words.

As if summoned, Allen Starling appeared, and the only English word Angelique could summon up was "dolt."

At twenty-four, five years older than Angelique, Allen was a tall, blunt-faced man. His hands were strong, his arms and torso brawny; however his hips, legs, and small feet looked as if they belonged to a different man, as if God had taken them from his workshop of leftover human parts and stuck them on at the last minute, having suddenly realized his creation was incomplete. Allen wanted to wed her in order to bed her, but she knew marriage was out of the question. She didn't love him, and she would only marry for love.

Her parents had died within three weeks of each other, Papa first. On her deathbed, her heart broken, Maman had confessed that she had a sister, to whom she'd written a letter. The sisters had been close once, and Maman had no reason to believe that Auntie Bernadette would not welcome her only niece with open arms. The *dilemme* was that those open arms would have to extend across an ocean, for Maman's sister, Bernadette Browning-Hale McCoy, lived in Connecticut, America.

"*Petite Ange,*" Allen cried. "*C'est magnifique! C'est un triomphe!*"

"She twigs English, you great booby," Gertrude said.

"*Merci,* Allen. However, I am . . . how you say? . . . deliberating a new act, something more daring. Perhaps even . . ." Angelique paused in an attempt to keep her passion under wraps; too much of a boast would negate her declaration. "Perhaps even the forward somersault."

"No girl can do the forward," Allen said. "It is impossible."

"God-a-mercy, no *man* can do a forward somersault on the rope, and what could be more daring than your costume?" Gertrude wrinkled her nose, which in turn crinkled the brown eyes that matched the color of her long, straight hair—hair she could sit on and frequently did. "If there weren't beads sewn at your bosom and between your legs, people below would think you was in the nuddy."

"Mon *doo*, who cares what *they* think?" Allen waved his arms expansively. Like his sister, he had oversized hands that easily caught Gertie's wrists during their brother-sister trapeze act. Known far and wide as "The Flying Starlings," Allen and Gertie had perfected their act in London before joining the Cirque de Délices.

Angelique smiled for a second time. Her flesh-colored tights and leotard, beaded for propriety's sake, had been an inspiration. She had heard the indignant, astonished, and admiring gasps from the audience, and a few gallery faces were beginning to look familiar, enhancing her bid to be held over another month. Or two. Perhaps—*dare she hope?*—six months.

Oh, if only she could perform the forward. Her future would be settled. Secure. The Cirque de Délices would never let her go; no circus would.

In the back-flips she performed with *élégance*, her shoulders flexed naturally, and her swinging arms gave her additional momentum. However, somersaulting forward reversed natural reflexes, and the body experienced what her papa had called a "gravitational pull."

She wasn't certain what "gravitational pull" meant, but she knew her arms were no help because they got in the way. Unless they were wrapped about her chest. Otherwise, they'd catch between her legs. Consequently, her papa had adamantly insisted that the forward was *très* dangerous, and he would not allow his beloved daughter to attempt it.

Angelique had obeyed her papa, of course, but she didn't agree. In her mind, the forward was *difficile* but not impossible.

Speaking of familiar faces, the young man from yesterday was

here again today, visiting the horses. Yesterday she had caught
sight of him before her performance. Today he had waited until
after her performance.

As Angelique stared at the man, she thought about her
parents. She knew they had fallen deeply, irrevocably in love
during their first meeting. Papa, a musician who played several
different instruments, was employed by a traveling *cirque* that
had been performing in London. Maman's papa, a prosperous
shopkeeper, had been occupied when Papa entered the shop, so
Papa had asked Maman for the white satin braces, embroidered
with forget-me-nots. Maman had melted at Papa's grin, but she
did not understand French and became confused until an
elderly gent said, "Galluses, Miss, to hold your breeks up by."
The second time Maman and Papa met, Papa had learned
English, Maman, French. Almost immediately, Maman accepted
Papa's bouquet of forget-me-nots and his marriage proposal.

Maman's parents had disapproved, had, in fact, locked Maman in her small attic bedroom until Papa's *cirque* left London.
However, Maman then made what she called a journey of the
heart. Except for one gown, one petticoat, one pair of calico
drawers, one pair of shoes, one pair of gloves and one bonnet,
she had knotted together every other piece of clothing she possessed. Adding a dozen petticoats, a couple of bed sheets, and
several cambric pantalets that fluttered like the tail of a kite, she
had tossed her homespun rope out the window, wormed her
way through the window's wee opening, and followed Papa's
cirque to Paris.

Until now, Angelique had never quite believed the romantic
tale.

Briefly, she stood motionless. Then she abandoned Gertie
and Allen and walked, as if pulled by a puppeteer, toward the
dark-haired stranger.

In his deep-green eyes was a kind of lazy amusement, which

made Angelique speechless and a little angry. For how was she to impress him if she could not think of anything to say? She felt an uncharacteristic sense of inadequacy, a fear that whatever she said or did would seem foolish to him.

As he stared at the blue silk robe that concealed her costume, his absorbing gaze seemed to undress her. In truth, she could almost swear that his eyes were *discarding* her costume.

She found herself studying the face around those eyes, noting his expressive brows, bold nose, mobile mouth, and deeply cleft chin. Handsome but not handsome, she thought illogically, wondering how he would look with a mustache and beard. He possessed a pirate's arrogant demeanor, and she imagined him bare chested, wielding a cutlass, lithe as a panther.

And, in all probability, just as dangerous.

"Do you comprehend English?" he said, his voice as mesmerizing as his eyes. "I guess you do not, *mademoiselle,* so perhaps you will not take offense when I say you're the prettiest lass I've seen in the divil's own time, and I've a mind to lay with you."

Angelique's bones turned to water, and she cursed herself for her tongue-tied torpor. She usually had a pert remark for any man, no matter what his age, and this young man deserved nothing less than a slap across his smug face.

"I would imagine you did not sleep well last night," he continued, his voice a lilting croon. "Nor did I. To tell the God's honest truth, I did not sleep at all. But I've a perfect cure for that, *mademoiselle.* A carriage awaits my return, and the parson lives but a short ride away."

Parson? Still speechless, Angelique allowed him to lead her outside the building.

He halted, lightly caressed her face, and smoothed the wind-tousled hair away from her forehead. "Sean Breandan Kelley is me given name, lass."

She finally found her voice. "I am Angelique Marie Bernadette Aumont, *monsieur,* and you are a rude, insufferable—"

"Connoisseur of beauty," he finished in perfect French.

They stood there, staring at each other, and Angelique understood that he had been teasing her all along. She did not know if she should slap him, sputter indignantly, or laugh, so she followed her only other impulse and swayed toward him, her eyes shut. His hands closed about her waist, drawing her closer, and she felt his powerful leg muscles. Without conscious thought, her mouth parted to receive his kiss.

It was several moments before he released her, but when he did it seemed too soon, and she felt cheated. Opening her eyes, she saw him gazing at her tenderly.

"You must go back now, me precious darlin'," he said. "Your family would be troubled to have you disappear with no word of warning. And I would not be troubling your family, for I might have need of their blessing."

Impulsive words sprang to her lips. *I have no family. I do not care if I never return to the Cirque. I do not care about the forward somersault. I do not care about anything except you.* Instead she said, "Blessing? Do you intend to wed me, *monsieur?*"

"Aye, lass." He smacked his forehead with the heel of his hand. " 'Tis a swell-headed mooncalf I am, niver bidding your consent. We shall talk more tomorrow, if that pleases you."

Talk more? His Irish-green eyes had done most of the talking.

"Does that please you?" he pressed.

She nodded, thinking about her mother and father.

As he walked away, she could still smell the masculine sweat on his clothes and the scent of leather from his boots, and she felt both dizzy and lonely.

He stopped mid-stride and made an about-face. With a glance that took her in from head to foot, *Monsieur* Kelley smiled. His thumbs snapped the galluses that held his breeks up, and Angelique fell deeply, irrevocably in love.

CHAPTER SIX:
HORTENSE SCHEMES TO GET RID
OF ANGELIQUE

Hortense knew exactly what she must do. Her faint two days ago had been far more beneficial than a mere loss of consciousness, for upon awakening, her mind had been crystal clear, and her scheme had been conceived as quickly and easily as Charlotte.

Impatiently, she served the café's customers. Soon she needn't perform the hateful chores that secured her lodgings above the café, if one could call them lodgings. The room she shared with Charlotte boasted a feather mattress, a chiffonier, a wooden tub, and a tiny parlour. Hortense yearned for the spacious interior of her parents' home, where she wouldn't have to elbow her daughter or the garlic-onion woman—or even her darling Sean—out of the way every time she walked down a hallway on her way to the kitchen. Or the loo.

Her usual mode of transport, a carriage, would have been more comfortable, but a hackney was more prudent, and as soon as her despicable café tasks were accomplished, she set out in all haste. Thankfully, she'd reached her destination in the nick of time, before rather than during the Cirque's opening spectacle. She had clothed herself in a severe black gown. A heavy black veil fell from the top of her head to the tips of her toes. Now all she had to do was enter the bloody building's cellarage and find *Petite Ange*.

Early this morning, while preparing the café's daily fare, Sean had told a delighted Charlotte all about his propitious meeting with the Cirque's *danseur,* but Hortense had no way of knowing if his puffery had been the truth, half a truth, or merely a flight of his imagination.

The orchestra had been playing a song called "Open Thy Lattice Love" by American composer Stephen Foster, Sean had said, and forever more that would be his favorite song. *Petite Ange,* whose real name was Angelique Aumont, had been in the basement with the horses. Surrounded by a mob of admirers, all of whom toted bouquets of flowers, sparkling jewels, and boxes of *chocolats,* she had left her wealthy suitors to stroll with Sean.

"Did she swoon and did you catch her?" Charlotte had asked.

"No one can catch a falling star," he had replied. "But sometimes, if you're virtuous and very, very good, you can capture a dream."

In Hortense's opinion, Sean was neither good nor virtuous, but perhaps God did not consider Sean's weaknesses imperfections. After all, God was a man.

The smell hit Hortense as soon as she spied her first horse. Withdrawing a handkerchief from her beaded reticule, she pressed the small square of linen against the piece of veil that hid her long, sharp nose. In doing so, she dropped her reticule.

"You fell your *porte-monnaie,* Madame."

The voice was engaging, musical, heavily accented. The hand that held out the reticule looked large, young, and strong, with fingernails buffed to a soft sheen. Hortense felt resentment build anew. After years of washing and chopping vegetables, her nails were as coarse as the bark on a tree.

"Dropped, not fell." Extending her hand for the reticule, Hortense silently thanked God for gloves.

"*Oui,* dropped," the young girl said. "Are you in mourning, Madame?"

"What? Oh, my gown and veil. Yes, *mademoiselle.* I mean *oui.*

My . . . uh, father recently expired." Directing the handkerchief toward her eyes, Hortense gave what she hoped was a convincing sniffle. "But one must take the good with the bad, *mademoiselle*, for I inherited a small fortune."

"I have suffered a recent loss, too. My papa never earned a fortune, but he died happy."

"How did he die?"

"He played music, Madame, but one day he followed Maman up to the very top of the *Cirque* and fell, I mean *dropped* from a rope."

"Why on earth would he do that? I mean, follow her to the top?"

"He wanted to give her a kiss," the girl said. "Maman soon followed him to heaven."

"Your mum fell from a rope, too?"

"No, Madame. She died of a broken heart. You see, she was part Irish, and the Irish can only love once."

Totally nonplused, Hortense stared into the girl's gray-green eyes, now shiny with unshed tears. "You are Angelique Aumont, are you not?" Hortense finally managed.

"*Oui*, Madame. And you are . . . ?"

"Hortense Downing-Cox Kelley," she said, then took a deep breath. "My husband told our daughter all about how he met you yesterday, after your performance. He sang your praises, *mademoiselle*."

"Your husband? Your daughter?"

"My husband, Sean. Our darling daughter, Charlotte, is five years old. We saw your rope act the day before yesterday, and I have to admit my husband was smitten, one might even say infatuated, beyond belief."

With satisfaction, Hortense saw the tart's face turn white as a bed sheet. Even though it hurt her pride, Hortense continued with the words she had rehearsed inside her parlour. "Only last month my husband became infatuated with a young girl who appeared in a production of Mr. William Shakespeare's *A Midsummer Night's Dream*."

That was the whole of the speech Hortense had practiced, but she was enjoying her stellar performance and couldn't resist adding more details. "The young girl played a queen, or perhaps it was a princess. No, it was definitely a queen, named Anna or Fantasia or Janet, something like that. My goodness, how I do run on. You've probably never even heard of Mr. Shakes—"

"Titania, Madame."

"I beg your pardon?"

"You said *A Midsummer Night's Dream*, did you not? The queen, she is called Titania. 'Come, wait upon him; lead him to my bower. The moon methinks looks with a watery eye; And when she weeps, weeps every little flower. Come, wait upon him; lead him to my bower. Lamenting some enforced chastity.' "

"How on earth—"

"My mother read Mr. Shakespeare to me when I was a *bébé*. I read him myself when I got bigger, in order to grow my English."

"How very clever of you, my dear. But we were talking about my husband, Sean, who has a . . . shall we say fondness? . . . for performers." Hortense hoped she didn't sound as desperate as she felt. "I, myself, once considered the stage, but a well-bred lady . . ." She shrugged.

Had she gone too far? The girl's eyes were more green than gray, jade rather than slate.

"If you are such a well-bred *lady*, Madame, why do you endure your husband's indiscretions and forgive his misdeeds? I am merely a lowly performer but—"

"I remain loyal to my husband, *mademoiselle*, because, deep down, he loves me. As you say, the Irish can only love once."

Hortense felt her heart pound. She knew that beneath her veil, her face was bright red and splotchy. Mentally reaching into her bag of tricks, she withdrew her last weapon. "Sean will never leave me, *mademoiselle*, for I am once again with child. We hope and pray that this time I shall birth a healthy son."

"A healthy son," the girl echoed.

Hortense nodded and patted her belly. The onion-garlic woman's food, not pregnancy, had caused its roundness, for she and Sean had never shared a bed. Momentarily, she felt ashamed of her fib. Then she remembered what she had told Charlotte: *sometimes it is all right to pretend.*

"Perhaps you should sit down, Madame Kelley. I did not know he was married, I swear! You look unwell. Please sit down. There is a bench—"

"No. No, thank you." Hortense did indeed feel shaky as relief washed over her. Still, she had one more piece of business to negotiate. At five feet six inches tall, she topped *Petite Ange* by a good three inches. And although she desired nothing more than to sit, once seated she'd be at a disadvantage. "Sean will return to you, *mademoiselle*. He will tell you lies, just as he did with his Shakespearian actress. He will say he is not married. He might even swear that our Charlotte is not his beloved daughter." Yanking off her glove, Hortense flaunted her wedding band. "Charlotte is a Kelley, and so am I, and may God strike me dead if that is not the truth."

"Madame, you are upsetting yourself for nothing. I will not see your husband again."

"I appreciate your sincerity, Angelique, but that is one promise you will never be able to keep. So here is what I propose." Hortense reached inside her reticule and retrieved a wad of banknotes as thick as two bricks. "Yesterday I received a substantial inheritance from my, uh, dead father. I have brought it with me and shall give you a share, enough to settle someplace far away from your *Cirque*. You could find yourself a husband or set sail for America, where I've heard the streets are paved with gold."

"Truly, that is not necessary. Only today I received a letter from my Auntie Bern—"

"No, please, I insist. Perhaps you might leave tonight. Should my husband discover that I have paid you this visit, he will beat me. He has a violent temper, and I could lose the baby."

Shamed anew by the monstrosity of her lies, in particular her father's imaginary demise and Sean's imaginary abuse, Hortense saw a toad-faced man race toward them.

"*Petite Ange,* here you are! We are celebrating Gertie's birthday. There's cake and—"

"A moment, Allen. I am conducting important business, and then I have some good news about my upcoming . . . how you say? Proposal?"

"Proposal?" A smile split his face in two and lit up his eyes. "Or do you mean prospects, Angelique? Your future prospects."

"*Mais oui,* prospects," she said, and Hortense watched the young man's smile gradually disappear, his eyes become less bright.

"Madame here has decided me," Angelique added.

"Thank you." Hortense prayed she wouldn't sink to the ground in a grateful heap. She realized her face was not only red and splotchy, but slippery with perspiration. If she really were with child, she'd no doubt miscarry. "*Merci,* Angelique."

"*Bonne chance,* Madame Kelley."

"Good luck to you, too."

Sometimes luck had nothing to do with anything, Hortense thought. Nor did good behavior. Catching a dream was easy. Holding on to it required duplicity. And sweat.

CHAPTER SEVEN:
CHARLOTTE HAS A GIFT FOR SEAN

Charlotte Kelley possessed a lisp that would doubtless be considered an asset one day. For now, it made her words too large for her tongue, and more often than not her attempts to converse, especially in French, were misunderstood.

Desperate, she switched to English. "Sean, you must listen. Mum made *Petite Ange* leave the Cirque de Délices. I do not know what Mum told *Petite Ange,* but I do know that Mum gave *Petite Ange* some of Grandfather's money. Mum showed me the leftover banknotes, bundled inside her beaded reticule."

Sean hunkered down and stared into the child's owl-round eyes. "I understand what you're sayin', me little darlin'. What I cannot understand is why *Petite Ange* would accept your mum's payoff."

"I do not think it was the money. I think it was what Mum told *Petite Ange.*" Anticipating his next question, Charlotte shrugged her thin shoulders. "I do not know what Mum told *Petite Ange,* Sean, but it must have been something terrible bad."

"And why do you tell *me* all this, sweetheart, knowing full well that I shall be leaving you? For I could niver stay after hearing of your mum's fiddle-tinkering."

"You shall leave anyway, once we return to England," Charlotte said in a matter-of-fact voice, "and you must find *Mademoiselle* Cinderella."

Heartsick, his hopes for the future dashed, Sean managed to

give his stepsister a lop-sided grin. "And when I find *Mademoiselle* Cinderella, what must I do?"

"You must kiss her awake."

"It is the sleeping princess who was kissed awake, Charlotte."

"*Mais oui*, but Mum benumbed *Petite Ange*. And that is the same as sleeping, is it not?

"Where did you learn that word, sweetheart? Benumbed."

"From Mum. She looked and sounded like a black crow, all show-off and braggy."

"And did your mum happen to mention where Angelique . . . where *Petite Ange* would be goin', me darlin'?"

"She said something about America," Charlotte lisped.

Sean could feel his face settle into new lines of despair. " 'Tis a podgy place, America."

"As big as London?" Charlotte's eyes grew even rounder. "Mum says London is bigger than Montparnasse, and Montparnasse is lolloping big."

"I've niver visited London, sweetheart, but I've heard America is a wee bit bigger."

"Perhaps that is why my papa is lost."

"Perhaps." Sean tried to keep the anger from his voice. "If I should happen to trip over our papa, do you want me to kiss him awake, too?"

Charlotte giggled. "In the fairy tales you have read to me, no man kisses another man awake, though I do not know why that is. In any case, I do not believe my papa is asleep. He is just lost. Please, Sean, you must promise to look for *Petite Ange* and kiss her awake."

"I promise to try." He fixed his gaze upon an overfed vase whose gaping mouth vainly endeavored to contain its cargo of fleurs de lys and roses . . . without doubt Hortense's triumphant bouquet, fashioned after her visit to the *Cirque*. "But I am now thinkin' my pretty rope walker was only a dream," he said with a sigh.

"No, Sean, for I dreamed the same dream. I saw her on the rope with my own two eyes, as did my mum."

"Your mum," he said, striving to keep the bitterness from his voice.

"And you said if you are very good, you can *capture* a dream."

"Then I shall try and be very good. But first I must find the means to reach America. It takes money, and . . . why do you stare at me like that? Have you another secret?"

"*Mais oui.* I have been naughty."

"You? Naughty?" Sean couldn't help grinning at the absurdity of a badly behaved Charlotte.

"I have been *très* naughty," she insisted. "Close your eyes."

Perhaps he should be kissed awake, Sean thought, as he suddenly realized that Charlotte's hands had been behind her back ever since they had begun their conversation.

"Do you have a going-away present for me, sweetheart?" he asked, squinting through his dark scrim of lashes and wondering if she planned to present him with her favorite toy, a floppy-eared, yellow rabbit she had named Fromage.

"*Mais oui,* a going-away present," she said. "My gift is very heavy, Sean, for it is filled with America."

Withdrawing her hands from behind her back, Charlotte thrust forth her mother's beaded reticule.

CHAPTER EIGHT:
TIMOTHY KELLEY LANDS IN AMERICA

Boston, Massachusetts
Upon reaching Boston Harbor in the year of our Lord, 1846, Timothy Kelley took one glance at the ferret-faced men who boarded the ship and swarmed the dock like locusts, promising jobs and cheap lodging, and his gut told him they were acting the maggot—not to be trusted.

He trusted his gut.

"Feck off!" he shouted at the first three who approached him.

The fourth scurried away, looking fearful, as Timothy yelled, *"Téigh trasna ort féin"*—go fuck yourself!

Timothy would have wagered all he owned, which wasn't much, that the fourth man did not understand one word of Gaelic. However, the worthless piece of scum had easily translated Timothy's beetled brows, angry eyes, and tense, knotted fists.

A shame angry eyes and clenched fists hadn't frightened the insects that fed on the Irish Lumper, the wet, knobbly potato that could be grown in garden beds as well as fields. By 1831 the diseased potatoes, too blighted even to boil, had caused a good many families to go begging, just to stay alive. At which point Timothy had stated a prophetic, "I'd rather starve than beg!"

By the time he'd swallowed his pride, there was nothing left to solicit. Except prayers.

As luck would have it, Timothy's uncle, who owned a café in France, had managed to liberate Timothy and his wife, Molly, and their son, Sean, shortly before the family, on the brink of out-and-out starvation, shook hands with the Angel of Death.

Then Fate dealt Timothy a disastrous hand. They had barely reached France when his beloved Molly began to cough. Soon her relentless coughing spewed blood, so they saw a doctor, who used an ear trumpet, what he called a stethoscope, to listen to Molly's chest. Whereupon, the learned doctor puckered his brow and patted Timothy on the shoulder, and, in no time at all, his young wife was gone, buried in a French cemetery rather than the family plot.

Timothy shook his head to clear away images of shriveled potatoes and Molly, his one true love, forever young, forever beautiful, forever dead. Instead, he settled his expression into what his son Sean would have called a stone face. He did not want to reveal one scrap of emotion. Not fury, not relief, not pleasure, most assuredly not the intelligence he knew lurked behind his green eyes. He was well-read in both French and English. He could write a passable hand. He had learned English—even learned to *think* in English—when he'd worked as a dustman, and he had refined his English by conversing with Hortense—his bloated, penniless wife—and his son Sean, who spoke English as if it was his first, rather than third, language.

What Timothy desperately needed to control was his frame of mind.

It fueled his surly mood.

The long crossing on the "coffin ship" had been nothing short of a nightmare. By his admittedly inconclusive count, one in seven steerage passengers had not survived the voyage.

In good health before making his way to Liverpool and boarding the Boston packet, Timothy now believed that the road to hell was paved with water rather than land. He had barely been aboard the ship five weeks when he began to doubt he'd be able to endure three months of insufferable conditions without leading a revolt against the ship's officers. The only thing that kept him from performing the deed was possible failure, leading to a punishment called "keel-hauling." He had heard keel-hauling was awarded for serious offences.

A stout line, he had been told, was woven through a block on the lower yardarm on each side of the ship. One end was secured under the arms and around the chest of the wrongdoer, whose wrists were then secured behind his back. The line went under the ship, as a bottom line, and was secured around the offender's ankles. On the word of the captain, the boatswain ordered the man hoisted off the deck and clear of the bulwarks. Slack was taken down on the bottom line, and as it was hauled in, the line around the man's chest was slacked away, and he was hauled under the ship. He came up on the other side feet first. With both lines taut, the man was slung in such a way that his stomach, chest, and face were dragged across the barnacles of the keel, and he partially drowned.

Timothy didn't know if what he had heard was true, but it was not worth a shite to find out, so he suffered the steerage compartments, where the overhead timbers were no more than five feet high, a foot shorter than Timothy when he stood up straight, without his boots on. Not that he ever removed his boots, especially since the timbered floors of the compartments were awash with seawater and vomit. Furthermore, if he turned his head for more than an instant, his boots could—and most certainly would—be stolen.

The steerage compartments had two tiers of beds, where men, women, and children were crowded together with scarcely enough room for themselves and their few belongings. Cots were provided, but they were so narrow Timothy couldn't turn over. Worse, the beds and bedding were not aired out or washed, and the only air and light came through a hatchway that was closed during stormy or rough weather, making the air more foul week by week, day by day. The bogs, or as Hortense would say, loos, were almost all broken and too few for the number of people aboard, and the stench . . . *Jaysus!*

Half-starved, Timothy could scarcely swallow the food provided: grain, hardened and served in lumps, and what his steerage mates called "bow wow mutton"—meat so bad it looked and tasted like dog flesh. At night, trying to sleep, waking in fits and starts, he dreamed about the French café's food, and more often than not, he pounded the ship's timbers, furious with the world, furious with humankind, furious with himself, bloodying his knuckles and swearing aloud in Gaelic, English, and French that he'd made a mistake. A colossal mistake.

If he ever traveled aboard a ship again, perhaps going back to the Ireland he both loved and hated, it would *not* be in steerage!

Timothy knew he was resourceful as well as smart. He knew he'd never again make a *faux pas* like the *faux pas* he'd made by marrying the disinherited Hortense Downing-Cox. He had journeyed to America to earn his fortune and to escape a proletarian destiny, and, by God, he'd let nothing stand in his way. Not hunger, not thirst.

Not even ferret-faced maggots!

CHAPTER NINE:
TIMOTHY MEETS MR. AND MRS. CLUTTERBUCK

The one light in Timothy Kelley's tunnel of darkness was the buxom lass who stood cowering by his side.

At least she'd been buxom at the start of the journey. She had to have lost two and a half stone, but that didn't devalue her creamy skin, her dark, cherry-red hair, her smoke-colored lashes and sky-blue eyes. Despite the deplorable shortage of fresh air and sunshine during the seemingly endless voyage, her cheeks were patched with crimson.

A shawl helped hide her gown's threadbare bodice, which, had it fit her, would have barely constrained her once bountiful breasts. At this very moment her feet performed a graceless cé-lei reel upon the cold, teeming dock, and her hands, like a kitten's paws, kneaded his arm. She had flinched at his rough language, especially when he shouted in Gaelic at the worthless piece of scum, but she had not moved away from him.

Annie Laurie Cloncannon looked innocent, and Timothy knew for a fact that she was innocent. Because she had told him so, and he believed her.

He also believed that language was a tool for concealing the truth, but he would swear on a stack of bibles that Annie Laurie didn't have a dishonest bone in her body.

If she said she was pure, she was pure.

Not that he had tried to bed her. Instead, he had become her protector, her Irish *Aingeal coimhdeachta*, or in English, her "guardian angel"—keeping the other young wolves at bay.

49

Not that he was a young wolf.

However, as an older wolf, he had one advantage the feckin' young wolves did not. He could speak both English and Gaelic. Annie Laurie could only speak Gaelic.

To that end, Timothy had formulated a plan. He had told Annie Laurie, in Gaelic, that when they set foot in America he would pretend to be her *fear céile*, her husband. On the grave of his dead mum, he swore, he would not abandon her to the American wolves. And some day, when they were settled and safe, they would visit a priest and wed.

She had been so grateful, she had kissed him, a deep mouth-to-mouth, tongue-to-tongue kiss, and he realized he could bed her . . . if only he'd had a decent bed.

Along with the keel-hauling rumors, Timothy had heard that American landowners were always on the lookout for Irish *émigrés* to clean house, to work in their kitchens, to serve meals, even, in many cases, to play nursemaid.

A colleen who looked like Annie Laurie would not go unnoticed.

Sure enough, a short, plump moneybags and his tall, skeletal wife trotted straight toward the lass. Close on their heels, another man and woman pumped their arms like grounded graylag geese as they tried to outdistance the first couple. Timothy hid a grin.

The first moneybags wore a black frock coat, striped waistcoat, and gray trousers. A cravat had been knotted in front and puffed up to create a pigeon-like neck. Above small eyes and the barest hint of eyebrows, he sported a top hat, what Timothy's London mates would have called a chimneypot. The woman, swaddled in black from her shoulders to her shoes, wore a winter-white fur stole that Timothy could have sworn belonged to the weasel family.

The man and woman looked to be somewhere between forty

and forty-five years of age, and, although he knew he'd never met her before, Timothy thought the woman looked damned familiar.

"You there!" the plump man shouted, staring at Annie Laurie.

Timothy felt her go from kneading his arm to plowing a furrow in his arm.

"Yes, you," the man said, lowering his voice as he captured Annie Laurie's frightened gaze. "I am James Clutterbuck and this is my wife, Caro—"

"No need to give her our Christian names, Mr. Clutterbuck." The woman, thin as six o'clock, stood ramrod straight.

"—line," he finished. "You may . . . I mean you must call us Mr. and Mrs. Clutterbuck or 'sir' and 'ma'am.' " Despite a cold wind that stained Annie Laurie's cheeks a darker red, sweat streamed down the man's face, forming puddles above his full lips and in the folds of his chins. "You see . . . the thing is . . . Caroline, I mean Mrs. Clutterbuck, here, is in need of another maidservant."

He spared a quick glance for his wife, then once again caught Annie Laurie's gaze. "Would you like to work for us, Bridget?"

"Beggin' your pardon, Mister," Timothy said, doffing his cap, "but my wife, *Annie Laurie,* does not speak English."

If possible, Mrs. Clutterbuck stood even straighter. "Your wife?"

"Yes, Missus."

"No, no, that will never do," she said, her fingers buried in a handful of fur before she fretfully pulled the front of her weasel across her flat, black bodice.

Timothy blinked. Here, now, why would she want to hide a bosom that was already well and truly out of sight? Could it be a tribute to his tallness, taking into consideration that her husband only came up to her nose? Perhaps it was an homage to Timothy's hair, as black as a moonless, starless night, or so

51

he'd been told by Hortense, his poetic heiress who was neither poetic nor an heiress. Had Mrs. Clutterbuck been favorably affected by his eyes that, according to Hortense, were the color of emeralds, and a torso that week after week, day after day of near-starvation had not severely weakened?

He had managed to scrape the filthy, three-month beard from his face with his knife so that he'd appear shaven, assuming one did not look too closely, but he'd given any water on hand to Annie Laurie, and he could smell his own odor.

"The girl looks awfully young to be his wife," Mr. Clutterbuck mused aloud. "If truth be told, she reminds me of Diana, goddess of the hunt. Diana had the power to talk to animals. Control them, too. She was a *virgin* goddess, one of the three maiden goddesses, along with—"

"We have need of a maidservant," Mrs. Clutterbuck interrupted, glaring at her husband. "We do *not* need a manservant. A man and wife? Good gracious, no. No, no, no! We will take the biddy, Mr. Clutterbuck, but she will have to leave her paddy behind. Surely he can find employment building a canal. There is always unskilled work to be had . . ."

She paused to appraise Timothy. "Assuming a mick like this one is not slothful," she continued in a scathing tone, "and will truly look for work."

Timothy stared back, meeting her gaze with disdain. Had he been able to do so, he would have turned up his nose. "Would you separate a man from his lawfully wedded wife?" he finally asked, then blinked once again when he realized why Mrs. Clutterbuck looked so familiar.

She wore a black bonnet that hid all of her hair and both her ears. Had the skin on her face been stripped to the bone, she'd have looked like one of the illustrations in a story Timothy had read—a story called *The Vampyre* by someone named Polidori.

"Our servants have rooms at the back of the house, in the

servants' quarters," Mrs. Clutterbuck said, ignoring Timothy's lawfully wedded remark. "You and your *wife* would not be welcome there. The other servants would never allow it. They know very well we would give the boot to any domestic who dared to marry. Rules are rules. And where, may I ask, is your *wife*'s wedding band?"

"My beloved wife's ring was stolen during our passage from London to your grand land of Boston. 'Tis my hope to buy her a gold and diamond marriage band as soon as—"

"Silence! Enough of your rubbish." Mrs. Clutterbuck turned to Mr. Clutterbuck. "Rules are rules," she repeated. "If the paddy is part of the bargain, this biddy is unacceptable."

"Rules are made to be broken, my dear."

She gasped. "Rules are *not* made to be broken, James! Rules are made to be followed."

"Ah, but what about the rule of thumb, my dear? The rule of thumb is not intended to be strictly accurate or reliable for every situation. It is an easily applied procedure for recalling some value or for making some determination."

"Mr. Clutterbuck, have you lost your mind?"

"I only meant that perhaps the girl's husband would agree to sleep in the stables," he said. "Joshua left for Johnson's fields at cock's crow. Cook knew but decided it was good riddance to bad rubbish and kept mute. So, my dear, we need a stable boy."

"This man is no boy!"

"Have you worked with horses, Paddy?" Mr. Clutterbuck asked Timothy.

Timothy pictured his dustman's wagon and the draft horse with its muscular back and powerful hindquarters. Then he pictured the horse he had owned in Ireland. Molly had named it Saint Padraig and called it Paddy, he thought with a wry twist of his lips. Unfortunately, "Paddy" had been devoured during the famine.

"Yes, sir," he replied. "I have worked with horses." *I have even eaten one.*

Momentarily defeated and smart enough to know it, Mrs. Clutterbuck said, "Very well, Mr. Clutterbuck, you may have your paddy and your biddy, but here are *my* rules, and if the paddy disobeys, he will be out on his ear. And his *wife*"—she all but spat the word—"will be sent packing, as well." She turned to Timothy. "Do you understand?"

He nodded.

"You will sleep in the stables and eat your meals with Cook and the other servants. My housekeeper rules the roost, and Cook rules the kitchen, although, like all of the other domestics, they follow *my* rules."

"Yes, ma'am."

"I am not finished. You will enter my domicile by walking into the back of the house, *never* the front of the house. Mr. Clutterbuck and I are god-fearing Christians. Presbyterians. And since I am fairly certain you and your biddy are Cat-licks, you may spend time together on Sundays when Mr. Clutterbuck and I attend church services. Bog trotters like you breed like rabbits, or so I've been told, but there will be no . . ." She paused as if searching for a word. "No dancing the kibbles or having your corn ground. Do you understand?"

Timothy gave Mr. Clutterbuck a puzzled glance.

"Mrs. Clutterbuck means there will be no horizontal refreshment," said Mr. Clutterbuck. He made a V with the first and second fingers of his left hand. Then he inserted the first finger of his right hand between the two left-hand fingers, whereupon he moved the right-hand finger back and forth, back and forth, faster and faster.

Even Annie Laurie recognized the crude gesture. With a startled *oomph,* she clutched Timothy's arm tighter.

Mr. Clutterbuck began to pant as the sweat streamed from

his face to his cravat and dripped, like raindrops, from below his ears to his padded shoulders.

Mrs. Clutterbuck forcibly pulled his hands apart. Her eyes seemed to shoot daggers at Mr. Clutterbuck, still struggling to catch his breath. Burying her hands in her weasel again, as if the white fur strengthened her resolve, she turned toward Timothy and met his gaze straight on. "I was trying to be discreet, Paddy, but I should have said 'no fornication' so that a green nigger like you would understand."

Seething inside, Timothy nevertheless managed to regain his stone face. "Beggin' your pardon, Mrs. Clutterbuck," he said, "but *fornication* between an unwed lad and lass is a sin, be they Catholic or Calvinist, so 'tis fortunate, indeed, that my Annie Laurie and I are wed good and proper. 'Tis also fortunate that Catholics keep the eighth day, Sunday, with joyfulness."

"You . . ." Mrs. Clutterbuck snapped her mouth shut. If she had been a turtle, she would have snaked her neck sideways and hidden her head underneath her weasel.

Timothy thought he heard a muffled laugh from Mr. Clutterbuck.

Gently removing Annie Laurie's fingers from his arm, Timothy then used the same arm to encircle her shoulders, and, with an obvious display of affection, she snuggled against his side. In doing so, her shawl slipped, revealing a bosom that was, even in its diminished state, twice the size of Mrs. Clutterbuck's.

Mrs. Clutterbuck's face turned the color of fresh blood. It was not a pretty sight.

Her mouth opened and closed, as if she was mimicking her husband's loss of breath. Or a grounded fish. Finally she said, "Are my terms . . . my *rules* agreeable, Paddy?"

Timothy's mind raced as he eyed the harbor, glancing hither and yon.

The graylag-goose man and woman were chinwagging with another lass, a comely but nearly toothless girl, who was eagerly bobbing her head and, at the same time, picking up her small bundle of possessions. Timothy silently cursed his luck.

He noted a well-clothed gent, as smartly garbed as Mr. Clutterbuck, holding a sign that had *NINA* scrawled across its front.

Momentarily discarding his indifferent expression, Timothy raised one eyebrow, looked at Mr. Clutterbuck, then nodded toward the man with the sign.

Mr. Clutterbuck followed Timothy's gaze. "The sign?"

"Yes, sir."

"It means 'No Irish Need Apply.' So you would be well advised to accept Mrs. Clutterbuck's offer and agree to abide by her rules."

"Mr. Clutterbuck, you have my sworn oath that Annie Laurie and I will obey your *wife*."

Timothy couldn't resist giving Mrs. Clutterbuck a taste of her own medicine, and he swallowed a grin at her expression when he laid emphasis on the word "wife."

He was suddenly anxious to see Mr. and Mrs. Clutterbuck's estate. A servants' entrance as well as servants' quarters meant a sizable house and, possibly, an equally large stable. If he could not own such a place himself, it would suit him fine . . . for now.

He was so hungry he felt he'd keel over if he didn't eat something soon. Cook would be a woman, of course, and except for Mrs. Clutterbuck—and he wasn't from tip to toe certain about her—he'd never had a problem charming, nor taming, a colleen. He envisioned double portions and swallowed hard.

Then he smiled at Annie Laurie and said, *"Tá mé chomh ocras go raibh mé a ithe capall agus chase an marcach."* He had a feeling Mr. Clutterbuck would have laughed at his jest, since in Gaelic he'd said, "I'm so hungry I could eat a horse and chase the rider."

Annie Laurie giggled.

"What did you say to her?" Mrs. Clutterbuck snapped.

"I said that you were her new mistress, and she should do everything you told her to do."

"And she found that amusing?"

"Yes. I mean no." Timothy thought fast. "She is simply happy to work for such a fine lady as yourself, so she laughed. In good humor, you might say."

"May I presume it's settled, then?" Without waiting for a reply, Mr. Clutterbuck pounded Timothy on the back with a heavy hand. "*I'm* happy to hear that you and Bridget will obey Mrs. Clutterbuck's rules. Here are mine, Paddy. You will muck out the stalls every day without fail. You will keep the tack polished. And mended, if need be. You will attend to *all* of my horses, making certain they are exercised, groomed, and fed. You will take special care with the thoroughbreds that belong to my sons, Lucky and Emperor."

"Your sons are named Lucky and Emperor?"

"No, of course not. The horses are Lucky and Emperor. My sons are James—we call him Jamie—and Robert. We call *him* Robin. They are fourteen and twelve years of age."

"The biddy may ride inside our carriage," Mrs. Clutterbuck said, her voice somewhat muted by the loss of her nostrils as she pressed a handkerchief against her nose. "Your mick will ride on top, next to the driver. I cannot, and will not, tolerate his odor."

"There is a trough outside the stables where Paddy can wash up, my dear. He shall cleanse himself before he is allowed to enter the house for his evening meal. Will that be satisfactory?"

"I suppose it will have to do. What about his clothes?" She gestured toward Timothy's legs. "His unmentionables are filthy.

I have clothes for the biddy, but . . ." She shrugged.

"I shall give him Joshua's trousers." Mr. Clutterbuck's plump cheeks flushed. "I mean Joshua's unmentionables. They were left behind, along with one or two shirts, when that good-for-nothing took off for the bloody fields. As you can plainly see, our new paddy is taller than Joshua. Otherwise, they are the same size."

Timothy wondered what bloody fields had lured the missing stable boy. He recalled a song, "Clare's Dragoons," that his da used to sing when he was gee-eyed.

> *When on Ramillie's bloody field,*
> *The baffled French were forced to yield,*
> *The victor Saxon backward reeled*
> *Before the charge of Clare's Dragoons.*

"Step lively," said Mr. Clutterbuck, interrupting Timothy's train of thought before he could, impulsively, break into song.

A good thing, too, Timothy mused, hiding yet another grin behind a discrete cough. He had been told he could "sing like the sighing of a tempest spent," but now was not the time, nor the place, to display that particular gift.

As he urged a timorous Annie Laurie to step lively from the dock to the Clutterbuck carriage, he had a sudden thought.

Mrs. Clutterbuck had birthed two sons.

Which meant she had danced the kibbles and had her corn ground . . . twice.

CHAPTER TEN:
SEAN KELLEY MEETS P. T. BARNUM

New York City
August, 1850

Thanks to Hortense, Sean Kelley knew more about Tom Thumb than he did his own father. Following the untimely death of Sean's mum, Timothy Kelley had blown in and out of Sean's life like a black squall, while Tom Thumb remained a constant source of discussion.

According to Hortense, Tom Thumb was a relatively large baby, weighing nine pounds, eight ounces at birth. She always laughed when she said that, thinking it a great joke—on whom, Sean wasn't sure. Furthermore, he didn't know if Hortense's "factual account" was the God's honest truth. She had heard it from a café customer who had heard it from an American cousin who lived in Bridgeport, Connecticut, America, not far from Tom Thumb's parents.

Hortense said that Tom Thumb had "developed and enlarged as normal for the first six months of his life."

Then he suddenly stopped growing.

He had visited England in 1844, and his popularity had been so extensive that his likeness was reproduced on plates, mugs and fans. Tom Thumb dolls were sold in the shops, a song was composed in his honor, and there was even a children's dance called the Tom Thumb Polka.

The "American Dwarf" had been accompanied by his guardian, P. T. Barnum.

Over the years, Sean had only half listened to Hortense's excited chatter about how she'd seen Tom Thumb sing, dance, recite poetry, and perform his clever impression of Napoleon Bonaparte. Sean had no doubts about that—after all, Barnum had exhibited his star attraction inside a public hall. But when Hortense lapsed into tales about Tom Thumb's visits to Queen Victoria at Buckingham Palace, Sean stopped up his ears. Hortense could not have been in attendance when the Queen's pet poodle charged Tom, and the boy brandished a tiny cane and began fencing with the dog. Yet Hortense made it sound as if she had been among the queen's guests, and her frequent brags would have made Timothy Kelley, a windbag of the highest order, flush a vivid crimson.

Finally, one fact penetrated Sean's fog-drenched brain. During his London visit, Phineas Taylor Barnum had earned a bloody fortune. Tom Thumb's appearances at Buckingham Palace had been rewarded with expensive gifts and gold coins. His public performances brought in hundreds of dollars a day, and Barnum had collected the proceeds from the Tom Thumb booklets and souvenirs that sold by the thousands.

Furthermore, Barnum didn't even have to perform.

Not that Sean was against performing. While watching an assortment of performances at the Cirque de Délices, he had recognized his own dormant desire to strut before an audience, the focus of everyone's attention, a manipulator of emotions, not unlike Napoleon Bonaparte.

Still, in Sean's admittedly biased opinion, P. T. Barnum had bested Napoleon. Why commission armies and structure expensive wars when you could hire the talent that would, eventually, make you as memorable as your hired talent? In other words, Barnum had a green *thumb* when it came to finding "freaks."

In years to come, people would no doubt remember Tom

Thumb, but they'd also speak, with awe and admiration, about the man who had turned a child with a defective growth gland into a vast, worldwide star.

Sean had learned even more about Tom Thumb from P. T. Barnum himself, during a nighttime visit to Sportsmen's Hall, a Water Street crimp house owned by a member of an Irish street gang known as the Dead Rabbits.

Water Street ran parallel to New York's East River, and many of the houses had a saloon, dance hall, or house of prostitution on every floor. Sportsmen's Hall occupied the whole of a three-story frame house at 372 Water Street. The lower half was painted a vivid, bilious green. The main room on the first floor was arranged as an amphitheater. In the center was a ring enclosed by a wooden fence, where huge gray rats from the wharfs were sent against terriers and, sometimes—when they had been starved for a few days—against each other.

One of the most notorious Water Street saloons, a drinking den that Sean had not yet visited, was called Hole-in-the-Wall. Located at the corner of Dover Street, it was managed by One-Armed-Charley and his trusted lieutenant, Gallus Mag, a giant Englishwoman, well over six feet tall, so called because she kept her skirts up with galluses. Barnum said she'd stomp through the saloon with a pistol stuck in her belt and a huge bludgeon strapped to her wrist. Should she fell a quarrelsome customer with the bludgeon, she'd clutch his ear between her teeth and drag him to the door amid the frenzied cheers of the onlookers. If her victim protested or struggled, she'd bite his ear off. After she had tossed the customer into the street, she'd deposit his ear in a jar of alcohol behind the bar, where she kept her trophies in pickle.

Although Water Street was the locale of the most vicious drinking dens in New York's Fourth Ward, there was little choice between it and Cherry Street, where, Sean learned, John

Hancock and George Washington had once strolled. Cherry Street was the headquarters of the crimps who operated boarding houses where sailors were robbed, murdered and shanghaied.

Barnum and the chums who accompanied him were safe on Water Street and Cherry Street because the gangs knew P.T. liked to look in both places for new acts for his American Museum. He had missed out on a woman nicknamed Shakespeare, who claimed she came from an aristocratic family and in her youth had been a celebrated London actress. In return for a bottle of swan gin, she'd recite every female role in *Hamlet, Macbeth,* and *The Merchant of Venice.* Unfortunately, she had been cut to pieces before Barnum could hire her.

Another thug who liked to visit Sportsmen's House was a man named Snatchem. Barnum had described Snatchem as a "beastly, obscene ruffian." He plied his trade as a river pirate, but he was also a "bloodsucker" at bare-knuckle fights. When one of the fighters began to bleed from cuts and scratches, Snatchem would suck the blood from the wound. He proudly described himself as a "rough and tumble stand up to be knocked down son of a gun."

The exact opposite of P. T. Barnum.

Snatchem had also described himself as a "kicking in the head, knife in a dark room fellow."

The exact opposite of me, Sean had thought with a grin.

After downing a mug of beer inside Sportsmen's Hall, Barnum had held up the mug and winked at Sean. "Please don't tell Charity," he'd said. "She's a teetotaler, as am I, but beer is merely a cereal grain." Then he had introduced Sean to Hell Cat Maggie, a female member of the Dead Rabbits.

"I have it on good authority that she's filed her teeth into points," Barnum had stated, once he and Sean had returned to their rough wooden benches. "And that she wears long nails of brass when she battles rival gangs from the Bowery."

Barnum had then pointed out a man named Jack the Rat, who would bite the head off a mouse for ten cents and, with his teeth, behead a rat for two bits. Barnum had wanted to employ Jack the Rat, but Jack was the son-in-law of a Dead Rabbits leader who used Jack's special bent to recruit gang members, so Jack the Rat had turned down Barnum's generous offer.

As luck would have it, Tom Thumb's parents, Sherwood and Cynthia Stratten, had *not* turned down Barnum's offer.

Barnum's half-brother had shown him a small boy named Charles Sherwood Stratten, who was four years old, stood twenty-five inches high, and weighed only fifteen pounds.

"After seeing him and talking with him," Barnum told Sean, "I determined to exhibit him in public. I secured his services from his parents and paid him three dollars a week, plus room and board."

"Tom Thumb was only four years old?" Sean had asked.

"This is between you and me, lad," Barnum replied, raising his first finger and aiming for his mouth in the age-old gesture for "it's a secret." Missing his mouth completely, his finger landed on his left cheekbone, somewhere to the right of his ear, and Sean realized that his new friend and benefactor was as drunk as Davy's sow . . . on *one* beer. Or was it two?

"Yes, sir," Sean said, sincerely. "You have my word on it. I won't tell a soul."

"I changed Charles Stratten's name to *General* Tom Thumb and billed him as eleven years old." Barnum gave Sean a loopy smile and a sly wink. "New York's fascination with the child was unbelievable and, after a month, I raised his salary to seven dollars a week, then twenty-five dollars and . . . well, you know the rest."

"But they say Tom Thumb, I mean General Tom Thumb, wasn't your first exhibit, sir."

"No. That honor goes to Joice Heth, a blind slave I touted as the one-hundred-and sixty-one-year-old nurse of George Washington. I billed her as 'the most astonishing and interesting curiosity in the world.' People lined up to hear her stories about 'dear little George.' "

"I take it she wasn't dear little George's nurse."

"No." A laugh bubbled up from Barnum's chest.

"And how old was she really, sir?"

"Following Joice Heth's death, an autopsy was performed. It showed that she was no older than eighty." Barnum laughed so hard, his bench nearly toppled over.

Sean joined in the laughter. When he was able to speak again, he said, "There's a sucker born every minute."

"I disagree, lad. I have not duped the world, nor attempted to do so, and I've generally given people the worth of their money twice told. It costs two bits to enter Barnum's American Museum, and you cannot tell me that people don't get their money's worth. The bigger the humbug, the better people will like it. Take the Feejee Mermaid. I've never heard one complaint about my mermaid being a cheat. Have you?"

The Feejee Mermaid was the top half of a small monkey's skeleton, including its head, sewn to the large body of a fish that was missing its head. "No, sir," Sean replied. "I have not."

In truth, people had not even complained about Barnum's museum sign that read: THIS WAY TO THE EGRESS. Since egress was another word for exit, visitors would have to pay an additional twenty-five cents to reenter the museum.

"More persons on the whole are humbugged by believing in nothing than by believing too much," Barnum had added before calling for another mug of beer for Sean, and then joining Hell Cat Maggie, Jack the Rat, and the rest of the Dead Rabbits who were singing Stephen Foster's "Open Thy Lattice Love."

Which was followed by a rousing chorus of Foster's "Oh! Susannah."

Sean remembered that the Cirque de Délices orchestra had been serenading people with "Open Thy Lattice Love" when he had descended into the basement and wooed his *Petite Ange*.

The Dead Rabbits sang, "Oh, Susanna, oh don't you weep for me."

Quietly, Sean wept into his beer.

CHAPTER ELEVEN:
THE AMERICAN MUSEUM

Sean stood beneath the American Museum's *Egress* sign. Although he was situated inside the museum, he shaded his eyes with his hand as the object of his recent musings came into view.

A spotlight seemed to shine down upon P. T. Barnum. Exceedingly bright, the spotlight tended to blind any observers who watched him approach. And to add to his mystique, an unseen hand appeared to maneuver the imaginary spotlight so that it followed him from place to place.

Today he was clothed in his customary black. The hair that framed his balding forehead was in its usual disarray, but the deep nose-to-mouth lines that dominated his bulldog-like face revealed a smug smile.

"She agreed to the tour," Sean guessed, greeting his benefactor. Together they strolled past one of Barnum's most popular attractions, the Happy Family, a very large cage filled with animals considered natural enemies—cats and dogs, owls and mice, hawks and sparrows—all living together in harmony.

"She did, indeed," Barnum replied, "but the girl drives a hard bargain, lad. Aside from her fee of one hundred and fifty thousand dollars, payable in advance, I'll be responsible for the salaries of her musical director and a male singer to accompany her in duets. She also requires a lady-in-waiting who will travel with her."

"Lady-in-waiting?"

"Another name for a lady's maid, I believe. My daughter says it's another name for a *femme de chambre*. I'll be damned if I know what a *femme de chambre* is . . . or does. I'm thinking she washes out the knickers of her mistress every so often, assuming Miss Lind wears knickers."

Sean swallowed a grin. "I'll find out, sir." He felt his face flush. "I mean I'll find out what the lady-in-waiting does. It is, of course, none of my business if Miss Lind wears knick—"

"Needless to say, I agreed to pay all travel and hotel expenses for the entire entourage."

"You take a huge gamble, sir, bringing Jenny Lind to America. She's a concert singer, not a music hall singer, and there's no evidence that she'll appeal to a widespread populace."

"When I want your opinion, I'll ask for it!" Almost immediately, Barnum's face relaxed into a second wreath of a smile. "We must whet the public's appetite, Sean, and I would guess you have some tricks up your sleeve."

"Yes, sir. I've been thinkin' you could use the average punter's adherence to religion and morality since the lass herself regards her voice as a gift from God."

"Splendid."

Encouraged, Sean continued. "I've also been thinkin' we could auction the first ticket."

Barnum's brow furrowed. "Please explain that scheme."

"First, you must convince your chums that high bids will be good for their own businesses. Then we inform the press."

Barnum snapped his fingers. "If my friend John makes the outstanding bid, the newspapers will print the story, and he'll sell more hats."

"It is that very notion I had in mind," Sean said, relieved that his benefactor required no further explanation.

In truth, Barnum was a mastermind when it came to promotion.

"Small doses of advertising," he had once told Sean, "result in nothing. It's like giving a sick person half the medicine he needs. It just causes more suffering. Give the whole dose, and the cure will be certain and decisive."

One of his most ambitious uses of the "whole dose of medicine" had to be the wooly language he'd used for his "What Is It?" exhibit.

"It" was, in point of fact, an African-American man named William Henry Johnson. William Henry Johnson's mother had sold him into show business at a young age. He was between four and five feet tall and appeared to suffer from smallness of the head, a condition associated with incomplete brain development.

By far one of the American Museum's most popular exhibits, aside from the Happy Family, Barnum liked to describe "What Is It?" as the world's first quasi-man, like Quasimodo in *The Hunchback of Notre Dame*. Except, Barnum claimed, his quasi-man had been born a "brute" in the African jungle but was now beginning to take on "human" and "civilized" features. Colorful posters asked the public to determine whether the creature was man or animal.

Sean slanted a glance at the museum's WHAT IS IT? poster, which read: "Is it a lower order of man? Or is it a higher order of monkey? None can tell! Perhaps it is a combination of both. It is beyond dispute THE MOST MARVELOUS CREATURE LIVING."

Even though he'd seen the poster more times than he could count, the corners of Sean's mouth turned up, splitting his face into an ear-to-ear grin. Because Barnum had touted William Henry Johnson's physical description by adding: "It has the skull, limbs, and general anatomy of an orange orangutan and the countenance of a human being." In Sean's opinion, that was the very definition of an American politician!

In Sean's estimation, Barnum was a genius who knew more about marketing and staging than Sean could learn in a lifetime, and yet every night Sean tried to stay awake and think up new schemes that would impress his employer.

Upon arriving in New York City, he had sought out Barnum straight away, confident that the famous promoter could use an artist of Sean's caliber.

Overconfident, as it turned out.

Unimpressed by Sean's sketches, paintings, even his obvious zest for a position at the museum, Barnum had coldly informed Sean that there were no openings of any kind unless Sean wanted to "shovel shit from the animal cages."

Although the last six words were flavored with equal helpings of contempt and ridicule, Sean doffed his cap and politely thanked Barnum for his time.

As he was leaving, he mentioned his desire to own a traveling circus some day.

That did impress the consummate showman. Barnum offered Sean a drink, a cigar, then said that he, Barnum, had studied circuses and planned to put together one as soon as it was feasible. He said there were big differences between a traveling circus and the older, city-bound shows. While most city circuses relied primarily on trick riding displays, the smaller traveling shows depended more on acrobatics, exotic animal displays, juggling, and specialty acts.

And clowns.

The best example of the power of the clown, Barnum insisted, was what he called "the most famous man you've never heard of"—a man named Dan Rice.

Sean snapped his fingers. "I've heard of Mr. Rice. Is he not a singer of Negro songs?"

Barnum nodded. "Dan got caught up in the popularity of singing songs in blackface, but his first opportunity came earlier, when he worked with a pig named Sybil, a pig who could do many tricks, including the ability to tell time."

"A pig named Sybil? 'Tis a strange name for a piggy, sir."

Barnum tapped his forehead. "I may be wrong about the name, lad. Seems to me I heard the name 'Lord Byron' at one time or another, so perhaps the pig was a male pig, named for this Lord Byron fellow. I don't recall for sure.

"However, I do recall that Dan, with his wife, Maggie, joined a traveling puppet show and was paid four dollars a week to perform his comedy pig act," Barnum continued. "I know for a fact that, early in his career, Dan Rice was down on his luck and only had one horse. His competitors mocked him. They said Dan's show was a 'one-horse show.' But Dan was able to turn the expression around by putting on a high-quality show, and his rivals were forced to eat their words . . . along with crow." Barnum chuckled at his own pun. "In addition to his 'clowning,' Dan is a songwriter, an animal trainer, a strong man, and a dancer."

"I want to mold my own circus along the lines of the Cirque de Délices in Paris, France, rather than a one-horse show," Sean said, "but I'd sure like to meet Dan Rice."

"If you can catch him," Barnum replied with a grin. "His circus travels by wagons in the north and by river barges in the south. Right now I believe he's in New Orleans."

Returning to the present and Jenny Lind, Sean said, "I needn't state the obvious, sir. Dishes, fans, flasks, trivets, and—"

"Figurines. Yes. Before I forget, Charity told me *not* to forget to invite you to a small dinner party. You've quite won her over, Sean. My daughters, as well. Charity said that hiring you to promote my museum was one of the best ideas I've come up with in . . . what's your favorite expression? . . . oh, yes, donkey's years." Barnum winked.

70

Sean had a great deal of respect and admiration for Charity Barnum, and during another long night at the Water Street saloon, he had asked Barnum how he'd met Charity and if he'd known from the start that she was the girl he wanted to marry.

"I've met the girl I want to marry," Sean explained, "but then I lost her and I fear I'll niver again find her. There's an Irish turn of phrase, 'We only part to meet again,' and I pray it's the God's honest truth. Still, I'd like to hear your story, sir, if you don't mind the telling."

"I don't mind. I was nineteen years old. I owned a store in Bethel, Connecticut, and of all the young people with whom I associated in our parties, picnics, and sleigh rides, Charity stood highest in my estimation and continued to improve upon acquaintance."

Barnum paused to pour from their pitcher of beer. "In the summer of 1829 I asked Charity for her hand in marriage," he said, and even in the dim light of the saloon Sean could see that his eyes were bright with memories. "Although my suit was accepted and a date appointed, I could not wait. I applied myself closely to business while Charity went to New York in October, ostensibly to visit her uncle. I followed in November, to purchase goods for my store, and the evening after my arrival we were married. And," Barnum boasted, thumping his chest with his fist, "I became the husband of one of the best women in the world."

One of the best women in the world. Sean agreed wholeheartedly. Charity Barnum's stern appearance was a sham, as deceptive as the American Museum's Feejee Mermaid, for Charity possessed a lively sense of humor and always had a witty backchat, no matter how transparent or insensible the tease. Furthermore, she had taught him how to speak like a gent, even though his blasted tongue frequently betrayed him by revealing his provinciality. If he could find a lass like Charity Barnum, he'd seriously consider giving up his bachelor status.

Out of the blue he heard the echo of little Charlotte Kelley's voice: *Please, Sean, you must promise to find Petite Ange and kiss her awake.*

Upon reaching the shores of America, Sean had settled in Brooklyn, across the East River from New York City. Whereupon, he had initiated a search for the beautiful yet elusive rope walker. Weeks later, after listening to Sean's effusive praise, Barnum had renewed the search, vowing he'd hire a "live angel who walked on air" for one of his many exhibits.

However, it soon became apparent that the lovely, golden-haired *danseur de corde* had no desire to walk an American rope, much less be kissed awake by a specter from her past.

CHAPTER TWELVE:
ANGELIQUE DRESSES FOR A PARTY

Angelique Aumont sighed twice. She might as well get her wiffles over with now. Soon her corset strings would be knotted so tightly that deep breathing—in fact, any breathing at all—would be virtually impossible. Or, at best, painful.

Seated directly in front of her bedroom dressing table, barren except for a basket filled with sewing goods, a hairbrush, a comb, and a small cedar box that held gewgaws for her hair, she darted a glance toward the gown Auntie Bernadette had selected for tonight's dinner party.

Several unladylike ruminations filtered through Angelique's brain, most having to do with defecation, but the word she chose to murmur was, "Drab."

"Wot did you say?"

"I said my gown is drab." Angelique stared up at her friend and maidservant, Gertrude Starling. Auntie Bernadette had sent Angelique the funds for her journey to Bridgeport, Connecticut, while Madame Kelley's generosity had paid Gertie's way, with several banknotes left over to give her brother Allen a start toward the nest egg he had begun for *his* voyage to America.

Angelique had laughed at the term "nest egg" until Gertie told her, in all seriousness, that it came from a farmer's practice of placing real or fake eggs in the nest of a hen.

"And why would he be doing that?" Angelique had asked.

"To fool his hens into laying more eggs, you silly goose. More eggs means more money."

Once here, Allen would join his sister and, together, they'd perfect their flying trapeze act, then perform it for Dan Rice's circus or Spalding's North American Circus, or for the great P. T. Barnum himself. It was said that Barnum presented specialty acts every Saturday afternoon, inside his famous museum. The acts were for children, who watched free of charge. Their parents paid. Meanwhile, thanks to Angelique's gentle persuasion, Gertie had joined Auntie Bernadette's staff of maidservants.

"My gown is dull, dreary, colorless," Angelique snapped.

"But the black'll make your hair shine more yella'," Gertie said as she combed a short fringe across Angelique's forehead. Her skilled fingers then drew Angelique's hair into a coiled plait, worn high, decorated with tiny stars and white silk flowers drawn from the cedar box atop the dressing table.

A contrite Angelique jumped to her feet, nearly upsetting the box but, luckily, not her complicated hairdo. "*Merci*, Gertie. Auntie Bernadette says no one should have hair the color of mine. Of course, she is also displeased with my mouth, my eyes, and the 'holes in my cheeks.' Too bold, I suppose."

"The holes are called dimples, *Petite Ange,* and you cannot alter what God has provided."

"True, but we can alter that hideous gown."

Twenty minutes later, a froth of lace, pinched from Angelique's pink-and-white petticoat, decorated a bodice that was now décolleté. Long, fitted sleeves had given way to puff sleeves, and artificial flowers enhanced Angelique's waistline. Angelique's sewing skills left much to be desired, so despite her large hands, perfect for trapeze flying, Gertie's nimble fingers flew across the drab dress material, stitching row upon row of pleated ruffles, adding invisible stitches to secure the white lace and colorful flowers.

Once she had finished flouncing the gown, it was no longer floor length, so a red taffeta crinoline peeked from below the modified hemline.

"God-a-mercy," Gertrude said. "Your auntie will put on a tantrum when she sees wot you've done."

"What *you've* done," Angelique replied, her chastisement belied by a wink.

"For wot *I've* done, I should be rewarded."

"Very true. Hmmm . . . what should your reward be?" Angelique pretended to deliberate.

As a McCoy house servant, Gertie wore a taminy petticoat under a black, floor-length gown, interrupted at the waist by a plain white bib apron, the black gown's only embellishment, not counting the apron's strict, but more often than not wilted, bow in the back. All of Auntie Bernadette's female servants dressed alike, except for the housekeeper, who wore several keys at her waist that jangled when she walked. And Cook, who wore a white gown and a white hat that looked like a hollowed-out popover.

In Gertie's kit were her circus costumes, of no use to anyone, including Gertie. However, when her day's work was done and her dinner eaten, Gertie retired to her room, which she had once told Angelique was "nothing more than a monk's cell." There, she untied her apron strings, shed her shapeless black dress and woolen petticoat, and changed into one of the fancy, ruffled dressing gowns she had managed to sew from the material she'd begged off Angelique.

Clothed in her finery, she'd often duck in and out of hallway shadows and make her way to Angelique's bedroom. So far she hadn't been caught, but it was only a matter of time. Angelique had warned Gertie over and over to be careful, perhaps stop her nightly visits altogether, but she might as well talk to the wall. At any rate, a part of Angelique didn't want to lose Gertie's company. Gertie made her laugh, and there wasn't much laughter in the McCoy household. Auntie Bernadette believed "die laughing" was the God's honest truth, while Angelique preferred to quote Ralph Waldo Emerson: "The earth laughs flowers."

Gertie said that Angelique was a silly peagoose, and, if caught, Gertie would simply say that Angelique had sent for her. She was, after all, Angelique's groom of the chamber.

"*Non*, you are a lady's maid," Angelique had replied with a laugh. "A groom of the chamber is a valet, like Edward, my uncle's valet."

Angelique had provided her friend with several garments she knew she'd never wear, and she dreaded the day when Auntie Bernadette would fling open what she called her niece's "glory box" or "hope chest" and discover its missing cache. Uncle Alistaire paid for the contents; however, it was Auntie Bernadette who selected Angelique's *articles d'habillage*.

The chest contained various articles of clothing, as well as linens and blankets and quilts for Angelique's marriage bed. There was also a baptism gown—for Angelique's first baby—and an assortment of embroidered undergarments.

Useless items!

"Even though I have only spoken to *Monsieur* Sean Kelley once, I love him with all my heart," she had told Gertie. "However, he is already . . . how you say? . . . taken, *oui*, taken, by the woman in black. Since I cannot have him for my *mari dévoué* . . . for my devoted husband . . . I shall never wed."

In fact, kneeling inside her aunt's chapel until her aching knees could no longer support her, she had taken a solemn oath to remain a spinster until the angel of death claimed her.

Thinking about the glory chest, Angelique felt her lightly powdered shoulders tighten with dread. Because every time she gave Gertie a piece of clothing or an embroidered undergarment from the chest, she feared Auntie Bernadette would open the damfool box to place another *article d'habillage* inside, whereupon she'd discover the missing contents. And wouldn't that make the fur fly?

Gertie loved gewgaws, and the pink petticoat that had just sacrificed its froth of lace still had layers and layers of lacy trim. Gertie's skill with a needle would create a wondrous dressing gown. It made the perfect reward, and Gertie's excited thank-you was Angelique's reward.

"Did you not understand me, *Petite Ange?*" Gertie placed the material atop Angelique's four-poster bed and, almost reverently, caressed the lace. "Your auntie will have a tantrum at the sight of your altered gown. Or she'll faint dead away."

Gertie clutched at her heart—on the wrong side of her chest, Angelique noted with amusement—and mimed a dramatic swoon.

"Unfortunately," Angelique said with mock seriousness as she helped Gertie to her feet, "my dear aunt suffers from a gastric disorder and cannot attend Charity Barnum's dinner party."

"Aha! I was told by Henry, who heard it from Mary . . . Mary the chambermaid, not Mary the scullery maid . . . who heard it from Cook, who heard it from Mr. McCoy's flunky, that Mrs. McCoy had overeaten herself and suffers from the belches."

Although she tried hard to maintain a stern expression, Angelique couldn't help laughing, aware that her aunt's recurrent bouts of indigestion were a constant source of amusement for the servants and frequently led to forbidden festivities like the Servants Ball, patterned after the less risqué British Servants Ball. She was also aware that Gertie and her most recent suitor, Henry the coachman, usually played the ringmasters—the ring *leaders*—when those festivities were sampled, swallowed, and rued the next morning.

The festivities and their aftermath had to be carefully hidden from the watchful eye of Auntie Bernadette. If discovered, a disobedient servant would be dismissed. Or worse.

Bernadette Browning-Hale McCoy favored floggings as the ultimate reprimand. More often than not, the soles of a servant's bare feet were used as a target. And, as a warning, a cat-o'-nine-tails—along with a cane and a coiled whip—decorated the hallway in the servants' quarters.

Angelique often wondered why Auntie Bernadette's servants did not up and leave, find work elsewhere. Surely kindhearted families needed good house servants. Gertie dispelled that notion quickly. Almost all of the McCoy servants had signed contracts to work off their passage money. The contracts, Gertie said, were for five to seven years. Mrs. McCoy had threatened "debtor's prison" should an "indentured" servant run off before fulfilling his or her contract. Gertie pooh-poohed Auntie Bernadette's threats, but the assortment of young servants, all of whom had emigrated from England, believed they'd be locked up behind prison bars if they tried to run away from Mrs. McCoy's settling of real, or more often imaginary, scores.

Right now it appeared that Auntie Bernadette's acts of vengeance, including her threats to cane or flog a disobedient servant, were the outermost thing from Gertie's mind as she hooted with laughter and clapped her hands and stamped her feet and then joined Angelique in whirling 'round the bedroom, spinning to a silent *Valse à Deux Temps*.

Gertie partnered Angelique, who played the dance music inside her head. It was, she remembered, the same way she had practiced her Cirque routines. Until the actual performance, all of the music had been played inside her head.

Truth be told, she felt incredibly festive, the same feeling she experienced when she saw a loose balloon skim the rooftops and float toward the sun; the same feeling she experienced just before she tiptoed onto the rope and performed a difficult *saut périlleux.*

She only hoped that tomorrow morning she wouldn't rue tonight.

CHAPTER THIRTEEN:
ANGELIQUE ATTENDS CHARITY BARNUM'S DINNER PARTY

Escorted by Uncle Alistaire, an astute businessman who was nevertheless overwhelmed by his acerbic wife and her seven cats, Angelique entered P. T. Barnum's ornate mansion.

Like everything Barnum set out to do—and more often than not accomplished—his mansion had been designed to attract attention. Called Iranistan, or Oriental Village, it looked like a sultan's palace, executed in rust-colored sandstone, capped with domes and spires, adorned with intricately carved arches that framed the broad piazzas on each of its three floors.

A London architect had developed the overall design, and then Barnum had engaged an American architect and builder, giving him instructions to proceed with the work, not "by the job" but "by the day," and to spare neither time nor expense in erecting a comfortable, convenient, and tasteful residence.

Once begun, the construction continued during Barnum and General Tom Thumb's tour throughout the United States and Cuba. Appropriate, elegant furniture was made expressly for every room in the house. The stables, conservatories, and outbuildings were perfectly put together. A profusion of trees were set out over the seventeen acres.

Iranistan also had a greenhouse from which Barnum would gather flowers for Sunday services at the local Universalist church. He had imported a variety of choice livestock and took pride in having been elected president of the local agricultural society.

According to Angelique's uncle, *Monsieur* Barnum had said, "The whole was built and established literally regardless of expense, for I had no desire even to ascertain the entire cost."

Despite his wife's outspoken contempt for *Monsieur* Barnum, or possibly because of it, Uncle Alistaire said that by the time the house was completed, it had cost over one hundred-fifty thousand dollars. Upon hearing that, a stunned Auntie Bernadette had choked on her mouthful of Chateaubriand. Clothed in a feathery gown that had a tendency to shed feathers, her hands had flailed, and her crystal goblet, filled with red wine, had fallen to the dining room floor.

With a feeble moan she had clutched her stomach and vomited wine, broth, beef, shallots, butter, tarragon, mushrooms, and something else Angelique had no desire to identify, although she thought it might be the smelly *petite poisson* . . . little fish . . . Auntie Bernadette had devoured at teatime. What had she called them? Oh, yes, sardines.

Eyes shut, arms flapping like a graylag goose, Auntie Bernadette had plunged toward the polished floorboards. As she lay in a vomitous swoon, red wine marinating her feathers, Uncle Alistaire had rung for the servants, but first he'd winked at Angelique.

What did that mean?

Upon reaching Connecticut and settling into her aunt's house, it had taken less than a fortnight for Angelique to discover that there was no love lost between Auntie Bernadette and Uncle Alistaire. She could almost swear they hated each other.

Had her uncle waited until his wife took a mouthful of Chateaubriand before he mentioned the cost of Monsieur Barnum's property, knowing how she'd react?

And why had he looked so crestfallen, so bloody disappointed, when Auntie Bernadette *vomited* the Chateaubriand that was stuck in her throat, nearly choking her to death?

Angelique was quite certain she had imagined that look. And quite certain she had not.

Before she could ponder her uncle's odd behavior any further, two of *Monsieur* Barnum's daughters, Caroline, eighteen, and Helen, eleven, greeted her with air kisses that narrowly missed the dents in her cheeks. What had Gertie called them? Ah, *oui*, dimples.

Helen Barnum's eyes shined. Obviously elated to be included in a grown-up party, she was a tall girl for eleven, perhaps an inch and a half shorter than Angelique. She wore a dark green silk and velvet gown with full sleeves and pleated skirts. Her sister wore a more somber gown of black velvet, its sedateness belied by an exquisite necklace of rubies and pearls.

Following the girls, Angelique ascended a carved walnut staircase, leading to a huge central dome at the very top of the three-story mansion, where the sitting room boasted a circular divan that, Helen said, could accommodate forty-five people. Diamond-shaped windows were set with panes of colored glass, casting an unusual glow, turning the room into an implicit fairyland.

Charity Barnum approached. Her warm welcome could just as well have been uttered in Greek or Hindi, yet somehow Angelique managed to stammer an acknowledgment as she stared at the man who stood beneath a window. The pane cast a reddish hue, but the sun had already begun its descent, so the flickering color merely tinted his thick, ebony hair.

Deciphering her guest's avid gaze, Madam Barnum laughed and said, "Would you like an introduction, my dear?"

"*Mais oui*," Angelique replied, her head bobbing like a child's teeter-totter while several strands of hair escaped from her neatly coiled plait. At the same time, a portion of her brain sternly told her heart to stop swinging like a pendulum.

She maneuvered the room carefully, as if she trod a lofty rope, but her mind raced. Would *Monsieur* Sean Kelley call her *Petite Ange* and reveal the circus background Auntie Bernadette had tried so hard to hide? Would *Monsieur* Kelley even recognize the Cirque de Délices girl he had wooed so briefly? Angelique's lips tingled with the memory of his kiss.

Madam Barnum accomplished the introduction, but once again Angelique did not hear one word through the cloud of imaginary bees that seemed to buzz around the gilt curls that now obscured her ears.

Instead, she focused on *Monsieur* Kelley's ice-green eyes, until his eyes were hidden by his elaborate bend at the waist, which, in her opinion, was nothing more than a mock bow.

Perhaps his arrogance was indifference. Perhaps he did not recognize *Petite Ange* after all, for he raised her glove-clad hand to his lips, kissed her cotton knuckles, and murmured, " 'Tis a pleasure to make your acquaintance, Mrs. Aumont."

"*Miss* Aumont." Madame Barnum smiled wickedly and gave *Monsieur* Kelley a wink, just before she excused herself to welcome three or four new guests.

Angelique stifled a gasp. Madame Barnum had cast herself in the role of . . . what was the English word? Matchmaker? Yes, matchmaker. Did Madame Barnum not know that this blasted snake in the grass, this man who looked so *bon* in black trousers, starched white shirt, and gray vest, was already married?

"Our host has spared no expense on his home," *Monsieur* Kelley stated, his voice low. "Marble fireplaces, gilded ceilings, elaborately carved doors, and all sorts of paraphernalia."

Angelique blinked, surprised by his choice of subject. "Do you envy *Monsieur* Barnum his possessions, *Monsieur* Kelley?"

"Not at all. But I do envy him his business acumen. While he was in France . . ."

Monsieur Kelley paused, as if waiting for her reaction to the word "France." Angelique kept her face expressionless.

"While he was in Paris," Monsieur Kelley continued, "the estate of a Russian prince was auctioned off. There were many valuable pieces, including silver flatware, a gold tea set, and some rare china. The items could have commanded enormous bids, but their value had been diminished by the fact that they bore the prince's monogram and coat of arms."

Angelique stifled a second gasp. Bloody oath! Lulled by the snake's deceptively hushed tone, she suddenly realized that his hand cradled her elbow.

Snakes have no hands, she thought incoherently. And yet this reptilian rascal was expertly guiding her toward the walnut staircase.

His fingers were as gentle as she remembered, and the gesture felt familiar, even after all this time. She wanted to pull away, express indignation at his assumption that she would yield to his grasp, but curiosity overwhelmed her. He hadn't finished his anecdote, and she suspected he was leading up to something profound and personal. She would not admit that she enjoyed his warm palm against her elbow, his fingers lightly, almost negligibly, stroking her arm.

Truth be told, she could no more sever *Monsieur* Kelley's silky filaments than a bee could sever the complex filaments of a spider's web. She hoped that, once she found her voice again, she'd be able to *sting* her way free.

"Barnum bought the prince's entire lot," *Monsieur* Kelley said, leading her out onto the third-floor piazza. "The prince's initials were P. T., so Barnum had an engraver add a final B."

"What about the coat of arms?"

"It could have been created with Phineas Taylor Barnum in mind, for the motto on the escutcheon read 'Love God and Be Merry.' "

"Is that your motto as well, *Monsieur* Kelley?"

"Yes. But I have not been very merry."

"May I ask why you have not been merry?"

"Because a rope walker whom I loved with all my heart did a moonlight flit."

"Equilibrist."

"I beg your pardon?"

"Equilibrist, not rope walker."

"What, may *I* ask, is the bloody difference?"

"A rope walker walks. An equilibrist performs. And what is a moonlight flit?"

"Moonlight flit, my beautiful *equilibrist*, means she disappeared. Like a puff of smoke."

Raising her chin, Angelique asked the question that had burned her tongue ever since Charity Barnum's introduction. "Could you not love God and make merry with your wife?"

"Ah," Monsieur Kelley said.

"Do you mean 'ah, the equilibrist discovered my secret' or 'ah, it is the reason she did a moonlight flit'?"

Her venture into idiomatic English caused *Monsieur* Kelley to emit a burst of laughter that could surely be heard by the couples below, circling *Monsieur* Barnum's opulent fountain. "Hush!" Angelique stamped her foot. "Why do you laugh like a peagoose?"

"I have niver heard of your peagoose, darlin', but I would imagine a peagoose honks. A peafowl is an ornamental pheasant, the peahen is the female peafowl, and the *peacock* has a greatly elongated tail that can be erected and spread at will. I am fairly certain they niver laugh, either. It is the hyena that laughs."

Angelique tried to maintain her composure. She had, of course, learned the word peagoose from Gertie, and now she felt like one. "Why, may *I* ask, does my misery incite a chorus of snickers and snorts, *Monsieur* Hyena?"

"It is happy I am that you're miserable, *Mademoiselle* Peahen."

"Oh!" Enraged, she turned to leave the piazza, but he gently grasped her shoulders and pulled her against the length of his body. With her back against his chest, she could not see his face, yet she felt his tense thigh muscles and wondered how that was possible. Wouldn't her skirt and petticoats ensure an impenetrable obstacle?

"I have been disconsolate too, Angelique," he huffed into her ear. "Niver knowin' how my stepmother accomplished her flummery."

"I did not say I was disconsolate . . . your stepmother?"

"Aye, lass."

"The lady in mourning was your stepmother? She said her papa had died and left her a small fortune. She gave me a portion of her inheritance. I did not want to take it, but she became so upset I thought she would swoon if I refused."

"Hortense swoons at her convenience, and the only thing she mourned was my neglect, once I had seen you. Her papa is alive, or at least he was, though I suspect he became a bit paddy-whacked when his daughter Hortense, my *stepmother*, discovered the loss of her favorite reticule. I pray daily that my five-year-old stepsister, Charlotte, was able to maintain an innocent demeanor, for it was little Charlotte who pinched Hortense's beaded reticule, filled with her da's guilt money. Charlotte gave the reticule to me. She said I must search for the small angel who'd stolen my heart."

"But the lady in black said God would strike her dead if she was not a Kelley. *Mon Dieu,* that wicked woman wed your papa."

"Aye, lass. That pawky witch wed my father, Timothy Kelley. Hortense and Timothy were made from the same tattered cloth. 'Tis lucky you and I were cut from a stronger fabric, Angelique, for I swear by all that's holy that I'll not be losin' you again."

Sean's beguiling brogue whiffed inside her ear. Her back was still against his broad chest, and she felt his fingers trace her bodice, as though he contemplated the fit of her gown. Apparently satisfied, he circled her heart breast with his first finger. Her nipple grew taut and quivered, not unlike the magic jumping beans sold to Cirque patrons. Angelique shivered with delight, even as she realized that she must immediately annul this *affaire*.

Bloody oath, but she missed the Cirque, missed her freedom, missed her independence. Just like her corset, she was now restricted to drab ladylike activities and drab gowns. Auntie Bernadette had even picked out a drab, wealthy fiancé, although Angelique openly scoffed at the idea of a husband and repeatedly whispered her vow to remain chaste and unwed.

However, all thoughts of her suitable suitor fled when Sean turned her around and traced the soft, moist, inner edges of her lips with his tongue. Quick as a wink, she dismissed her vow to remain chaste. Eagerly, she opened her mouth and shut her eyes and pressed herself so close to his body, she could smell whiskey, tobacco, and boot leather. A moan forced its way up her throat. Her heart felt the gravitational pull of a forward somersault. She had never performed the forward, and that very thought caused her to pull away.

"I am a virgin," she confessed in French, her cheeks hot, her eyes downcast.

"I niver doubted that for a moment," he said, tucking one of her errant curls behind her ear. "We shall be wed before we—"

"*Non.*"

"What do you mean, no? Are you sayin' you'll not marry me?"

"I am saying that our marriage would be a . . . what is the bloody English word? Hindrance? Obstacle?"

He snorted. "I cannot be dissuaded, if that is what's fretting you."

"Sean, you know nothing about my family, my life, my corset!" she cried.

"Your corset?"

"My aunt, who is my guardian, merely tolerates my uncle's friendship with *Monsieur* Barnum. She admires and respects wealth, but she abhors *Monsieur* Barnum's menial background. And his fame. Especially his fame."

"This is America, lass. Your aunt can refuse to bestow a blessing on our marriage. That is her God-given right, but she cannot forbid it."

"You would wed me without permission? Without a marriage portion?"

"Who has been filling your head with such twaddle, Angelique? In Brooklyn, where I reside, one does not speak of marriage portions. Still, you bring me a great gift." He gave her the most beautiful smile she'd ever seen. "Someday I shall own a circus, the finest in all the world, and you shall perform. But only if it pleasures you to do so. If it does not, you can run our household and raise our daughters, like Charity Barnum does for her husband."

"Suppose we have sons?"

"We shall have daughters, but they'll not play the equilibrist."

"What will they play, *mon* Sean?"

"Equestrians. Should our wee lassies fall from their horses, it is not such a lengthy journey to the ground."

"I would rather be high enough to count the stars."

"And so you shall be, lass, as soon as we are wed."

Angelique looked up at his face, at his earnest expression revealed by the capricious moonlight. *I would follow this man to the ends of the earth,* she thought. She heard music—*Monsieur* Barnum's pianist, Old Blind Joe, who could hear a song once and play it perfectly. She knew that *Monsieur* Barnum's entertainment, prior to Charity Barnum's sit-down dinner, included excerpts from a melodrama called *The Drunkard,* which portrayed the evils of alcohol.

"This time I have the carriage, *Monsieur* Kelley," she said. "My uncle drove us here in a brougham. I propose that we leave *Madame* Barnum's 'small' dinner party, congested by so many people that we shall not be missed, and find a secluded place to plight our troth, perhaps return one half an hour later."

"*Non, mademoiselle,*" he said. "What I have in mind for you would take longer than half an hour." A solemn expression transformed his face. "In truth, we must say our marriage vows first."

"After we prove how much we love God, may we be merry, *mon* Sean?"

He let loose with another delighted whoop of laughter, just before he lowered his head and gave Angelique a kiss that seared her lips and sealed their bargain.

As Sean encircled Angelique's waist and guided her back toward the dinner party, he wished he could tell little Charlotte that he had found *Mademoiselle* Cinderella and kissed her awake.

At the same time, he wondered how his stepsister fared. He fully intended to bring her over to America as soon as he could, even if it took donkey's years. Hortense wouldn't give a shite, would in fact be delighted to be rid of the girl.

One again he heard the echo of Charlotte's voice: *I do not believe my father is asleep. He is just lost.*

Asleep or lost, America was too vast a territory to search for Timothy Kelley.

Nonetheless, Sean couldn't help wondering what his rogue of a father was up to.

He pictured Timothy slapping the gob. In other words, kissing someone.

Most likely a hatchet-faced spinster.
With an inheritance.

CHAPTER FOURTEEN:
TIMOTHY KELLEY BEMOANS HIS FATE

Boston, Massachusetts
April, 1849

Timothy Kelley made a sound that was half grunt, half sigh. It had been three long years since he'd first set foot upon the cobbled path that led up to Buckingham Manor, James and Caroline Clutterbuck's estate.

Upon alighting from the top of the carriage on that fateful day in 1846, he had been thunderstruck by his first sight of the Clutterbuck house. Three stories high, the carved decorations included trefoils, flowing tracery, and, at prominent lookouts, gargoyles. The large gargoyles, he later learned, directed water away from the building. Most people thought them ugly. Timothy thought them beautiful.

The grounds surrounding the house were as breathtaking as the house itself. They included a walled garden, a shrub and rose garden, a bowling green, an outdoor tea room, and a stairway zigzagging along a rough-cut limestone wall that led to a grassy slope topped with a statue of Diana, the goddess of the hunt. No wonder Mr. Clutterbuck had compared Annie Laurie to Diana. Annie Laurie could have posed for the sculptor.

A creek-fed millpond and a man-made, brick-lined reservoir, located behind the statue of Diana, provided water for the estate. The greenest grass Timothy had ever seen—and that included Ireland—was interrupted at intervals by flower beds.

Once winter had reluctantly melted into spring, song

sparrows perched on birdbaths, in harmony with horned larks and red-winged blackbirds. Leafy shade trees looked like parasols, and clipped hedges separated the lawn from a path that led to the stables—which, for the last three years, had been Timothy's home.

Three years! Time seemed to fly as speedily as the chimney swift, a bird Timothy found fascinating. Chimney swifts ate entirely in flight, dining on flies, beetles, termites, flying ants, bees, wasps, and moths. The Boston chimney swift was the only bird that built its nest and raised its young in chimneys. Mr. Clutterbuck, who seemed to know more about birds than Timothy knew about horses, had once told Timothy that chimney swifts "copulated on the wing."

Three years! And here he stood, giving off an odor of dung while brushing scratchy hay from his perspiring face, no further along in his plan to become wealthy than he'd been when his two feet first landed on American soil. Or, in his case, the Boston dock.

Right now, his future seemed to *be* American soil. And dirt. And mud. And manure.

He smelled polished leather, hay, oats, and, of course, dung and heard the horses snorting, their hooves striking their stalls. They could have been striking a death knell for Timothy, otherwise known as "Paddy." Mr. Clutterbuck had never given him a last name, and every once in a while Timothy wondered if he'd ever had one. Long ago, upon reaching France, Molly had posed for a daguerreotype, but Timothy had lost it on the coffin ship, and the nighttime and daylight dreams of his lost love grew shadowy, along with the fading image in his mind's eye.

Instead, he dreamed of freedom.

Timothy heaved a deep sigh. Three years of hard labor and boredom, only relieved by an occasional Sunday morning rendezvous with Annie Laurie Cloncannon, now and forever called "Bridget," who did not have a last name either. The first Sunday subsequent to his arrival, while Mr. and Mrs. Clutterbuck were attending church services, Timothy had managed to steal some grog, most of which he gave to Annie Laurie, who shyly confessed she'd never swallowed a drop of hard liquor before. Then, up in the hayloft, he caressed every inch of her bountiful body, carefully holding his own desire back until, tight as Dick's hatband, she eagerly urged his entry.

Her owl-wide stare and glassy eyes were a bit disconcerting, but not as disconcerting as her high-pitched scream when he finally entered what Hortense had called her "thatched cottage" or, on more than one occasion, her "cupid's arbor."

Wondering if Annie Laurie's scream had been a cry of pain or delight, his self query had been answered by her litany—in Gaelic—of *"Níos mó, níos mó, níos mó."* He'd been thrilled by her "more, more, more" and had mounted her anew, but as soon as his *péineas* penetrated her *faighean,* she'd turned her head and vomited grog.

Luckily, none of her spew had stained his unmentionables. That would have been hard to explain. So would a pregnancy, so Timothy always pulled out before spilling his seed.

Come to think of it, Annie Laurie had not paid him a visit in a month of Sundays. Startled by the thought, he realized that he preferred to use the Clutterbucks' "church time" to read one of the books he'd pilfered from Mr. Clutterbuck's vast library. He had especially liked The *Last of the Barons* by E. Bulwer Lytton and, to his surprise, *Jane Eyre,* by Charlotte Brontë, not his usual fare. He tended to avoid books written by women. Even if he hadn't kept away from books written by females, the Clutterbuck bookshelves were heavily inhabited by males.

The name Charlotte Brontë brought to mind his daughter, and he wondered how she was getting along. Would Hortense be a good mum? He thought not. Someday he hoped to bring Charlotte to America.

Timothy shook his head at that idea. *Jaysus*, he didn't even have enough of a stake to ride away from Buckingham Manor. And unless some sort of miracle occurred, he never would.

With another heavy sigh, he walked toward a high-pitched whinny that sounded eerily like Annie Laurie's ecstatic screams when she and Timothy indulged in what Mr. Clutterbuck called horizontal pleasures. The whinny stemmed from the Dutch-style door of the third stall. Inside was a Piebald mare. Timothy's mare.

As always, he felt the pride of ownership, carefully hidden when Mrs. Clutterbuck was nearby. She didn't take kindly to his right of possession and was loudly vocal in her disapproval, screeching that a green nigger had no right to own property, be it land, house, or horse.

Mr. Clutterbuck had won the piebald in a game of cards. The man who'd lost the mare to Mr. Clutterbuck's full house, ace high, was not overly dismayed. Because the piebald was a kicker.

Mrs. Clutterbuck wanted Mr. Clutterbuck to sell the horse. Or kill the horse. The hair, hide, bones, and organs could be used for fertilizer, she said.

Mr. Clutterbuck said he'd sell the piebald or give it away—assuming someone would take it—if it continued to kick. On the other hand, if Paddy could cure the kicking, he'd give *him* the horse.

Timothy was tempted to get down on his knees and thank God. Instead, ignoring Mrs. Clutterbuck's squeal of dismay, he thanked Mr. Clutterbuck.

He could scarcely believe his good fortune. Molly's Saint Padraig had been a kicker, too, and Timothy had listened and learned well when an elderly Irish jockey, his face hidden by pipe smoke, had related the reason for the kicking and then taught Timothy what to do to stop it.

Horses were an instinctive herd animal, the old jockey, who looked like a leprechaun, had said, and they behaved according to a "herd pecking order." Therefore, horses fighting for dominance often displayed aggressive behaviors—like kicking—until the other horses backed down and showed respect.

Timothy began by placing the black-and-white mare in a round pen and moving her around it, changing directions several times. If she turned to face him or came toward him without his permission, he used a rope at her hindquarters but didn't hit her. Eventually, and patiently, he employed a rope halter with a long lead—until she accepted him as dominant.

The same color as the plumage on a magpie, the mare looked like she had been splashed with black and white paint. Timothy named her Meaige, Gaelic for magpie. Mr. Clutterbuck, who had trouble remembering much less pronouncing Meaige, called her Maggie.

Meaige continued to kick in her stall, to get attention or demand food. Timothy shaped a leather bracelet with a chain attached and fastened the bracelet to her kicking leg so that, when she kicked, the chain hit her in the leg.

That completed the cure. Mr. Clutterbuck kept his promise. And despite Mrs. Clutterbuck's rage, Meaige, or Maggie, was well and truly Timothy's mare.

CHAPTER FIFTEEN:
MR. CLUTTERBUCK HAS A REQUEST

Huddled in the corner of the barn, his knees up, his back against the wall, Timothy sang a song he had learned from Cook. "Den lubly Fan, will you come out to night, will you come out to night, will you come out to night; den lubly Fan will you come out to night, and . . . dance by de light ob de moon." Cradled on his lap, facedown, was the latest book he'd filched from Mr. Clutterbuck's library.

Suddenly a voice said, "Have you finished with the horses, Paddy? And I believe the 'lubly Fan' is now a Boston girl."

Timothy had been so engrossed in his song, he hadn't heard Mr. Clutterbuck's footsteps; had not even smelled the soap the laundress used to scrub Mr. Clutterbuck's clothes.

"Boston girls will you come out tonight?" he asked, as he desperately searched for a place to hide the book.

"Yes, only it's 'gals,' not 'girls.' The song was written by a blackface minstrel named John Hodges, who performs as 'Cool White.' Because of the song's popularity, minstrels have changed the lyrics to suit local audiences, so it might be performed as 'Buffalo Gals' in Buffalo or 'Boston Gals' here in Massachusetts. And please don't bother."

"Sir?"

"Don't bother trying to hide *The Three Musketeers*. I know you steal books from my library."

"Borrow, sir. Borrow, not steal."

"I know that, too. Because of your honesty, I told Cook to allow you access to the room."

Why that sly minx. Cook made it sound as though she'd lose her position if—

"Do not, under any circumstance, let Mrs. Clutterbuck catch you. It would be instant dismissal. For Bridget, as well. Do you understand?"

As Timothy rose to his feet, he placed his finger alongside Athos, Porthos, Aramis, and d'Artagnan, to hold his place in the book. "Yes, sir, I understand. And yes, Mr. Clutterbuck, I have finished tending to the horses." *But not the barn. I still have to shovel—*

"Mrs. Clutterbuck and I are hosting an important dinner party tonight, and I need you to help serve."

"Serve? You need me to serve?" Timothy couldn't have been more astonished if Mr. Clutterbuck had said he needed Timothy to bathe a butt-naked Mrs. Clutterbuck.

"I need you to keep the water glasses full and the wine flowing, and then perform some of the same duties for the gents in the smoking room, immediately following the meal."

"But Mrs. Clutterbuck—"

"Has no choice. My butler is attending a family funeral and will not return until Monday. My underbutler, who is my butler's bloody son, is also attending the funeral, and my groom of the chamber is—"

"Groom of the chamber? Beggin' your pardon for the interruption, sir, but what is a groom of the chamber?"

Mr. Clutterbuck scowled. "A valet, Paddy. You know what a valet is, do you not?"

"Yes, sir." *Someday I plan to have one!*

"Mrs. Clutterbuck prefers the designation 'groom of the chamber.' At any rate, while my groom of the chamber has impeccable taste in men's clothing and knows everything, true or false, about the latest fashions from abroad, he is addicted to absinthe and could not hold a dinner tray steady if his life depended on it. Unfortunately, Bridget, who has served my gentlemen guests on two or three occasions, is . . . indisposed."

"Indisposed?" Timothy felt his heart clench as he remembered how his beloved Molly had coughed her heart out. "What's wrong with Annie Laur—with Bridget, sir? Is she very ill? I beg of you, please tell me what's wrong with her. Is she dying?"

"Tarnation, Paddy, you look as if you're about to keel over. Bridget has a debilitating belly ache, that's all. From her 'flowers.' She's in her flowers."

"Her flowers," Timothy echoed.

"Her monthly visitor, you numskull! Cook, an indelicate soul, calls it 'the red tide.' "

"Oh. *Oh.*" Timothy felt relief wash over him. Then a second feeling of relief when he realized that meant Annie Laurie wasn't with child. He had tried to avoid spilling his seed, but he was never certain he'd pulled out in time. After all, he could have sworn he'd pulled out of Hortense in time, even though she was so tight, her "thatched cottage" captured what she called his "silent flute" and wouldn't let go. His wife . . . his true wife . . . wasn't much to look at, was in fact as plain as a hole in a grindstone, but he had to admit she copulated like a cat on hot bricks.

"I will be happy to help serve at your posh dinner, Mr. Clutterbuck," Timothy said. "However, my trousers, I mean my unmentionables—"

"Are not at all appropriate. Cook will provide you with the necessary attire." He screwed up his nose like a rabbit. "She will also provide you with soap and hot water."

"For me to wash up. Yes, sir, I appreciate—"

"It doesn't really matter what you wear, Paddy, as long as your garments are dark and your feet are suitably shod. And, of course, you must smell clean. I promised Mrs. Clutterbuck you'd be 'invisible,' and the odor of the stables would undoubtedly negate that promise. I know you are smart, a great deal smarter than you let on would be my presumption, but if you say one word to my guests in the dining room or the gents in the smoking room, I will dismiss you myself. Immediately! Do you understand?"

"Yes, sir." *Yes, I'll stay mute, Mr. Clutterbuck, but there's nothing wrong with my ears. You cannot stop me from listening, and I might hear something of value. In fact, this could be the opportunity I've been waiting and praying for.*

Mr. Clutterbuck took *The Three Musketeers* from Timothy and flipped through its pages. "It's a damn shame Bridget is indisposed," he finally said, shutting the book with such a distinct thump, Timothy cringed.

"Damn shame," Mr. Clutterbuck repeated. "The men like to look at her, and the women appreciate her demeanor. My wife trained her well. Bridget is docile but won't be bullied. She's gentle yet spirited. She knows when to hold her tongue and when to use it."

And how to use it, thought Timothy, hiding a grin within a discreet cough.

"In fact," Mr. Clutterbuck continued, "if it was Mrs. Clutterbuck who was indisposed, Bridget could easily play hostess, and no one would think she did not belong at the foot of the table. In one sense she reminds me of Pygmalion's statue. In classical mythology Pygmalion was a sculptor who carved an ivory statue of a maiden and fell in love with it. When Aphrodite's festival day arrived, Pygmalion made offerings at the altar of Aphrodite and wished for a bride who looked like his statue. When he got home, he kissed his statue and found that its lips felt warm. He kissed it again and found the ivory had lost its hardness. You see, Aphrodite had granted Pygmalion's wish. I've read Ovid's narrative many times, Paddy, and the ivory statue with the warm lips? The statue that came to life? I'd take an oath that Ovid had Annie Laurie in mind when he wrote his poem."

Timothy had no idea who Ovid was, but as he retrieved *The Three Musketeers* from Mr. Clutterbuck's outstretched hand, he stored the name away in the recesses of his mind.

"Yes, sir, I'm sure that's true," he belatedly replied as Mr. Clutterbuck left the stables.

The sun was beginning to set when Timothy finished his despicable chores. Walking toward the manor, eager to serve Mr. Clutterbuck's "gents" and perhaps hear something of great importance, or at least something useful, he tripped over a rut in the path, a small groove he habitually stepped across with long-legged ease. Because it suddenly occurred to him that Mr. Clutterbuck had called "Bridget" Annie Laurie.

CHAPTER SIXTEEN:
TIMOTHY SERVES MR. CLUTTERBUCK'S
DINNER GUESTS

Miserable and shaky, Timothy stood in the dining room, next to an ornately decorated sideboard.

He was wobbly from exhaustion, having mucked the stalls and pitched fresh hay to all of the horses as soon as Mr. Clutterbuck had left the stables. Both chores had stretched Timothy's muscles to the limit, and he'd swear on a Calvinist bible that it was easier to deliver a foal than balance a large silver tray on an uplifted hand while trying to look invisible.

Every time he bent from the waist to refill a glass or goblet with water or wine, he was certain his borrowed shirt, his borrowed black frock coat, and his borrowed trousers would rip apart at the seams. Mr. and Mrs. Clutterbuck's butler was as tall as Timothy, but he had to weigh two stone less. According to Americans, that would be twenty-eight pounds.

White silk stockings trussed Timothy's legs and rose to his knees, or rather just below his knees, and the only black shoes that could be found pinched something awful. He felt as if his toes were on fire.

Furthermore, he had not heard one thing of interest.

Slowly, carefully, he moved his head from side to side, afraid it would be forever fused in one place, like the sculptor's statue before Aphrodite granted his wish. What was the sculptor's name again? Pig something.

Evidently Mrs. Clutterbuck considered a bare room to be in poor taste, so she had filled every empty space with furniture and bric-a-brac. A looking glass dominated one wall, making the room appear larger than it was, not that it was a small room. The ceiling boasted a crystal chandelier with so many candles, Timothy couldn't count them all. Wooden planks, like the deck of a ship, had been applied below the chair rail and above the skirting board, and—

Timothy dismissed the décor. He was more interested in the table settings, which he filed away in the same place he'd filed Ovid—for future reference, if needed.

Each place setting included a small plate atop a large plate, two large knives, a small knife and fork for fish, three large forks, a big spoon for soup, a small oyster-fork for raw oysters, a wine glass, and a water goblet.

The knives and oyster fork had been placed on the right side of the plate, the other forks on the left. Bread had been sliced thin and laid on a *serviette* to the left of each plate, while glasses had been placed at the right of each plate.

The dinner itself had started with raw oysters, followed by a choice of two soups: hare soup and something yellow. The soups had been followed by fish and vegetables, then meat—a roast joint in front of Mr. Clutterbuck, a fowl in front of Mrs. Clutterbuck. Plates of kidneys, sweetbreads, and cutlets had been carried around the table by servants, who then served jellies, creams, trifles, and confections. Finally, the salad greens from Mr. Clutterbuck's own paddock were offered, along with cheese, celery, radishes, and cucumbers.

Timothy imagined himself carving the roast joint, his own servants silently clearing the plates from each course. However, despite Mr. Clutterbuck's rapturous admiration for Annie Laurie, Timothy couldn't picture her carving the fowl. To his surprise, he could envision Hortense not only carving the fowl, but conversing with the other ladies. She'd talk about P. T. Barnum and General Tom Thumb's visit to London, of course, but he had a feeling the ladies would be captivated by her tales. Perhaps the men, as well.

Before he hosted *his* dinner, he'd treat his guests to a performance by Cool White, that fellow Mr. Clutterbuck had mentioned. *Boston gals won't you come out tonight, come out—* He swallowed a heavy sigh.

Before taking up his post next to the gleaming mahogany sideboard, a beautiful piece of carved wood—though its appearance was spoiled by four oversized, crocheted doilies on top— Timothy had heard Cook say two vegetables would be served with the fish and two vegetables with the meat, but potatoes should never be offered with fish. Yet another fact to be stored away, even though Timothy had no idea when, or even if, he'd ever use it. Or, for that matter, why potatoes with fish were forbidden. He had a feeling it had something to do with the bible.

Right now the guests were being served fruits, bonbons, and anchovy toast.

He had strained so hard to hear something of importance, he was certain his ears would soon fall off and land on the silver tray, in between the decanters of wine and water. Or, even worse, plunge to the marble floor where they'd be stepped on by his too-tight shoes.

Mr. Clutterbuck's gents talked endlessly about politics, about President Polk, who, true to his campaign pledge to serve only one term, had returned to Tennessee in March and, unfortunately—or as one man put it, deservedly—died of cholera three months later.

All but two of the men did not like President Taylor, who differed with Democrats over the concept of a strong national bank and opposed the extension of slavery into areas where neither cotton nor sugar could be grown. One man said that President Taylor did not support strong protective tariffs, while another man with a deep southern accent said that Taylor's opposition to secession as a means of resolving the nation's problems was "culpable." A third man said that someone should poison the cherries and iced milk that President Taylor liked to drink at outdoor events. All of the gents, including Mr. Clutterbuck, laughed at that implication.

The women sounded as if they'd been let loose from a hen house. They clucked on and on about magazines called *Graham's* and *Peterson's* and *Miss Leslie's*. Another magazine, called Union-something, included two to three fine art engravings every month, designed to be pulled out and displayed, featuring the work of a group of American artists.

Timothy remembered seeing *Graham's* and *Miss Leslie's* in the library, but, needless to say, he'd never opened them.

One woman with a glittering necklace and a sagging bosom went on, endlessly, about a play she'd seen called *Glance at New York,* an "entertaining look at life on the streets" with street gangsters known as the "Bowery B'hoys." The show, she said, offered several musical numbers that included barroom ballads and other popular tunes. Once again, Timothy was reminded of Hortense and her innumerable P. T. Barnum and Tom Thumb tales. He could hear her relating the tale of Tom Thumb fencing Queen Victoria's pet poodle. She would have been feted and adored.

Finally, when he was certain he'd either yell, "Go fecking home, you waggish, lean-witted prigs!" or melt to the floor in a puddle of water, wine, and sweat, the men and women stood up, stretched, belched, emitted several farts, and adjusted their clothing.

Mrs. Clutterbuck then said the ladies would "retire" to the drawing room while the men held "an important meeting" in the smoking room.

Cook had shown Timothy the smoking room before the

guests were due to arrive. His first impression was: *velvet.* Velvet curtains. And furniture upholstered with velvet. Cook said that, when he was by himself, Mr. Clutterbuck "wore a velvet smoking jacket." The velvet absorbed smoke, she said, and kept its odor from the rest of the house.

The room also boasted a gun collection, several books—what Cook called "worldly books"—and a tall pile of newspapers at the head of a long table.

Were the newspapers important? Timothy thought they might be *very* important, but Cook had shooed him out of the room before he could take a look.

Timothy shook his head, brought his attention back to the task at hand, and followed the eleven guests and Mr. Clutterbuck through an arched doorway, into the smoking room. Atop that room's sideboard were bottles of hard apple cider, Old Crow Bourbon, and a decanter of water.

After filling glasses, Timothy stepped back and leaned his hips against the sideboard. Mr. Clutterbuck, who stood at the head of the table, nodded at Timothy and told him to "place the potable liquids on the table and leave the room."

No! Jaysus, no! Please, Mr. Clutterbuck, not after standing all night, clothed in too-small attire and too-tight shoes. Your order to leave the room shows me that something of great significance is sure to be discussed, and I want to hear what it is.

Although his plea had been silent, Mr. Clutterbuck quirked one of his sparse eyebrows and said, "Are you hard of hearing, Paddy?" Turning to the men, he said, "Caroline and I have a devil of a time finding good servants."

"I know what you mean," said the man with the deep southern accent. "The missus and I have a hell of a time findin' good slaves. We are, however, well pleased with Joshua, the stable boy I stole from under your nose. He's grown some and is bigger than Theo, the brother who begged me to hire him. I promised Joshua he could work the fields, an' he's become a hell of an overseer who can manage my darkies with one or two flicks of the whip. He has a habit of gettin' my prettiest negresses too heavy with child to carry out their duties proper-like, but you take the good with the bad, eh?"

Mr. Clutterbuck's look of disgust mirrored Timothy's, but before Mr. Clutterbuck could respond, a man with a chain of hair under his chin and hair on each side of his mouth, forming, with his moustache, something that looked like a door-knocker, curled his lips in what passed for a smile. "I'll be happy to take Bridget off your hands, James," he said. "Name your price."

"She's not for sale, Tom, not for any price."

"Who the hell is Bridget?" asked a gent with the grotesque face of a drinking mug, a face Timothy's London mates would have called a "meanmug."

"When last I dined at this fine establishment," the gent named Tom said, "a young woman with the most beautiful cat-heads and, in my knowledgeable opinion, the sweetest derrière I've ever seen served me kidneys, cutlets, and whiskey."

"How could you see her derrière?" Meanmug's eyes gleamed. "Was she unclothed?"

"Certainly not," Tom replied, "but servants don't have to wear those repugnant wire frameworks that hide their apple cheeks."

Mr. Clutterbuck said, "The man who came up with wire 'bird cages' and stuffed pads to be worn under a woman's skirt should be hanged from the highest tree."

Timothy silently agreed.

"But you were not invited here to discuss women's fashions," Mr. Clutterbuck continued. Still standing, he turned and said, "Paddy, place the bottles on the table and leave the room straight away, before I give you the boot."

"Yes, sir. Without delay, sir."

As Mr. Clutterbuck circled Meanmug's shoulders and led him toward the corner of the room, Timothy laid the silver tray on top of the stack of newspapers. He carefully placed the bottles on the table and then, even more carefully, wriggled his fingers underneath the stack's top pages. He could feel his heart pounding too fast, like the thundering hooves of a thousand wild horses, but Mr. Clutterbuck was still conversing with Meanmug and had now been joined by the doorknocker-faced man named Tom.

Mr. Clutterbuck said, "Shut the door behind you, Paddy."

"Yes, sir," Timothy called over his shoulder, his heart still pounding, even though a thousand thundering horse hoofs had become ten or twelve.

If Mr. Clutterbuck discovered the theft of his newspapers, Timothy was done like a dinner, although he was more than half certain Mr. Clutterbuck would keep Annie Laurie in his employ. After all, he had told the doorknocker-man she wasn't for sale, "not for any price."

On the other hand, any downstairs maid or houseboy could have stolen the pages. Timothy need only say, "You saw me the whole time, Mr. Clutterbuck, and you know I'm not a thief, so please tell me how I could have got clean away with anything except your silver tray. And I assure you, sir, that Cook has your tray in her possession. Just ask her."

Upon reaching the door, Timothy turned and gave Mr. Clutterbuck a mock bow, a needless gesture since Mr. Clutterbuck was still deep in conversation.

As Timothy's bowed head reached his knees, he felt his too-tight unmentionables give way in the arse.

The next morning, after watching Mr. and Mrs. Clutterbuck and their sons ride off toward the road that led to their god-fearing Presbyterian Church, Timothy climbed the ladder to the loft, where he sat with his back against a bale of hay, underneath the hayloft's large opening that looked like a glassless window.

Very carefully, he laid out the stolen newspaper pages.

Despite his exhaustion, despite an aching body that cried out for relief from his hours of standing and pretending to be invisible, he had barely slept. Instead, more often than not, he had paced up and down the stable floor. Paying no heed to the nervous nickering of his piebald or the equally nervous whinnies of Lucky, Emperor, and Mr. Clutterbuck's chestnut gelding, Zeus, Timothy had cursed the dark, moonless sky and waited impatiently for the sun to come up.

Upon discovering Timothy's ruined trousers and the sight of his exposed buttocks, Cook had laughed, swatted his rump with a lingering hand and then dismissed him, so he'd lost any chance to read Mr. Clutterbuck's newspapers by the light of the dining room or kitchen. The stable was too dim, and he dared not stand at the well-lit entrance to the manor, nor linger in front of the servants' entrance with its one oil lamp outside and too few wall sconces inside.

Annie Laurie would not be paying him a visit today if she still had a belly ache, and if she was in perfect health, rather than "indisposed," she had hoodwinked Mr. and Mrs. Clutterbuck and would not chance a walk away from her room or the manor.

Why would she hoodwink Mr. and Mrs. Clutterbuck? Perhaps during the last dinner party, the doorknocker-faced gent who told Mr. Clutterbuck he wanted to buy Annie Laurie had groped her breasts—what he'd called her cat-heads—or cornered her between the smoking room and the kitchen for further exploration, and she had devised a scheme to escape his scrutiny.

He needed to stop pondering the absence of Annie Laurie and read the stolen pages.

The first page was from a newspaper called *The California Herald,* dated 17 March, 1848. In large letters it said: GOLD FOUND! But the bottom of the silver tray had been too damp, if not out-and-out wet, because the smaller print was blurry, unreadable—

Gold?

The second page was from the *New York Herald,* dated 7 April, 1849, and the print was legible. Lowering his head, Timothy read:

"Hurrah! Here we are at last! The Land of Promise—*El Dorado* of the West. Our own bright, beautiful, bountiful California lies before us, her lap full of riches. Any strong, able-bodied man who is willing to labor five or six hours a day in the broiling sun can make from $10 to $20 per day for three or four months in the year."

Ten to twenty dollars a day?

Timothy discarded that page and almost ripped apart the next page in his eagerness to read what it said. It began in the middle of an article, so there was no date. The print danced before his eyes. He blinked several times to clear his vision.

". . . to enable our distant readers to draw some idea of the extent of the gold mine, we will confine our remarks to a few facts," the article continued. "The country from the Ajuba to the San Joaquin Rivers, a distance of about one hundred and twenty miles, and from the base toward the summit of the mountains, as far as Snow Hill, about seventy miles, has been explored and gold found on every part. There are now probably 3,000 people, including Indians, engaged collecting gold. The amount collected by each man who works ranges from $10 to $350 per day. The publisher of this paper, while on a tour alone to the mining district, collected, with the aid of a shovel, pick, and tin pan, about twenty inches in diameter, from $44 to $128 a day—averaging $100. The gross amount collected will probably exceed $600,000, of which amount our merchants have received about $250,000 worth for goods sold; all within the short space of eight weeks. The largest piece of gold known to be found weighed four pounds."

Four pounds? Four fecking pounds?

The last stolen page had a map of the California gold fields and two advertisements for clipper ships leaving from New York harbor, bound for San Francisco.

Timothy's heart sank when he saw the amount of money he'd need to book passage on a clipper ship, and of course there was no steerage, not that he'd ever endure steerage again.

How the bloody hell can I get passage money? Or, for that matter, the funds I'd need to travel overland?

He climbed down from the hayloft and walked outside the building. He made sure no servant was idly watching him. Cautiously, he peered left and right, making certain, in his own mind, that no servant was lingering *anywhere* in the vicinity of the stables. He shouted, "G'day," and then waited to see if anybody answered him. When nobody did, he burned all but one of the stolen pages. The page with the map he hid inside his bedroll. While doing so, he had to laugh at the notice on the bottom of the page. It said: "Edward Giles, of Norlunga, is requested to return or write immediately."

CHAPTER SEVENTEEN:
TIMOTHY CONFRONTS ANNIE LAURIE

Monday, while currying young Master Clutterbuck's horse, Lucky, one word ran through Timothy's mind: GOLD!

Tuesday, while attending to a sore above Emperor's right fetlock, Timothy dipped his first two fingers in the salve and spelled out GOLD across the thoroughbred's heart girth and barrel.

Wednesday, while riding his black and white mare, Timothy was very nearly unseated by a low-hanging branch, his mind miles away in California.

Thursday, Friday, and Saturday, as he pitched hay to the horses, he established a rhythm of continuity sustained by a whispered chant of "California, California, California," followed by a litany of "gold-California-gold-California-gold."

And now, once again, it was Sunday, and—once again—Annie Laurie had not appeared.

She had managed to avoid him during mealtimes by sitting next to the housekeeper, Michaela Pence, a religious fanatic who ruled the roost and did not like Timothy because, she said, he was godless and smelled of the stables, no matter how carefully he washed up at the trough. So he sat apart from the others, atop a hard wooden bench, at a small table not far from the doorway. Furthermore, Miss Pence always told him to leave as soon as he finished eating. Except for his furtive trips to the library, he obeyed Mrs. Clutterbuck and Miss Pence. He had never even questioned their "rules." *But now, today, enough was enough!* He needed to know why Annie Laurie's Sunday visits had stopped. And if that meant visiting her rather than the other way around, so be it.

He also wanted to hear what the servants had to say about Mr. Clutterbuck's "important meeting." After reading the stolen papers, Timothy was more than certain the gathering of Mr. Clutterbuck's big-wigs had something to do with the discovery of gold in California, and he was fairly certain Mr. Clutterbuck was trying to arrange some sort of expedition to the gold fields. However, during the past week, meal after meal, all Timothy ascertained was that Mr. Clutterbuck had appeared at breakfast the next morning "cranky as a bear with a sore head" while Mrs. Clutterbuck kept looking at Mr. Clutterbuck "like a lizard regarding a fly."

Another servant said, "Mr. C was crabbit as a cat."

Perhaps Annie Laurie, often a personal maid to Mrs. Clutterbuck, had discovered the source of Mr. Clutterbuck's cranky mood.

Even if she hadn't, Timothy missed her. He missed her supple body under his, missed her ecstatic whinnies when his "silent flute" found her "thatched cottage," but most of all he missed her companionship. Except for Cook, he had no friends among the servants. In fact, he led a lonely life, a solitary exist—

Now don't you be gettin' all maudlin and self-pityin', Timothy Kelley. Soon you'll be holdin' an Irish wake for yourself whilst you are still alive and kickin'.

He recalled his frequent tavern excursions when he and Hortense had lived in France, at his auntie's café. He remembered fondly the drinking and the gambling and, in particular, the whores who had welcomed him with open arms . . . and open legs.

Briefly, he wished he'd stayed put.

No, he did not!

Because he knew without a single doubt that the California Gold Rush was his destiny!

It took Timothy less time to think up a scheme to visit Annie Laurie than it had taken to grieve over Annie Laurie's strange behavior.

Despite a chill April breeze, he bathed at the pond, then donned a clean shirt and trousers. All of his clothes were second-hand and so worn out, his nipples showed through during a rain. Mr. Clutterbuck had promised him new clothes, or at least better clothes, but then Timothy overheard Mrs. Clutterbuck tell Mr. Clutterbuck that "the green nigger's shirts and unmentionables were serviceable and sufficient."

Next, Timothy placed a sharp knife, in its sheath, around his waist.

He strode toward the manor, only stopping long enough to un-sheath his knife, sever the stems from a few daffodils, rhododendrons, and azaleas, then fashion the stems into a love knot.

Entering the kitchen, he saw Cook sitting in a chair by a long wooden table, her fingers busy snipping the ends of snap beans. He didn't want to startle her but had little choice. Walking up behind her, he gently laid one hand on her shoulder and, in a voice little more than a whisper, said, "G'day, me darlin'. 'Tis Paddy, with a favor to ask of your kind heart."

She leapt to her feet, spilling his hand from her shoulder and beans from her apron-clad lap. "My word, Paddy, do not sneak up on a person like that. I swear I've aged ten years!"

He cocked his head. "In that case, you look thirty rather than forty."

"Get on with you. I'm not one to be taken in by your smooth talk, your . . . blarney," she said, her red cheeks and ear-to-ear smile belying her scold. "And what, may I ask, are you doing here? The library is locked, Paddy. Somehow Mrs. Clutterbuck discovered—"

"I have no need of the library today, darlin', thank you just the same, but I do need your help in another matter."

"Are those flowers for me?" she asked, fiddling with her apron strings.

"They are for my wife, my Annie Laur—my Bridget. You see, today is our wedding anniversary. I had hoped, somehow, to replace the wedding band she lost on the boat when we came to America, but since that's impossible . . ." He paused, trying to keep the bitter taste of his words out of his voice, for it was Molly's picture, not a fake wedding band, that had been lost.

"Since you cannot give your wife a new wedding band, you wish to give her flowers," Cook said with another smile. "That's nice, Paddy. Sweet. I will give them to her."

"Thank you, but I wish to give them to her in person, perhaps steal an anniversary kiss. Do you know where she is?"

"I do not. She could be asleep in her room, or taking a walk, or even completing a task for Mrs. Clutterbuck, who has said many times that she does not consider Sunday a 'day of rest for *Cat-licks.*' "

Timothy caught the bitterness in Cook's voice. "Are you Catholic, darlin'?"

"I am, and proud of it!"

"Then perhaps you'd let a fellow Catholic sneak up to his wife's room and lay flowers on her pillow. I promise I will do it very quickly, making sure no one can see me."

"Very quickly, making sure no one can see," she repeated, and Timothy could sense her mind racing like a jog cart.

"Mr. and Mrs. Clutterbuck and their boys are at church," he said, striving to keep his voice a sincere plea, his frustration at bay, "and they will not return home until the midday meal, which you and your parlor maids are busy preparing. If an upstairs maid catches sight of me, and I swear no one will, I'll make sure she knows you had nothing to do with my trespass. Please, darlin'?"

"All right, if it's that important to you. But be quick about it. If you are caught, I shall lose my position. Bridget's bedroom is on the third floor, second door on the right. For now I am going to visit the scullery, where I cannot see you come or go."

"Nor hear me come . . . and go," he said with a wink. "Unless I sing, 'Boston gals will you come out to night, and dance by de light ob de moon.' "

"Hush! Be off with you. And it's 'lubly Fan,' not 'Boston gals'."

Clutching his bouquet of flowers, Timothy took the back staircase two steps at a time. If Annie Laurie wasn't in her bedroom, he'd search for her in the rest of the house, and then, if necessary, outside the house, leaving no stone—nor bale of hay—unturned.

I'll damn well find her, unless she's gone with Mr. and Mrs. Clutterbuck and their two sons to the family church.

As he approached the second door on the right, he heard a whimper, a moan, then another moan, and he stopped in his tracks. He had oft heard those whimpers and moans up in the hayloft. Soon she'd cry "More, more, more."

What the bloody hell!

"Oh, my God, more, more, more!"

Timothy kicked the bedroom door open and strode inside. "Well, well, well," he said, and was surprised at how unflustered he sounded. "If this isn't a sight for sore eyes."

Annie Laurie opened her mouth to scream and had let out a mousey squeak before Mr. Clutterbuck moved the palm of his hand beneath her nose and squeezed her cheeks with his fingers and thumb. "Be quiet," he said. "The door is open, and if you scream, my groom of the chamber and the upstairs maids are sure to hear you and come running."

Timothy said, "Does she not scream when you dance the kibbles? She does when I . . . what's Mrs. Clutterbuck's other favorite expression? . . . oh, yes: grind her corn."

As Timothy's gaze took in the whole room, he saw a near-empty bottle of Old Crow on the floor. He squinted at Mr. Clutterbuck, who looked sober as a judge, and he was instantly reminded of a jest he'd heard when he lived in London: *Prisoner: "I was drunk as a judge." Court: "Surely you mean 'drunk as a lord'?" Prisoner: "Yes, my lord."*

For some reason that settled Timothy's composure even more. "Better watch out, sir," he said. "Annie Laurie appears scuttered, and she cannot hold her grog."

The words had scarcely left his mouth before she fumbled at Mr. Clutterbuck's hands, clawed his fingers free, turned her head, leaned over the side of the bed, and vomited on her knickers. Mr. Clutterbuck didn't look at all appalled, nor did he appear disgusted, so Timothy knew this wasn't the first time.

"You'd better put your unmentionables on, sir," Timothy said. "We need to have a talk."

Mr. Clutterbuck rolled off the bed, stepped into his trousers, and yanked them up. Then he pointed to the doorway with his first finger and said, "Leave the room, Paddy. This very instant!"

"No, I will not, and the name is Timothy, just like Bridget's name is Annie Laurie." Timothy pulled his knife from its sheath and commenced to clean under his fingernails. "Yesterday I wondered why you called her Annie Laurie," he continued. "Now I know. And soon *Caroline* Clutterbuck will know how you and Annie Laurie spend your Sundays—"

"You wouldn't dare!"

"—when you do not attend church. And why would I not dare, *James*?" Since Mr. Clutterbuck did not seem intimidated by the knife, Timothy re-sheathed it.

"Because you shall leave my property immediately," Mr. Clutterbuck said, "or I will have you punished severely and then jailed."

"No, you will not have me punished, nor will you lock me up. And I will not leave until I've spoken to your *wife.*"

Mr. Clutterbuck cracked a smile. "It is your word against mine, Paddy. Who do you think my wife will believe?"

"I think she'll believe *my* wife, who you know, and I know, and Mrs. Clutterbuck knows, cannot hold her pish or talk shite to save her soul. In other words, Annie Laurie cannot tell a lie."

"Annie Laurie is not your wife!" Mr. Clutterbuck roared. "She is not Annie Laurie Kelley. She is Annie Laurie Cloncannon."

"By God, you know our surnames," Timothy said with a lift of his eyebrows. "I would not have believed it. Did Annie Laurie tell you she isn't my wife?"

"Yes!"

"Then that proves my point. Annie Laurie tells the truth. Should she try to lie, Mrs. Clutterbuck would not be fooled; would, in fact, ferret out the truth in less time than it would take your silent flute to invade Annie Laurie's thatched cottage."

"Silent flute? Thatched cottage?"

"Ask him what he wants, Mr. Clutterbuck," said Annie Laurie in a raspy voice.

"You still call him Mr. Clutterbuck, even after all these weeks of 'horizontal pleasures'?" Timothy gestured toward the bed with his flowers, then tossed the bouquet at Annie Laurie.

She didn't reply, merely blushed to the roots of her hair. Timothy's fresh-picked flowers landed on her breasts and shed their fragrant petals. She shook them off like a dog emerging from the water and pulled the coverlet up over her breasts until it reached her chin.

Mr. Clutterbuck scowled. "What do you want, Paddy?"

"Must I remind you that my name is Timothy?" For the first time since his arrival at Buckingham Manor, he allowed himself to openly glare at James Clutterbuck. "It feels mighty fine to have my name back," he added. "You have no idea—"

"What do you want?"

"A stake."

"A steak?" Mr. Clutterbuck shook his head as if to free it from a swarm of bees. "That's all you want? A steak? I will gladly tell Cook to prepare as many steaks—"

"Not a beefsteak, you *manky eejit*. A beefsteak would be as much use to me as a back pocket in a shirt. I want a money stake."

Mr. Clutterbuck grinned like a dead hare. "Of course you do. For what purpose?"

"That, James, is none of your business. But if you must know—"

"The California gold rush! It was you who stole my newspapers. Mrs. Clutterbuck was right. I should have left you to rot in the stables."

"I presume your gents didn't nibble at your bait. You wanted to kick off an expedition to the gold fields, did you not?"

"Manky eejits," Mr. Clutterbuck said, mimicking Timothy to perfection. "It's reasonable that they might not want to leave their comfortable homes, comfortable wives, comfortable *lives*, but they would not even consider the fortunes they could amass by contributing to my venture."

"Speaking of contributing, sir."

"How much do you want?"

When Timothy mentioned a sum, Annie Laurie's eyes widened while Mr. Clutterbuck shook his head again. However, Timothy couldn't determine whether Mr. Clutterbuck had negated the request or was simply admiring Timothy's bravado.

"I'll have the funds for you in the morning," Mr. Clutterbuck finally said.

"No, James. You'll have the funds for me now, as soon as we leave this room and before Mrs. Clutterbuck and your sons return from church. I presume you have money inside the wall safe in your library, hidden behind your Dumas collection. I've read *The Man in the Iron Mask, The Corsican Brothers, Chichot the Jester, The Forty-Five Guardsmen,* and I was looking forward to reading *The Count of Monte Cristo.*"

"You may take *The Count of Monte Cristo* with you to California, which is where, I presume, you intend to go. Do you plan to take Annie Laurie with you, as well?"

"For the past three years I've worn cast-off, second-hand clothes, a situation I plan to remedy as quickly as I can. For the last three years I've had to eat food scraps. I've eaten ice-cold porridge on ice-cold mornings, and sometimes, if Mrs. Clutterbuck isn't watching like a hawk, I've enjoyed leftover food from your majestic dinner parties. By observing how Cook prepares the food for your *grandiose* galas, I could contend with the best chefs in the land. Paris, as well. I've been fed and for that I'm thankful. I have a horse and for that I'm grateful, even though I have to tell you, James, I earned the food and my mare many times over."

"You have not answered my question."

"I believe I have. The thing is, I have no desire to cohabit with a cast-off, second-hand woman, especially when, just like my clothes, the woman has been worn so many times her stains cannot be gotten rid of, not even if I use lye soap and boiling hot water."

He heard Annie Laurie gasp and begin to cry.

"I do not want scraps," Timothy continued. "Nor leftovers. You may keep Annie Laurie, sir. Fair trade for the Dumas book."

CHAPTER EIGHTEEN:
ANGELIQUE BEMOANS HER FATE

"What am I going to do?" Angelique wailed. "Oh, dear God, what am I going to do?"

She gazed up at the ceiling, as if God clung to the large, round medallion above the oil lamp, placed there, her uncle said, so that when the soot rose from the lamp, it would dirty the medallion and not the ceiling. That way it spared him from having to repaint the whole ceiling each year when all he'd have to do was refresh the medallion.

Auntie Bernadette's "picture room," also known as Uncle Alistaire's billiards room, boasted ornately framed portraits of dead men. The deftly stroked men, none of whom cracked a smile, graced the oak-paneled walls and climbed toward the ceiling. In the middle of the room, a carom table and a billiards table, both rarely if ever used, were nevertheless *de rigueur*—or so said Auntie Bernadette. Angelique had a feeling her uncle didn't give a tinker's damn.

What's more, she had the feeling that the men depicted in Auntie Bernadette's paintings were not truly related, like her aunt said they were. And yet they had always imparted a strange sort of comfort to Angelique's oft-bruised heart.

This evening, however, they seemed to avoid her eyes.

Surrounded by Auntie Bernadette's seven cats, Angelique sat on the picture room's floor. Tears dripped from her chin, landing in the deep V of her bodice. If she had not been wearing a Bertha, her tears would have left stains on her satin, saffron-colored evening gown.

For this evening's "entertainment," one of her modest black gowns would have been much more preferable, or a day dress with a plain and simple chemisette, but Auntie Bernadette had insisted Angelique wear this horrible ball gown, even though there wasn't a ball, nor a dinner party, nor a celebratory gala in sight. Nor would there be.

On the other hand, her auntie would doubtless consider tonight a celebratory *occasion.*

Thank goodness Angelique had not yet handed over the saffron gown to Gertie. The full-skirted gown, worn over several petticoats, would have been perfect for one of Gertie's frequent, albeit secretive, servants' balls.

Angelique's stomach roiled. She wanted to rip the gown from her body, the drapes from their rods, the tightly-woven netting from the lone billiards table. With genuine tears in her eyes, she had complained of a croupy cough, an aching head, a throbbing tooth, even, somewhat desperately, a broken-winded gastric disorder, but Auntie Bernadette, unmoved, continued to insist she meet and dine with her "intended."

A hungry Tuesday meowed and rubbed against Angelique's drawn-up legs. Thursday was asleep across Angelique's lap. Friday nosed a billiard ball while Monday worried the fringe on the bottom of a red velvet settee—a piece of furniture that belonged in a drawing room and looked out of place in the midst of the "brawny" decor. None of the seven cats, including Sunday, Saturday, and Wednesday, seemed perturbed by Angelique's shuddering sighs and sobs.

She had been weeping steadily for two hours, and the cats, clever creatures, had most likely decided she had no tears left. They were "on the dot," as Gertie liked to say. After all, how much salty moisture could one person, even a woman, produce?

Enough was enough! Angelique shook her head, spraying the

last of her tears over Thursday and Sunday. A sleepy Thursday hissed, but Sunday gave Angelique a haughty glare and commenced to wash his whiskers with a dainty paw.

Flexing her fingers, Angelique allowed her mouth to quirk at the corners. After years of hauling herself up and down a rope ladder, her hands were neither dainty nor delicate. In truth, she possessed a man's overlarge hands. Perhaps Monsieur Gray would consider her paw too rough to flaunt his ring of engagement, a ring that bore his family crest and motto: *abusus non tollit usum*—"Abuse does not take away use."

She liked Sean Kelley's "Love God and Be Merry" much, much better.

It had been a fortnight since the Barnum dinner party. However, Angelique had only seen Sean once, during a tea given by Charity Barnum. Auntie Bernadette had attended the event, but Madam Barnum, still playing matchmaker, had managed to squire Angelique into her husband's private study, an orange-colored, satin-walled library.

There, Sean had given her a kiss that left her breathless. And yet he seemed preoccupied.

"Something is wrong, *Monsieur* Peacock," she had said, hoping he would smile at the pet name. When he didn't, she added, "Please tell me."

"Barnum will hand over the funds for my traveling circus," he replied, "should Jenny Lind prove to be a success."

"Jenny Lind?"

"The concert singer."

"*Oui,* I knew who you meant. My aunt says her character is 'simplicity and goodness personified.' Why would *Mademoiselle* Lind make a difference?"

"In order to pay her wages, Barnum mortgaged the contents of his American Museum and borrowed all he could."

"But why would she not be a success, *mon* Sean?"

"Barnum himself doesn't know, but Jenny has a host of . . . shall we say, qualities? . . . that might lead to the wreckage of his enterprise."

"Can she not sing? Uncle Alistaire said that Monsieur Barnum said that Jenny Lind would be adored even if she had the voice of a crow." Angelique attempted a smile "My auntie did not crow a response."

"Barnum can make that claim, aware that the glowing reviews from her Liverpool concert have been pushed into print. Do you know Jenny Lind's life story, Angelique?"

"Of course. Who does not know her story? A poor and lonely little girl, Jenny often sang in the street. One day she was overheard by a famous *danseur,* who arranged for her to audition at Stockholm's Royal Theater."

Sean remained silent for a few moments. "Jenny Lind is a bastard," he finally said. "The illegitimate child of a woman named Anna Marie Fallborg. Jenny was born in secrecy and taken, under cover, to the home of distant cousins. She was then given away to a childless couple. The *maid* of a professional dancer overheard Jenny singing to her cat, and the rest is common knowledge. Except . . ."

"Except what?"

"She has described herself as having piggy eyes and a big broad nose."

"Is it her appearance or her illegitimacy that bothers you?"

"Did you know that the Danish children's book author, Hans Christian Andersen, wrote stories about her and for her?" Sean asked, ignoring Angelique's question.

She shook her head.

"He wrote *The Angel, The Ugly Duckling,* and *The Emperor's Nightingale.* When he fell in love with her and she rejected him, he wrote *The Snow Queen.* In that story he portrays Jenny with a heart of ice. I must keep the newspapers busy with those very details so they will not dig up a scandal. I've also suggested that Barnum inaugurate a Jenny Lind song contest. Two hundred dollars shall go to the winning ode, which will then be set to music. I'd like for you to win that prize, my love."

"Me? *Mon Dieu*, I can barely think in English, much less write it."

"Your English has improved so much, you could be American-born of French parents," he said, then grinned. "I'll write the ode for you, Angelique, and your beauty will do the rest. I cannot imagine Barnum passing up the opportunity to display a beautiful woman."

"Is writing the ode for me an honest ploy?" she asked, blushing at his compliment.

"*Honest* ploy?" Sean roared with laughter, then held out his arms and pressed her face against his vest. "After Jenny Lind's opening night, we shall be wed. Does that make you happy?"

"*Non.*"

"You keep saying no to me, *Mademoiselle* Peahen," he teased, holding her at arm's length. "What bothers you now?"

"My aunt . . ."

Angelique could not find the words to tell him that Auntie Bernadette was already busy planning her niece's wedding to *Monsieur* Matthew Gray, who lived in a village called South Carolina and had a second house and farm in New York's Hudson River Valley. Jenny Lind's New York City performance was weeks away. Sean needed *Monsieur* Barnum in order to establish the Sean Kelley Circus. Angelique did not want to divert his attention from the task at hand—selling Jenny Lind to the public and keeping the details of Jenny Lind's birth a secret.

Even though they had only been in each other's presence three times, Angelique understood Sean well enough to know he'd give up his *cirque,* his dream, if he believed their future together threatened.

"I've told you before," he said, "that your aunt cannot dissuade me."

Angelique managed a nod and a smile, all the while thinking: *Somehow I must keep* Monsieur *Gray waiting for my answer. Somehow, I must poke my feet.*

"Mr. Gray is waiting, Angelique! For goodness' sake, pinch your cheeks. You look far too pale." Auntie Bernadette's strident voice interrupted Angelique's reverie, even though she had not yet arrived at the best part—the part where Sean had soothed her fears with his experienced hands and warm lips.

She shivered at the memory.

"Are you cold?" Auntie Bernadette picked up Thursday and cuddled the cat against her padded bosom.

Not sure whether the question had been directed at her or the cat, Angelique simply followed her aunt into the hallway.

Tossing Thursday back into the picture room, Auntie Bernadette set a brisk pace toward the staircase. "Don't drag your feet, Angelique," she called over her shoulder. "Mr. Gray admires punctuality and would not appreciate a slowpoke."

"I do not care what *Monsieur* Gray admires or appreciates." Trying to keep new tears at bay, Angelique took a deep breath. "I shall never marry him, for I am in love with another man."

Auntie Bernadette stopped so abruptly, Angelique very nearly plowed into her.

"Have you been playing the whore behind my back, niece?"

Angelique bit back her first response. Insulted, hurt, and furious, she wanted nothing more than to tell Auntie Bernadette that she looked and sounded like the stepmother in one of the stories by the Brothers Grimm . . . a story called *Aschenputtel*. Angelique's mother had read the story to Angelique from a book called *Grimms' Fairy Tales,* and Angelique, who had brought the book with her to Connecticut, had read it aloud to Gertie, who could not read.

In the story, an evil stepmother treated Aschenputtel horribly, favoring her own daughters, one of whom had cut off a big toe, another a part of a heel, in order to wear a golden slipper—left behind at a ball—and marry a prince. The sisters failed to fit the slipper on either foot and later had their eyes pecked out by birds. Which had appalled Angelique's mother and delighted a young Angelique.

Aschenputtel had been clever and brave, but she had a tree that helped her; a tree planted on her mother's grave; a tree she watered with her tears; a tree where, one day, Aschenputtel had discovered a beautiful gown to wear to the royal balls.

I do not have a magic tree, but I can be clever and brave.

"I ask you again, Angelique," Auntie Bernadette said. "Have you been playing the whore behind my back?"

"Oui," she fibbed. "And I am quite certain your *Monsieur* Gray would not look twice at a girl who is . . . how you say? . . . soiled? Yes, soiled, so this fine dinner is for naught."

With a sinking heart she realized her response might have been brave, but it wasn't clever. She wished she could hide in a pigeon coop or up a pear tree. That was where Aschenputtel had hidden from the prince when he'd followed her home from two of the royal balls.

But she had no pigeon coop. No pear tree. No helpful, tear-watered tree.

Underneath the lisle threads of her stockings, inside her lace-trimmed, patent leather boots, her soles tingled as she recalled Gertie's comment about Auntie Bernadette whipping a disobedient servant's feet.

The eye-opener about her aunt's mode of discipline hadn't been the least bit funny, but Gertie had burst out laughing when Angelique said, "Oh, how I wish I had some magic birds to peck Auntie Bernadette's eyes out!"

CHAPTER NINETEEN:
ANGELIQUE MEETS HER INTENDED

Monsieur Gray was old—forty-five, perhaps even fifty. Angelique felt a flush of anger color her pale cheeks, which had been pinched more than once in order to eclipse the splotch from her aunt's face slap.

The lie about playing the whore had slipped out like a false scent. The result had been a clout from her aunt's unmerciful hand, followed by a heavy application of Auntie Bernadette's face powder so *Monsieur* Gray would not see the bruise. Angelique, who had never been inside her aunt's bedroom, stumbled through the entrance and immediately felt her eyes widen. The room was so crowded with furniture and knick-knacks, there was barely room to walk.

Mr. Shakespeare's line from *The Taming of the Shrew* came to mind: "Why 'tis a cockle or a walnut-shell, a knacke, a toy, a tricke, a babies cap: Away with it."

The first thing Angelique spied was the carpet, a threadbare eyesore, with great sprawling green leaves and red blotches. She surmised it had once been downstairs, perhaps in the dining room. Furnishings consisted of a central table, a wardrobe, a toilette table, three chairs, and a chiffonier. Auntie Bernadette's clothes hung from pegs or were folded into boxes. The boxes sat on the floor or fought for space on the chairs. Angelique's gaze took in the four-poster bed with curtains, then a wash-stand, then a chamber pot with a lid. She had a sudden urge to use the chamber pot but managed to resist until the urge went away. Meanwhile, she swallowed a sigh when she thought of Gertie's room, cold and damp in the winter and hot in summer, with little light coming in from the one small window. Gertie had been given a thin blanket and a locked box in which she kept her circus costumes and a few personal items, but her room was subject to inspection by Auntie Bernadette, who could insist Gertie open the box.

When she heard about the thin blanket, Angelique had given Gertie the wedding quilt from her glory chest, a beautiful silk and silk-velvet quilt, with a variety of embellishments that included butterflies, owls, flowers, fruits, grapes, a girl with a bonnet, and sheaves of wheat. A large floral spray had been hand painted on wine silk, while another had been done in raised embroidery using silk chenille.

Angelique fully intended to retrieve the exquisite quilt from Gertie's room when she wed Sean. And retrieve Gertie, as well.

After dusting Angelique's face with powder and pinching her cheeks, Auntie Bernadette said, "That will have to do. The powder does not quite hide the discoloration, but perhaps Mr. Gray will not notice. Even if he does, he need only recall the words on his family crest. Abuse does—"

"Not take away use," Angelique finished, thinking Auntie Bernadette's cheek pinches hurt worse than the face slap.

Now she stared at *Monsieur* Gray. According to Uncle Alistaire, *Monsieur* Gray was of German descent and had changed his name from Matthaüs Trübe to Matthew Gray. Did Auntie Bernadette honestly believe that her niece, the daughter of her supposedly much-loved little sister, would marry this *grenouille*, this frog?

He was of medium height, with a head that seemed too large for his narrow shoulders. His body looked as if it had been hinged at the knees and elbows. His eyes bulged. His nose was beaky. His brown hair appeared too luxurious for his age, and he possessed wide, fat, froggy lips. Even if Angelique had not loved Sean, she would have been repelled by *Monsieur* Gray.

Perhaps, she told herself, his disposition did not match his frog's exterior. Perhaps she judged him unfairly.

Auntie Bernadette's hisses still echoed in her ear. "You must make certain Mr. Gray is charmed by your bodily assets. We need him to wed you within a few weeks, for you might be with child. Men put such store in breasts, my dear. I give you permission to strut and preen, in a ladylike fashion of course. Furthermore, I will see to it that you do not leave this house until the day of your wedding ceremony."

Once again Angelique wished her ball gown was more demure. She watched *Monsieur* Gray's gaze take in her bruised face, then linger on her décolletage as he bent to kiss the back of her hand, and she felt the urge to slap him senseless.

Speaking directly to Auntie Bernadette, *Monsieur* Gray said, "She'll do."

"I'll do what?" Angelique asked, with the knowledge that she was, once again, being imprudent . . . no, more like reckless.

"Her hips are too small," *Monsieur* Gray continued, ignoring Angelique's query, "but she looks strong. I am a widower," he told Angelique. "My second wife died giving birth to twins."

His voice contained a controlled anger; however, she did not know if his ire was directed at his wife's demise or at the fact that she had presented him with twins before she had conveniently, and probably exhaustedly, expired.

"How old are your twins?" Angelique asked politely, swallowing an impolite rejoinder. "Are they boys or girls?"

"Girls. They are ten months old. I need heirs . . . sons." He paused as his mud-colored eyes touched upon her hips again. "My first wife, who is also deceased, was barren," he said, strolling over to the piano. "Do you play, Miss Aumont?"

Had his first wife died from exhaustion, too? Angelique bit

her lip to keep from asking. "No, *Monsieur*, I do not," she said.

But I can dance across a rope, she thought, tempted to giggle at the absurdity of the situation. Her one saving grace, and apparently her only escape from this marriage of convenience, was small hips.

"The circus had a piano player and a man who played the calliope," Angelique added, "so I never bothered to learn."

"Did you say circus, Miss Aumont?"

"No, Matthew," Auntie Bernadette quickly replied, after sparing a swift, angry glare at Angelique. "You misheard. She said 'circle.' Her circle of friends had a piano player, so she never learned."

"I could have sworn . . . but then, as I age, my ears are not as sharp as they once were."

Angelique wondered if frogs had ears. She thought maybe they had ears on the inside, holes on the outside. From whom had she heard that? Gertie, of course, who had called Angelique a peagoose.

"Nonsense, Matthew," Aunt Bernadette said. "You don't look a day over . . . uh . . . thirty."

"That's what people tell me." He waved away a second compliment and walked toward Angelique. "You shall learn how to play the piano, Miss Aumont. I like music."

"I cannot learn," Angelique retorted, "for my hands are . . . how you say? . . . all thumbs. However, I compose verse and have written an ode for Jenny Lind, the 'Swedish Nightingale' brought to America by *Monsieur* Barnum. I hope to win *Monsieur* Barnum's contest, a two-hundred-dollar prize, since I am, at present, bereft of funds."

Despite Auntie Bernadette's loud gasp, Angelique said, "Would you care to hear my verse, sir?" Sean had not yet delivered the ode he had mentioned, but this morning Gertie had recited a poem that was circulating among the servants. "In my verse, I pretend I am *Monsieur* Barnum talking to *Mademoiselle* Lind, and this is what he says: 'They will welcome you with speeches and rockets. And you will touch their hearts, and I will touch their pockets. And if between us both, the public isn't skimmed, then my name isn't Barnum and yours isn't Lind.' "

Monsieur Gray's muddy eyes were cold, and he tapped his chin with his first finger. "I admire wit, my dear," he said, "as long as it is not directed at me."

"My niece meant no disrespect, Matthew," Auntie Bernadette cried. "She does not even know how you earn your living."

"How *do* you earn your living, *Monsieur* Gray?"

"I own a large plantation, Miss Aumont, where I have many slaves."

"I do not believe in slavery!"

"My niece was raised by genteel, albeit naïve parents who lived in the French countryside and, sadly, suffered a ghastly carriage accident that cut short their peaceful lives," Auntie Bernadette said, the lies escaping her lips as easily as falling off a log. "And just like her unworldly mother and father, she knows nothing of slaves or slavery."

Monsieur Gray did not respond to Angelique's bold statement, so perhaps his hearing *was* impaired. Or, more likely, he didn't give a fig if she did, or did not, believe in slavery.

"My slaves have been discombobulated recently," he said, once again tapping his chin with his first finger, an odd mannerism meant to display displeasure, "for I have purchased an elephant named Korella to plow one of my fields. It was P. T. Barnum who arranged the sale."

"You are acquainted with *Monsieur* Barnum? You are his friend?"

"He is not my friend the way you mean friend, Angelique . . .

may I call you Angelique? He is my business partner. In return for his advice and help with my elephant, I loaned him ten thousand dollars so that he could fulfill his contract with Jenny Lind." Monsieur Gray paused to smirk a grin that did not reach his eyes. "Do you understand?"

"*Oui, Monsieur.* I am no ninny." Angelique tapped her chin with her first finger and was pleased to see *Monsieur* Gray note the gesture and narrow his squinty eyes until they were mere slits.

"And although we have just met," she continued, "I realize that you are no altruist. What did *Monsieur* Barnum pledge in order to secure your loan? His museum? *Monsieur* Thumb? More elephants?"

"No, my dear. He pledged his soul."

CHAPTER TWENTY:
THE PEAHEN AND THE PEACOCK

True to her word, Auntie Bernadette kept Angelique a prisoner, although her jail cell was spacious, her fellow inmates one uncle, seven cats, and a bevy of servants.

Somehow, Auntie Bernadette had discovered that Sean was Angelique's "lover." Perhaps she had intercepted a letter before Angelique and Sean had begun using Gertie, or Gertie's lover Henry, as their two couriers, and before they had begun using false names.

Drawing a tiny peahen in a cage, Angelique now signed her letters "Mademoiselle Paonne." Sean signed his "Monsieur Paon." Having once tried to earn his living as an artist, his paon, or peacock, was the most beautiful pen-and-ink drawing Angelique had ever seen.

In his letters he tried to keep his pessimism hidden, but she could read between the lines.

Even though Barnum seemed well pleased with Sean's tireless efforts, Jenny Lind was a conundrum. "Solving the riddle of the Sphinx," Sean wrote, "would be easier than solving the riddle of the Swedish Nightingale."

Not knowing that she cringed from attention, Barnum, with Sean's help, had mounted an inspired campaign. As Jenny's steamship approached the docking area at the foot of Canal Street, every wharf, window and rooftop along the waterfront crawled with "a sea of humanity." Unfortunately, once Jenny had descended the gangplank, she was almost trampled. Then, safe inside Barnum's carriage, over two hundred bouquets were thrust through the windows, drowning everyone with perfume and petals.

"You would not think me a lad if you could smell me," Sean had written, "and poor Jenny Lind was frightened out of her wits."

She was now living at Irving House, the most elegant quarters in the city, and Sean hoped she would honor her contract since, apparently, she had gotten "cold feet" halfway through her voyage and begged to be taken home.

But, he wrote, all of this was not Angelique's concern.

Of course it was her concern. The colder Jenny's feet got, the longer it would take for *Mademoiselle Paonne* to escape from her prison and join *Monsieur Paon*.

Angelique heard the unmistakable footsteps of her aunt. Quickly, she thrust Sean's latest missive beneath her pillow. He had included the Jenny Lind ode on a separate piece of paper, but she had not read it yet, and she had a sinking feeling she'd have to decipher the poem tonight, by candlelight. Damn and blast!

"I want you to stay by my side," Auntie Bernadette said without preamble. "You must learn how to manage a household, my dear. Matthew Gray has many servants and will expect you to oversee their various duties."

"*Monsieur* Gray has slaves."

"Slaves are unpaid servants, Angelique, and Mr. Gray expects—"

"An heir. He wants sons, and my hips are too small."

"Fiddle-faddle. The next time he visits, we shall pad your hips."

"I suppose that is an *honest* ploy!"

"Of course it is. Just as your 'padded belly' will be an honest ploy."

"What makes you so certain I am with child?"

"The wages of sin—"

"I have never earned those wages. I lied about my *affaire*. I cannot offer you proof of my chastity, but this morning my bleeding began."

"Flowers," Auntie Bernadette said, her cheeks crimson. "In America we call it flowers. And if you are not with child, Matthew Gray will soon pad your belly."

"*Monsieur* Gray will *never* get the opportunity to pad my belly, Auntie Bernadette, for I would rather sleep with a toad!"

Angelique was prepared to endure another face slap. However, she was not prepared for her aunt's smug smile.

CHAPTER TWENTY-ONE:
ANGELIQUE AND CHARITY

Angelique had organized her escape from Auntie Bernadette with a finesse worthy of Macheath in *The Beggar's Opera*. One of her fondest memories was of her papa taking her to see a performance of *The Beggar's Opera*, and during her long walk to Iranistan she had hummed *"Bergers, écoutez la musique!"* over and over again, in an effort to keep her spirits up.

Now, disheveled and footsore, she sat in Charity Barnum's parlor.

Handing Angelique a cup of tea and a handkerchief, Madam Barnum said, "Warm your stomach and dry your tears, child."

"But why did Sean leave New York, Madam Barnum? Please tell me."

"It's really quite simple, Angelique. Jenny Lind's opening night was a success. My husband kept his promise and gave Sean the funds for his traveling circus. And please call me Charity."

"But why would he leave without me, Madam Barn—uh, Madam Charity?"

Angelique watched Madam Charity walk over to the window and look out, her head bent, as if she contemplated the verdant lawn below. Then she made an about-face and said, "Do you not know that your wedding is the talk of New York, child? Your aunt picked Grace Episcopal Church as the site, and a reception will be held at the Metropolitan Hotel, and my husband has promised to provide the entertainment."

As Angelique pictured her aunt's smug smile, she felt the color drain from her face. "I know nothing of this, Madam Charity. I never said I would wed *Monsieur* Gray. In fact, last night I incurred his wrath."

"And how did you do that?"

Angelique's hands were shaking so badly, she placed her teacup and saucer on a small table. "*Monsieur* Gray began to . . . to . . ."

"Engage in sexual behavior?"

"*Oui.* Auntie Bernadette made up some excuse to leave me alone with *Monsieur* Gray. He pressed his face against my bosom. I wore a gown that showed my décolletage, and *Monsieur* Gray's tongue snaked inside my bodice. That made him *agité* and . . . how you say? . . . *excité*."

"Sexually aroused?"

"*Oui.* He ripped my bodice and suckled my breasts . . ." Angelique swallowed the sob that rose in her throat. "I thought I'd be sick."

"Oh, my dear, I'm so very sorry."

"At the same time he was suckling like a big *bébé*, he reached underneath my skirt and began to pinch my derrière. It hurt something awful, but before I could move away he squeezed my behind very hard with both hands, and I was so startled and frightened I reached out blindly. The first thing my hand found was his hair. Only it was a . . ."

"Wig?"

"*Mais oui.* His pate is bald. I began to laugh. I laughed and laughed. He was terribly angry, Madam Charity, and my auntie came running, and she was angry as well. She told *Monsieur* Gray I would be a great deal more biddable during the wedding night. He said it did not matter since he had *médicament* that would make me *très* obedient. He said he had made use of the medicine before with great success. He left the room for the *toilettes,* and Auntie Bernadette said if I ever exhibited such disrespect again, she'd whip me where it would not show, even though *Monsieur* Gray had once said he did not care if the bruises from a whipping showed, as long as they did not spoil my face. Or cripple my body so badly I could not 'breed.' He wants an heir."

Madam Charity drew in her breath sharply, then let it out slowly. "My, my, Matthew Gray is a monster, and your aunt is an evil woman. I had no idea, child. I'm so very sorry," she repeated.

"*Merci,* but it is not your fault, Madam Charity."

"Nor yours. Come to think of it, Bernadette is the only person, at least the only person I know of, who followed the American Museum's *Egress* sign, walked out of the building, and then demanded to be let back inside. She called the sign a swindle, said she would not pay another fee, and raised such a fuss, Phineas came running. He allowed her to return, along with the others who heard her earsplitting howls. Alistaire was humiliated and offered to pay the new fee for everyone, but Phineas said no. He said that the noblest art was that of making people happy, so if Mrs. McCoy was discontented, she should return directly and take the other dissatisfied customers with her."

"Auntie Bernadette is my deceased mum's sister, Madam Charity. She felt she had done her duty, fulfilled some sort of obligation, I guess, by sending me the money for my passage to America. I thought she would welcome me with open arms. However, I believe she was jealous of my mother's love for my father. She does not seem to get along well with my uncle. In truth, I believe they hate each other." Angelique looked down at her shoes and whispered, "Last night I did not sleep, afraid I'd be beaten. I am such a *lâche* . . . a coward. I am so ashamed."

"No, Angelique, you are not a coward, and there's nothing to be ashamed of." If Madam Charity had been a dragon, she would have breathed fire. "Your aunt is no longer welcome in my home, nor the homes of my friends."

Angelique clasped her hands together until her knuckles whitened. "I am not a coward when it comes to walking across a rope, but I am afraid to have a rope walk across me." She shuddered. "So this morning I managed to make my escape."

Madam Charity gently lifted Angelique's chin. "And how did you escape, child?"

"I dressed like my maid, Gertrude Starling. We are the same height, and I hid my hair beneath her hooded cloak. Tonight Gertie will pack a few of my clothes and my letters from Sean, leave the house as Gertie, and meet me here at Iranistan. Gertie and I are good friends, and she is good friends with Uncle Alistaire's groom, Henry, who will drive her here as soon as everyone has gone to bed. I am truly sorry, Madam Charity, but I could not think of any place else to go. I have no money, and your house was nearby."

"My house is miles away. Your feet must ache. And my husband has money for you."

"He does?"

"Yes, dear. Two hundred dollars. You won the Jenny Lind song contest."

Madam Charity walked over to the piano and picked up some sheets of music. Then, in a small but clear voice, she sang Sean's "Ode to Jenny Lind."

> "Oh, Jenny Lind, oh, Jenny Lind,
> Your magic, angel's voice,
> Hath claimed the hearts of all our men,
> All smitten long past choice.
> We beg of you to stay with us,
> With always one more song,

For you have won our very hearts,
Your lilting voice so strong.
Fair tribute to your beauty, and
The angel's voice you own,
Your gift to us, beyond all doubt,
When nightingale hath flown.
All hail the Swedish Nightingale,
Of beauteous form and song,
Our favored choice, this angel's voice,
May she re-main here long."

Angelique watched Madam Charity smile sweetly. "Ordinarily I sing hymns and God does not care what I sound like, so I may have been somewhat discordant," she said, placing the music sheets on the piano. "My husband plans to make your last verse the chorus."

"Sean's last verse." Once again, Angelique looked down at her shoes, dirt stained from her long walk. "Sean wrote the ode," she said. "The money is his, not mine."

"I suspected as much. Nevertheless, Phineas will hand over the two hundred dollars if you give him permission to use your likeness on the posters and sheets of music." Madame Barnum smiled again. "You are much prettier than Sean."

Lifting her teacup from its saucer, Madam Barnum took a delicate sip. "I am glad you came here, child, but why did you not make your escape earlier? Did your aunt threaten you with more than a whipping? Look at me, Angelique. Was that a nod? What did Bernadette say?"

"She said *Monsieur* Gray would ask for his loan back, the ten thousand dollars he advanced your husband. *Monsieur* Gray said that *Monsieur* Barnum pledged his soul. I am not certain what he meant by that, but it must be something terrible."

"He meant Iranistan."

If possible, Angelique felt her face lose more color. "Oh, no! By running away I've ruined everything. *Monsieur* Barnum will lose his soul, and you will lose your home. Oh, Madam Barnum . . . Madam Charity . . . this time *I* am so very sorry. Perhaps they have not yet discovered my absence. Perhaps I can return and—"

"Nonsense! Matthew Gray's loan was repaid, with interest, after Jenny Lind's second concert. Still, I appreciate your sacrifice, Angelique. And so will my husband."

"I do not understand. Does *Monsieur* Barnum know where Sean is?"

"No. But Sean left a map, detailing his route. You see, Phineas promised to purchase an elephant for Sean's circus, from the dealer who supplies his wild animals. Unfortunately, the dealer cannot go to a store and say, 'An elephant, please,' so it might take some time."

"A map, you say? Then I shall follow the map to the man I love. I would follow Sean to the ends of the earth, Madam Charity. You see, back in France I . . . we . . . he and I had a misunderstanding, and I fled straightaway, without giving Sean a chance to explain. When I saw him at your dinner party, he explained the misunderstanding away. Now it is my turn. I am thankful that I do not have to travel all the way from France to America in order to explain. And when I meet up with Sean and explain away the misunderstanding—"

"You will do no such thing, Angelique! You cannot travel across the country unescorted. I have a better plan in mind, but I want to discuss it with my husband first. For now, you must rest in one of our guest bedrooms. I would imagine you are exhausted."

"*Merci,* Madam Charity. I will poke my feet until you talk to *Monsieur* Barnum."

Despite having spent a sleepless night, despite having walked the countless *millas* to Iranistan, Angelique wasn't at all tired. Her mother had made a journey of the heart and followed her father to Paris. She would make a similar journey, even though the ends of the earth might be a wee bit farther.

CHAPTER TWENTY-TWO:
MAD DOG ASSEMBLES THE
McCOY SERVANTS

Still stuck inside Alistaire McCoy's house, fervently wishing he could go home to his wife, his three sons, his twin daughters, a hot dinner, and, most of all, a nourishing glass or three of Old Crow bourbon, Mad Dog Connolly assembled all of the servants in the Tapestry Room, situated to the left of the entrance hall.

The Tapestry Room featured three 16th-century tapestries denoting *The Triumph of Virtue over Vice*. Its centerpiece was a marble and bronze fountain sculpture titled *Boy and Dog Herding Sheep* and a triple fireplace spanned one end of the hall.

The McCoys' housekeeper, Grace Morgan, had suggested they assemble in her room, known as the Pug's Parlor. Every night, after chores were completed, *her* servants would walk in for dinner, the butler leading the way. That was, she said, known as the Pug's Parade.

Grace Morgan was a tall, portly woman whose gray hair had been tucked into a hairnet, unsuccessfully hidden beneath a too-small dust cap. She wore a black gown without the requisite bibbed white apron. Instead, unlike the other female servants, her gown had a white collar and cuffs. Even when she stood motionless, the many keys fastened about her waist seemed to jangle a song of disapproval, implying that Mad Dog had not only turned down the Pug's Parlor proposal, an offer that would have allowed Grace Morgan to rule the roost, but he hadn't asked her permission to invade, much less occupy, Mrs. Mc-

143

Coy's unsullied Tapestry Room.

After dinner, she had added, her voice as cold as a hot water bottle in the morning, the *upper* servants would convene in *her* parlor for conversation. Mad Dog wondered what kind of "conversations" they convened for. Did they talk about ways to eradicate Mrs. Bernadette Browning-Hale McCoy?

At the moment there was no conversation. One third of the room, the third nearest the door, displayed the servants, all of whom stood in front of several floor-to-ceiling windows. They looked like human chess pieces. Except, unlike chess pieces, they were flexible, prepared to bend in a curtsy or, if male, acknowledge Mad Dog's presence by bobbing their heads.

There were five males: the butler, the underbutler, the flunky, the valet, and the groom. The rest were female, although Mad Dog wasn't certain about the scullery maid, who was as thin as the shadow of a hair—with no perceptible bosom. She could have been male or female, he mused, swallowing a smile, longing for his wife Katie to stand by his side so he could share his observation. Whisper in her ear, nudge her with his elbow, wait for her musical giggle, and—

The scullery maid tossed her head, her dust cap flew off, and bright strawberry-red curls tumbled down her back, leaving no doubt as to her femininity.

The scullery maid, in fact all of the servants, wore stone faces—

Wait! Not all of them. The groom, clothed in garments that were too big for his lanky frame, moved his feet restlessly and . . . what the bloody hell was he doing to his fingers? Ah, he was popping them. But his restless feet and fingers could be the result of an acute discomfort he hadn't been able to conceal. He was, after all, far from his natural habitat, the carriage house.

Furthermore, even though Mad Dog stood an abyss length from the servants and a few feet from the door, he could smell the manure on the young man's boots. So could the other servants, and they were keeping as far away from him as a tidy chess lineup would allow.

According to Mad Dog's list of servants, the groom's name was Henry. And he was both groom and coachman. Strange that Mr. and Mrs. McCoy would have a coachman who looked so slapdash. But then, Henry might have been mucking out the horse's stall when Mad Dog convened the servants. That would explain his appearance as well as his repulsive odor.

The easy-to-read list of servants had been given to one of Mad Dog's coppers by Grace Morgan. Alistaire McCoy, it seemed, was away on business and had been gone for six days.

Mad Dog studied the servants again. One pretty housemaid's long brown braid, thick as an adult's wrist, had worked itself loose so that several shiny strands framed a flushed face that looked guilty as sin.

He swallowed a sigh. Where to start?

The housekeeper was probably his best bet. Easy to pick out of the lineup.

But first he glared at the servants, one after another. He was searching for a man or woman who'd cringe. Or turn away from his steadfast and, he hoped, penetrating gaze. Or at the very least, appear uncomfortable.

Damn and blast! *All* of the servants shifted from foot to foot, wrung their hands, or looked as if they wanted nothing more than to flee the room, and the damned room was so silent you could hear a bloody pin drop. Not far from Mad Dog stood Thomas, the copper who'd found Bernadette Browning-Hale McCoy's body after the police had been summoned to the mansion by Alistaire McCoy's stately butler. Every once in a while Thomas would clear his throat or hack up phlegm and then spit it into a handkerchief. Thomas smoked. And smelled like the evil tobacco he fancied.

Some of the servants had shifted their gaze from Henry the Coachman's manure-encrusted boots and were staring angrily at Thomas. A few were even screwing up their noses. Mad Dog kept his hand from straying to the pipe in his pocket; the pipe that helped him think. Instead, he instructed Thomas to search the carriage house for "anything out of the ordinary." That would get him away from the room. A shame he couldn't send Henry the Coachman from the room, too.

Here now, what was this? Henry had looked momentarily startled, before he again stared down at the floor and popped his fingers. Mad Dog kept his face unresponsive, but he wondered what the hell Henry was hiding in the carriage house. Stolen goods from the main house seemed a good bet.

"Henry, you may approach," Mad Dog said.

The coachman didn't move.

"That ain't Henry," Grace Morgan said, this time her voice both smug as April and cold as a dog's nose. "That there is Nella."

"On the list you gave me—"

"Yes, sir. I forgot Henry left Mr. McCoy's employ, and Mr. McCoy hired Nella to take Henry's place."

Strange name, Nella. Obviously foreign.

"When did this occur, Miss Morgan?"

"Huh?"

"When did Henry leave Mr. McCoy's employ?"

"Three . . . no, two days ago. And it's *Mrs.* Morgan, if you please."

"Oh, you are wed. Does your husband work for Mr. McCoy as well?"

"Ain't wed. Missus is a curtsy name."

"Courtesy, not curtsy," mumbled the butler.

"My apologies, *Mrs.* Morgan. Did Mr. McCoy hire the new coachman right away?"

"Yes, sir."

"But Mr. McCoy has been gone six days, so how could he hire Nella two days ago?"

"It was Mrs. McCoy what hired Nella," said the girl with the untidy braid as she limped a few steps forward, favoring first one foot then the other. Her accent was distinctly British. "Mrs. McCoy said she could not move about without a coachman, and since Henry had done a moonlight flit, leaving without so much as a good-bye to them who cared for him . . ." The girl paused to take an angry breath. "Given that Henry had buggered off, Mrs. McCoy was in a pickle. Then Nella come along like the answer to a prayer."

As she spoke, the girl's cheeks flushed a vivid crimson, which Mad Dog had always associated with a liar, but why would the crippled young woman lie about a coachman being hired by Mrs. McCoy?

"Mr. Nella, you may approach." Mad Dog snapped his fingers.

Once again, the coachman didn't move.

"It's just plain Nella, sir, and he don't understand or speak English good," said Grace Morgan.

Neither do you, Mrs. Morgan!

"Sir, I knows a thing or two about a thing or two," said a pasty-faced servant. Katie might have whispered that her black dress appeared a *smidín* too small for her pear-shaped body.

Stop thinking about Katie! "And you are?"

"Mary, sir. Not Mary the scullery maid, or Mary the laundress, or Mary the other upstairs maid. And there was another Mary, but she left Mrs. McCoy's employ when—"

"Yes, yes, what do you have to tell me?"

The girl walked forward until she was almost nose to nose with Mad Dog. She winked. "And how much will you pay me, sir?" she said in a sly, whiney voice.

"Pay you?"

"For my earful."

"Young lady, it is your duty to tell me whatever it is you *think* you know."

She pouted and said, "In that case, I *think* I'll wait for Mr. McCoy."

"You will not wait." Mad Dog tried to keep his anger under control. "If you do not speak to me right now, this very minute, I will take you . . . *in chains* . . . with me, to the precinct, and I will hold you there until you do speak. And you had better speak the truth, the whole truth, and nothing but the truth. Do you understand?"

"Yes, sir."

"You said 'earful.' What did you overhear?"

"I ain't done nothin' wrong."

"No one said you did."

"I was cleanin' the hallway 'cause Mrs. McCoy, she likes it speckless, in apple-pie order, and I was mindin' my own bizness, like always, when I heard some foul words that gave me a bit of a turn—"

"Cut to the chase!"

"Huh?"

"Get to the point."

"Garn! I'm gettin' there." Mary spread her plump arms, then found her waist with hands that looked like the webbed appendages of a duck. "Miss Angelique's door was part open," she said, "because Gertie was with her and Gertie, she don't like it shut."

"Gertie?"

"She's Miss Angelique's lady's maid." Mary practically spat the last two words. "Gertie needs the door part open 'cause she's . . . what's it called?"

"Claustrophobic?"

148

"No. Tight. Not tight from drink, though it seems to me she oft gets lushy, 'specially at a Servants Ball."

"That's a lie!" said the girl with the long, untidy braid. "*You* are the one who gets lushy. *You* are the one who spreads your legs for any man who wants a go at you."

"Ah-ow-oo." Mary's webbed hands left her waist and turned into fists. "And you . . . you . . . *you* get tight-oh-pho-something . . . whatever the bloody hell the bloody inspector said . . . 'cause you don't like small rooms!"

The girl named Gertie looked scared to death, and her eyes kept finding the door. Just the same, she reacted to Mary's words by folding her fingers into tight fists. Mad Dog swallowed a sigh. "Miss Gertie, this is a large room, not a 'tight' room, so there's no need to be frightened or even to open the door partway. Stay where you are for the moment, please. Go on, Miss Mary."

"Well, sir, it ain't that I fancied bein' Miss Angelique's lady's maid, but garn, sir, I been here heaps longer than Gert—"

"What did you hear, girl?" Mad Dog roared.

"Bugger off, sir. You can holler all you wants, but I ain't no snitch."

"I'll count to ten, Miss Mary, before I put you in chains. One, two, three, four, five—"

"Hold your bloody horses! I'll be straight up with you." She gave Mad Dog another sly wink. "I swear on me mum's grave that what I'm gonna tell you is the truth, the whole truth, and whatever else you said 'bout truth."

"Yes? Go on."

"Well, sir, I heard Miss Angelique say . . . ." Mary made an about-face so that she looked toward the servants. Then she smiled and bellowed, "Miss Angelique said she wished she had some birds to peck her auntie's eyes out."

As Mad Dog digested Mary's words, the servants, as one, let

out a loud gasp and then began nattering like geese in flight. The girl named Gertie shut her eyes and fell to the floor in a heap, her braid finally coming wholly undone, her hair spreading across her shoulders and back like a mahogany shawl. Grace Morgan and Nella the coachman raced toward her while Thomas ran into the room, the smell of burnt tobacco following in his wake.

"Beggin' your pardon for the interruption, sir," he said breathlessly, "but there's another dead body in the carriage house. And this time it ain't the cats what done the dirty deed."

CHAPTER TWENTY-THREE:
SEAN KELLEY MEETS MAUREEN
AND BRIAN O'CONNOR

Sean Kelley celebrated Saint Valentine's Day by hiring an equestrian.

Despite the anguish that tinted her blue eyes a deep violet, Maureen O'Connor was a beautiful woman. Sean had a feeling his own eyes reflected her bottomless sorrow, except when they gazed upon her son. Sean was fully aware that his expression softened and his eyes shone, and it wasn't simply his love for children. He was impressed—and delighted—when the dark-haired, blue-eyed little boy didn't try to hide behind his mother's skirts.

Instead, Brian O'Connor stood directly in front of his mum, as if he'd fiercely attack anything or anyone who dared to threaten her.

Sean hunkered down. "And how old might you be, lad?"

The boy held up seven fingers.

"And what will you be doing while your mum rides the horses?"

"Whatever you wish me to do, sir."

"Can you ride?"

"Of course," he replied, as if Sean's question was laughable. Then he looked up at his mother. "But I want someone to learn me how to tame the cats."

"*Teach* you," Maureen corrected, "and we've gabbed about this before, Brian. It is why I left my last position," she said to Sean. "The owner of the circus believed it would be good for business, putting a wee lad inside a cage filled with lions and tigers. I told him what-for, and he sent me packing."

Sean felt his face flush, for he had been thinking the same thing. While no Tom Thumb, Brian O'Connor, even at seven, had a devil-may-care demeanor. He was, Sean concluded, a man inside a boy's body.

"Folks think I'm daft," Brian said earnestly, "but I can talk to lions and tigers, and they understand every word I say."

Maureen pointed to an ugly scratch on her son's arm, beneath his rolled-up sleeve. "One tiger did not understand your words!"

"Yes he did, Mum. Mr. Browne's whip made him forget."

"You must snap a whip to tame the cats, Brian," Sean said.

"True, sir, but Mr. Browne struck the tiger's nose."

"You were in the ring? Performing?"

The boy shook his head. "We were practicing. I know how to snap the whip, sir, but I'd never hurt a cat. Just like Mum would never hurt a horse."

"Which is why I hired your mum," Sean said with a grin. "And I believe I have more than enough chores to keep you occupied."

"I'm good at chores," Brian bragged. "But someday I'll tame your cats."

Watching Maureen and Brian O'Conner walk toward the cook top, the tent where his *chef de cuisine* prepared meals for his performers and crew, Sean hoped "someday" would come soon. He desperately needed a star attraction.

And he needed the elephant Barnum had promised to deliver.

Traveling from town to town by horse and wagon, Sean found that many roads were impassable, especially during rainstorms. If swollen streams blocked the road, an elephant could double as a wagon pusher. With an elephant, Sean could erect a huge canvas tent, much larger than the tent he'd purchased before leaving New York City. Right now, more often than not, he

presented his show outside, usually in a farmer's field. And
although his loyal troupe was willing, Sean would not allow
them to perform during turbulent weather.

He had heard about an elephant named Korella. It had first
been purchased by Barnum, who then sold it to a wealthy
plantation owner. The elephant had effectively been trained to
take the place of a stubborn mule and plow the plantation
owner's fields. But now the wealthy plantation owner wanted to
sell his elephant to the highest bidder and, to that end, had
taken out illustrated advertisements in several newspapers. The
advertisements showed a realistic likeness of Korella, drawn by
an artist's hand, and Sean figured the plantation owner's field
hands feared a human's punishment far less than they feared
the huge, four-footed, flap-eared mammal.

Sean just happened to see the newspaper advertisement inside
a feed store. He had been all set to visit the plantation and
make a bid. Then, reading further, he had learned the name of
the owner: Matthew Gray. Angelique's fiancé. The well-heeled
gent whom Barnum said would be marrying Angelique inside
the esteemed Grace Episcopal Church—a church where, according to Charity Barnum, "the stained glass kisses your face."

Surely Matthew Gray and Angelique were wed by now, and
Sean would die a thousand deaths or push a thousand wagons
across a thousand swollen streams before he'd set eyes on the
woman who had married for wealth rather than love.

While he suspected her aunt had something to do with
Angelique's decision, that didn't negate the fact that she had
betrayed him. He had *not* believed the newspaper story, had in
truth been writing a letter to "Mademoiselle Paonne" when
Barnum entered the room and announced that he would
provide the entertainment at Angelique's wedding reception.

"Do you think the happy couple would enjoy excerpts from
Romeo and Juliet?" Barnum had asked.

"I think the future Mrs. Gray would prefer excerpts from *Beauty and the Beast,* or perhaps 'Open Thy Lattice Love' by Stephen Foster," Sean had replied, hiding the bitterness in his voice, his pride overwhelming his despair.

Perhaps his new equestrian could mend his broken heart. Sean pictured the masses of red hair framing Maureen O'Connor's porcelain complexion and dark blue-purple eyes, aware that below her neck and shoulders, her breasts and hips were well-rounded, her waist as small as a whiplash popper.

While applying for the job of equestrian, she had said she was a widow. But a vivid blush had stained her cheeks, and something in her voice did not ring true.

The last thing Sean needed right now was an irate husband.

Of course, there was always Panama Drayton. The young, statuesque trapeze artist had made it very clear that she'd be willing to perform with Sean beneath the wagons. But even if he had been tempted, the equally young strong man, Bobby Duncan, had already staked his claim. Well structured with cast-iron muscles, each brain cell Duncan lacked was stored inside his powerful arms and shoulders. Sean did not want to tangle with "the strongest man in the world," nor did he want to lose him, for it was his Kid Show exhibits, also known as his Congress of Freaks, that kept his circus afloat.

After opening in Brooklyn, he had toured New England, and at one stop in Waterville, Maine, so many people lined up to buy tickets, his troupe had given continuous performances, starting in the wee hours of the morning, ending late at night.

But those early shows had been confined to buildings and, occasionally, his circus tent. People preferred to sit under a roof, even a canvas roof. In order to make a profit, Sean needed huge audiences, which meant an *oversized* tent, and it was difficult to raise up and tear down an oversized tent without the help of an elephant.

The one snag to staging a circus in an oversized tent was that the people in the back rows had difficulty seeing the show. Sean had discussed this with Barnum, who offered a solution. Enlarge the ring where the acts were performed. That, Sean insisted, was out of the question.

"The diameter for circus rings is thirteen meters," he had told Barnum. "Circus horses all over the world are trained to perform in rings of that size. If every circus had a different size, horses would have to be re-trained every time they appeared with a new company."

"Then add a second ring," Barnum had said.

A brilliant scheme, Sean had thought at the time. He planned to add a second ring. And perhaps a third ring. The most popular acts would perform inside the center ring.

But two or three rings would make it problematical to hear the clowns' silly gibber-jabber, so he would commence yet another daring innovation. His clowns would perform their routines with no dialogue at all—in pantomime.

First, however, he needed a star performer. And more exhibits. Barnum had promised to try and find Sean a couple of cameleopards. Cameleopards possessed amazingly long, spotted necks, but they also had long black tongues, allowing them to encircle tree branches and eat the leaves that would otherwise be out of reach.

I'll wager Americans have niver seen a cameleopard, Sean thought with a grin. *As a matter of fact, I've niver seen one myself.*

He shut his eyes as a headache galloped inside his skull.

Once, not too long ago, he had pictured Angelique as his star performer, her rope stretched tight across the tent's top, drawing every gaze toward heaven.

"If you are very good," he had told his stepsister Charlotte, "you can capture a dream."

Had Sean been able to "capture" Angelique, he would have

filled his circus posters with her likeness. And he would have introduced her to the world as *Madame* Kelley, otherwise known as *Petite Ange.*

Once again he heard Charlotte's voice: "You must find Cinderella and kiss her awake."

I kissed her awake, sweetheart, only to lose her again.

Unbidden, he heard Charlotte say, "I do not believe my papa is asleep. He is just lost."

Although he had sworn in his heart to ignore Charlotte's unspoken plea to search for her *papa,* Sean couldn't help looking for his father's name in every newspaper he read, which was how he'd learned about Korella the elephant . . . by purchasing a newspaper, hoping to come across a mention of Timothy Kelley.

Which was truly insane. Timothy was nothing more than a gambler and, for a short while, a London dustman. However, Sean had oft heard his father sing, and when Timothy sang, he had a voice that would make the angels turn green with envy. He could have risen to stardom by joining one of the traveling theatre companies, whereupon he might have had his name printed in a newspaper. Traveling theatre companies had become not only accepted but well liked all over the United States, in particular throughout the American West. Short musical revues—called "vaudevilles" in Paris—and American "comic operas" that included sentimental stories and original music were even playing in many of the small towns where Sean put on his circus acts.

He had attended one minstrel show and watched players who sported shiny black faces entertain with comic send-ups. He hadn't been overly impressed with the performances. Moreover, one of his closest chums was a member of his circus Kid Show, a Negro "giant" named Black Jack, who had more *panache* than Sean's hoity-toity stepmother, Hortense, and all of the perform-

156

ing minstrels put together. Sean had winced and flinched when a minstrel performer—in blackface and tattered clothes—sang:

"Listen all you gals and boys
I'se jist from Tuckyhoe,
I'm goin to sing a little song,
My name is Jim Crow
Fist on de heel tap,
Den on the toe
Ebry time I weel about
I jump Jim Crow.
Weel about and turn about
En do jus so,
And every time I weel about,
I jump Jim Crow."

Had he not been seated in the middle of a row, afraid he'd "weel about" and stomp on too many toes, Sean would have fled the theatre. He was only glad, and vastly relieved, that Black Jack had turned down Sean's invitation to attend the show. On the other hand, he could picture Timothy Kelley roaming up and down the stage while singing some of the more romantic and sentimental ballads.

As he left the theater, Sean knew, without a single doubt, that throughout the centuries Jim Crow would keep rearing its ugly head. It was human nature to blame someone or something for self-made mistakes and bad luck, and, unfortunately, the color of a person's skin was a convenient and very large target.

Chapter Twenty-Four:
Timothy Arrives in California

If Timothy had determined the Boston coffin ship a voyage through hell, the much longer journey to California could be considered a passage through purgatory.

Or, as Dante Alighieri might say, *"Purgatorio."*

Timothy recalled Mr. Clutterbuck leaning against a stall, watching Timothy curry his fawn-colored horse, Zeus. While Timothy made circular motions with the curry comb in order to loosen the gelding's hair, dirt, and other detritus, Mr. Clutterbuck talked about the first part of Dante's epic poem, *Divine Comedy*. Called *Inferno*, it told about the journey of Dante through hell, guided by an ancient Roman poet named Virgil.

"In the poem, hell is depicted as nine circles of suffering located within the earth," Mr. Clutterbuck had said. "As an allegory, the *Divine Comedy* represents the journey of the soul toward God, with the *Inferno* describing the recognition and rejection of sin."

"Allegory?" Timothy tasted the word and decided he liked the flavor.

"An allegory is a story or a poem that can be interpreted to reveal a hidden meaning," Mr. Clutterbuck said. "Have you read *The Faerie Queene* by Edmund Spenser? I have a copy in my library."

"No, sir, I have not read it. But if I understand your 'recognition and rejection of sin' correctly, an allegory is religious or moral, where characters represent virtues and vices."

"Exactly. I'm impressed. Your ability to grasp a concept is more comprehensive than Mrs. Clutterbuck's, which doesn't surprise me, but you seem to have more inborn knowledge than my business partners and the majority of my business acquaintances."

Mr. Clutterbuck had scowled and shaken his head, as if to clear it of debauched business acquaintances. "In the *Inferno*, Dante passes through the gate of hell," he continued, "which bears an inscription ending with '*Lasciate ogne speranza, voi ch'intrate.*'"

"Sir?"

"Sorry, Paddy. I forgot you don't speak nor understand Italian. It means 'Abandon all hope, ye who enter here.' Dante and his guide, Virgil, hear anguished screams from the souls of people who in life were neither for good nor evil. Naked, the people race around through the mist in eternal pursuit of an elusive, wavering banner. All the while, they are chased by swarms of wasps and hornets that continually sting them. Maggots and worms at the sinners' feet drink a mixture of blood, pus, and tears that surge down their bodies."

"Pus and tears? Maggots and worms?" Timothy couldn't repress an unmanly wobble, causing Zeus to snort and then whinny indignantly.

"Yes indeed, Paddy," Mr. Clutterbuck said, stroking the gelding's forelock. "Maggots and worms symbolize the sinners' guilty consciences. It may also be seen as a reflection of the spiritual stagnation the sinners lived in."

Abandon all hope ye who enter here would aptly describe the California Gold Rush, Timothy mused. *So would pus and tears.* He had not seen maggots and worms, but he had no doubt they lurked near the water where dozens, if not hundreds, of miners panned for gold.

And if the worms and maggots were hiding underground,

fleas and lice were not.

The newspaper articles he had read did not bother to describe a place called Hangtown, named for the three people who had been hanged for theft and attempted murder. The newspaper articles did not mention Sutter's Fort, an old looking heap of buildings surrounded by a high wall. The newspaper articles did not mention that, upon leaving the plains, the hills looked dry and barren, burnt by the sun and long droughts. For the first time during his fire-and-brimstone journey to what was fast becoming the California nether world, Timothy fondly recalled the emerald paddocks of Buckingham Manor.

The newspaper articles he had seen did not mention the unbelievably high prices for food. Although Timothy could have made more money mining gold than working an unskilled and most likely boring job in Boston or New York, the puffed-up prices for food and clothing and the shortage of goods would wipe out any profit he'd earn from "panning."

An onion cost one dollar. *One dollar!* Timothy pictured his aunt's café, where the smell of garlic and onions would instantly spark pangs of hunger as soon as you walked through the front entrance. He pictured the Clutterbucks' kitchen, pictured Cook standing by the stove, pictured her stew simmering merrily in a large pot filled to the brim with chopped up onions, carrots, beans, potatoes, and beef. And flour to thicken the sauce.

Here, flour cost thirteen dollars per bag.

Butter cost twenty-five dollars per pound, eggs three dollars each.

Luckily, Timothy still had money from Mr. Clutterbuck's generous stake, but it wouldn't last him long if he wanted to *eat!* He wished now that upon reaching Sacramento he hadn't purchased the diamond stickpin in the shape of a shamrock, which he'd bought for luck, or paid such a high price for the black stallion he had named Virgil. His mare had been sold long ago. Even if he had been able to take her all the way to California with him, she would never have survived what James Clutterbuck might have called Timothy's "California odyssey."

He quickly came to realize that many of the drifters who traveled to California were there not so much to mine gold but to mine the miners.

To that end, some of the men had built up high profits from the sale of picks, shovels, pans, blankets, shirts, pants, boots, and, especially, whiskey, and they were now purchasing numerous acres of land with an intent to build cattle ranches—in point of fact, *vast empires*!

Timothy itched to do the same. Mine the miners. But how?

In the months it had taken for him to travel from Boston to California, the easy gold had been used up, and it was becoming more and more necessary for several men to band together just to survive. Timothy had bought a shallow metal pan. All he had to do, he'd been told, was sit by a riverbed, scoop wet soil into the pan, swirl the pan, wash away the dirt, and he'd find his gold in a variety of sizes—from lumps as small as a man's thumbnail to nuggets as large as the knobby end of a woman's elbow.

Timothy heaved a deep sigh as he remembered his beloved Molly oft saying, "Timothy, me darlin', if it sounds too good to be true, it most likely *is* too good to be true."

Problem was, a simple pan no longer did the job, and most miners had turned to "rocking the cradle." Named for its resemblance to a child's cradle, when rocked by one, two, three, or more miners, the box sifted large amounts of ore. First a miner would shovel gravel onto an iron plate pierced with holes. Then he'd pour water over it, causing the finer material to drop through the holes and onto an apron that spread it across two or three slats, also known as riffles. As the material moved through the cradle, the gold was caught on the riffles to be

161

removed later.

Finally, there was something called a long tom, similar to the rocker but much more elaborate. A paddlewheel ensured a constant source of water. Again, gravel was shoveled into the top end, and water pushed it along a long wooden course, sometimes hundreds of feet long. Again, the slats collected the heavier ore, which was then further processed.

In every town, at every miner's site, there were countless shootings, stabbings, floggings, even lynchings. Timothy didn't have a rocker. He didn't have a long tom. He didn't have a gun, though he carried a knife in the sheath around his waist and a second, smaller knife in his boot.

Nor, he quickly discovered, did he fancy spending his days panning for gold. It wasn't that he was a stranger to hard work, not after his years as a potato farmer in Ireland, a dustman in London, and a groom at Buckingham Manor, but surely there was an easier—and safer—way to make his fortune.

Weary but not yet thoroughly discouraged, Timothy rode Virgil up a hill until they reached the ridge. The black stallion snorted and tossed his head. Timothy felt like copying Virgil's snort and toss. Instead, he dismounted and stared down at the town of Coloma, at the numerous shacks along the south fork of the American River. Though he knew it was impossible, it looked as if there were more people in Coloma than he'd seen in London or Paris. Or on the coffin ship. Or the busy Boston dock, teeming with ship personnel, immigrants, and ferret-faced maggots.

He remounted Virgil and slowly rode through the town. Counting days in his head, he reckoned it was Sunday. A colorful Sunday. Apparently miners used Sundays to wash their work trousers and red flannel shirts.

The main street was crammed full, swarming with men on foot and men riding or guiding mules and horses. Timothy did not see any women, although a few scantily-clad ladies waved from the open windows of what was, obviously, a whorehouse.

The jibber-jabber of incompatible accents sounded both soothing and confusing. German, Australian, French, Chinese, English, and Italian blended and clashed with a mixture of Spanish from the men who had traveled to the gold fields from South America and Mexico. The darkest Negroes Timothy had ever seen, had not even dreamed existed, sounded like they sang every word, even when they merely spoke in their everyday, normal voices.

Games of chance were ballyhooed on every corner by thimble riggers, Monte dealers, and string-game tricksters. There were tents set up for poker and other card games.

Timothy dismounted and led Virgil down the street until he found a smithy that boarded horses. It cost a fortune, depleting Timothy's stash even further, but the blacksmith promised to feed and rub down the stallion.

Once he knew his horse was being looked after, Timothy entered numerous gambling tents, all of them doing a brisk business. His purpose was not to gamble, but to see how they operated. He then continued strolling down the street, gently shouldering people out of his way, until he spied a gambling house and saloon whose bold black letters proclaimed ROSIE'S WATERING HOLE AND BETTING HOUSE.

A genuine building constructed of wood, its interior was spacious and well-lit. The gambling tables were crowded. Unlinked chains of men stood behind the tables and the seated players, waiting for a seat to open up. After watching for an hour, Timothy determined the dealers dealt fair. He knew dealers didn't have to cheat in order to make a profit for the house, but that didn't seem to prevent the more disreputable dealers from acting dishonestly, and Timothy had been surprised to see the owners of the gambling tents he'd visited earlier ignore their double-dealing swindlers. One of the owners had even nodded at a table and winked at Timothy. The wink meant: *I'll let you win.* Timothy had shrugged. His shrug meant: *No thanks, thanks just the same.*

He'd never work for men like that, nor would he play a "friendly" hand of cards, even though he had learned, years ago, in Paris, how to cheat a cheater.

Bringing his attention back to the saloon's interior, he saw that an upright piano dominated a spacious corner of the barroom. He couldn't even imagine how the piano had been moved to Coloma in one piece, but there it sat in all its glory, shining in the lamplight, its eighty-eight black and ivory keys beckoning like seductive fingers, even though Timothy had never learned to play any kind of musical instrument.

From the very end of the bar, he heard a female voice shout, "Don't you dare puke in my establishment, Earl," and watched a man swallow hard, cup his mouth with his hands, spin from his stool, and race for the door.

Timothy slid onto Earl's stool, warmed from Earl's backside. He ordered a beer from a young man with a spectacular spaghetti mustache—bushy with points at the end. The woman who had warned the miner not to puke in her establishment had disappeared and then reappeared a few minutes later. In her hands she clutched what looked like two whiskey bottles.

Timothy looked around again. Looked at the gamblers. Looked at the piano. Looked at the woman behind the bar. Even from a distance he could see that she had comfortable curves and a freckled face. He had a scheme in mind that didn't require him risking his own money. He felt peaceful. He felt at home. And, for the first time in his life, he felt as if he truly belonged.

CHAPTER TWENTY-FIVE:
ANGELIQUE MEETS A COWBOY

"Will you please, please be quiet."

"*Je suis désolé, Mademoiselle* Lind," Angelique said with a brief curtsy. "I am sorry."

"Not you, Angel, the bird." Jenny Lind pointed to a small birdcage. Inside, a canary was singing its heart out. "Get rid of that bird! It's giving me a headache. I want it gone from my dressing room before I return. Do you understand? Was that a nod, Angel?"

"*Mais oui, Mademoiselle.*"

"Good." Sweeping up her long skirts, Jenny Lind turned toward the dressing room door.

As Angelique leaned over to pick up a pair of abandoned knickers and a discarded shawl, she heard the door slam. She could usually determine Jenny Lind's moods from the strength of her slams. This evening Jenny was very angry.

"And what am I supposed to do with you?" Angelique said to the bird.

Thanks to Charity Barnum, Angelique had become part of Jenny Lind's entourage. *Monsieur* Barnum had been reluctant at first, even after Madam Charity told him about Matthew Gray's attempted seduction and Auntie Bernadette's reaction. But when Madam Charity reminded him of their difficult courtship, he'd boomed his big laugh and agreed to make Angelique one of Jenny Lind's two personal tour servants. He promised he'd take care of Gertrude Starling whenever she arrived. He'd find her another servant's position, or unearth a new trapeze partner and hire her to entertain at his museum. But, he said with a grin, it was up to Charity to put on her "best kid gloves" and "handle" Angelique's Aunt Bernadette.

"Cowardly custard," Madam Charity had said with a purr in her voice, just before she'd given Monsieur Barnum a kiss on the lips.

Witnessing the intimacy of the kiss, unable to leave the room without being spotted, an embarrassed Angelique had faded into the shadows. Whereupon she heard Barnum say, "When it comes to Mrs. McCoy, money is an excellent servant but a terrible master."

"There is little doubt that Bernadette is wealthy, my love," Madam Charity had replied. "However, she wants to 'belong' even more."

"Belong?"

"With her marriage to Alistaire, she's accumulated a great deal of wealth, even managed to climb the social ladder a few rungs, but her niece could ruin her social standing."

"I don't see how—"

"If her society friends find out her niece performed in a circus, even a prestigious circus like the Cirque de Délices, Bernadette would slide down that society ladder quicker than hell can scorch a feather. On the other hand, if Angelique weds Matthew Gray and moves far away, she cannot interfere with Bernadette's grandiose plan."

"Do you aspire to climb the social ladder, Charity? I ask that in all seriousness because, as long as you are married to me, you'll never climb above the first rung."

"No, Phineas. I only aspire to be a good person. In truth, I'm a minnow. You've always said one should never attempt to catch a whale with a minnow, but I caught you. And now we must help Angelique catch her whale, though I doubt she's a minnow. She's determined to find Sean, whom she loves with all her heart, which in my book means she's one hell of a whale."

"A whale who walks on air rather than water."

"Whales don't walk on water."

"They do if they are P. T. Barnum," he said with a wink.

The very next day Angelique met Jenny Lind.

Madam Charity had introduced Angelique to Jenny as "Angel Aumont." Jenny had been pleased. Many of her fellow performers preferred French maids, and Angel Aumont, who looked clean as a whistle and sounded humble, possessed a delightful French accent.

Furthermore, Jenny believed her own special angel had guided her career and now oversaw her success. Angels were good luck.

Angelique often wondered if she wouldn't have been better off setting out on her own. Jenny Lind was spiritual and devout, but she hated thanking people, disliked staying at a table after she'd finished eating, was wracked with headaches and rheumatism, and plugged up her ears with wool stoppers at night to "shut out the noises of the world." She could be sweet and generous—at Christmas she had showered everyone with gifts—but Angelique knew that, as the tour progressed, Jenny was growing increasingly distrustful of *Monsieur* Barnum.

Angelique also knew Jenny's advisors had pleaded with her to break her contract. After several months of touring, Angelique could speak English with only the smallest trace of an accent. But since she was a servant and French, everyone assumed she could not understand what they said, and she heard things she was not supposed to hear.

This afternoon Jenny was enraged because she did not care for her hotel room—too small; or the theater—too poorly maintained; or the theatre manager—too lazy, and he *spat* when he talked; or the town—too provincial; or her dressing room—

barely the size of a closet; or her dressing room mirror, which made her look fat! In addition, someone had told her the structure for her Tennessee concert would be a tobacco warehouse.

Jenny's contract gave her the option of withdrawing from her tour. If she did so, she'd have to pay *Monsieur* Barnum $25,000. Her tour had begun with a concert at Castle Garden—a promenade, beer garden, restaurant, exhibition hall, opera house, and theater—in New York City's Battery Park, and it was such a success, *Monsieur* Barnum easily earned four times his investment. Jenny had cut out a newspaper article where author Washington Irving was quoted as saying, "She is enough to counterbalance, of herself, all the evil that the world is threatened with by the great convention of women. So God save Jenny Lind," and Angelique had been told by Jenny's musical director that tickets for some of her concerts were in such demand, *Monsieur* Barnum sold them by auction, and oftentimes people had to pay to get into the auction.

Angelique toured with Jenny as the singer gave concerts in Boston, Philadelphia, and Richmond, Virginia.

From there, they went by ship to Charleston, South Carolina.

In New Orleans Jenny finished her concert with "The Herdsman's Song," a Swedish song, and "I know that my Redeemer liveth" from *Messiah*.

Twenty minutes ago Jenny had begun an angry letter to *Monsieur* Barnum, but she'd stopped in the middle, too infuriated to write. Instead, she had peppered Angelique and the canary with indignant epithets.

And yet Angelique gladly endured the singer's insults. Because she was close to Sean. She could feel it. Even better, she had overheard *Monsieur* Barnum, during a visit, teasing Jenny, asking if she would like an elephant to share her stage before he delivered it to a friend in St. Louis, Missouri. Jenny had not been amused, and Angelique had a feeling Barnum would soon lose his famous singer.

So, just in case, she had asked *Monsieur* Barnum if she could borrow the very latest map that Sean had sent, by post, to Iranistan. Then, using the back of one of Jenny Lind's promotional leaflets, she had drawn a copy, all the time thinking that Sean sketched peacocks better than he could depict lines on a map.

On the crudely drawn map, not far from St. Louis, Sean had inked a big black *X*.

The next stop on Jenny's tour was Topeka, Kansas. After the Topeka run, Jenny and her entourage would travel to Missouri, before going on to Tennessee. Angelique couldn't waste time, waiting for Jenny to finish her three performances in Kansas. By then Sean might be gone, his *cirque* on the road to a new city. Somehow, some way, even if she had to walk, ride, or fashion Icarus-style wings of feathers and wax and *fly*, she needed to find Sean before he left Missouri. She was so close, she could practically smell the masculine sweat on his clothes and the scent of leather from his boots.

During his visit, *Monsieur* Barnum had seemed uncomfortable in Angelique's presence, especially when she had politely asked after the health of her Auntie Bernadette. Angelique could have sworn he changed the subject on purpose.

Bernadette Browning-Hale McCoy was Angelique's legal guardian until Angelique turned twenty-one, so perhaps *Monsieur* Barnum believed she was breaking the law, and he did not want to be . . . what was the word her uncle oft used? Involved? Complicit?

Mais oui, complicit.

Meaning *Monsieur* Barnum, whom Madam Charity had called a cowardly custard, did not want any part of Angelique's wrongdoing.

Damn and blast! If *les autorités* wanted her brought back to

Connecticut, it was even more imperative that she hide herself amongst the performers of the Sean Kelley Circus, lest she be captured and—

A knock sounded at the door. Still deep in thought, Angelique said, *"Entrez,"* then repeated it in English. "Enter."

The furniture was suddenly dwarfed by a tall stranger whose over-large hands awkwardly clutched a bouquet of flowers and a cowboy hat.

Stifling a yawn, Angelique repeated the words she had said at least a hundred times before. "We thank you for your thoughtfulness, sir, but we prefer that flowers be delivered to a children's hospital. If there is no children's hospital, any hospital will do."

"Yes, ma'am. Pretty bird you got there. Problem is, these ain't my flowers."

And that canary ain't my bird, Angelique thought, her mouth quirking at the corners. "If you did not purchase the flowers," she said, "who did?"

"I dunno, ma'am. A gent outside the theater give me four bits to make sure these here blooms got brung to Jenny Lind's room. Are you her?"

"Yes, I am Jenny Lind," Angelique fibbed. "But please return those blooms to the gent and tell him what I said about hospitals."

"Cain't do that, ma'am."

"Why not?"

"I need the money."

"Suppose I give you six bits and . . . why are you shaking your head?"

"Ain't never took no money from a girl, ma'am, and don't plan to start now."

Intrigued, Angelique gestured toward a chair. "Won't you sit down, sir?"

"I'll sit if you take these here flowers, and I ain't no sir. Roy

Osborne's the name."

"I shall take your flowers if you take my bird," she said, gesturing toward the canary. "And please call me, uh, Jenny."

"Yes, ma'am."

"Jenny."

"Yes, ma'am."

Angelique swallowed a laugh and placed the cowboy's bouquet on top of the dressing table. Roy Osborne, now seated, stared at the canary. Angelique stared at Roy Osborne.

Harsh weather lines spun out from his sky-blue eyes. Deep furrows connected his nose to his mouth. His long, sun-streaked brown hair was tied at his nape with a piece of string, and he was perfect for what she had in mind.

But first, a few questions.

"How old are you, Mr. Osborne?"

"Dunno, ma'am. More than my fingers and toes put together, I reckon. How old are you?"

"As old as my fingers and toes put together," she said. "Why do you need money so badly, Mr. Osborne? Are you not employed?"

"I was, ma'am, but my horse died."

"Oh, I am sorry."

"Me too, ma'am."

"How much does a horse cost, Mr. Osborne?"

"Reckon I could git one for fifty, ma'am, a good horse for seventy-five."

"Dollars?"

"Yes, ma'am."

"I think I'd want a good horse," Angelique said, watching Roy Osborne squirm in his chair.

"Ma'am, I'm sorry, but I gotta' git. You see, I'm in a hurry, a big hurry."

"And why are you in such a big hurry?" She watched his face

redden. "Oh. There's no need to be embarrassed, Mr. Osborne. The water closet is down the hall."

If possible, his weathered cheeks turned redder. "No, ma'am, it's not that," he said, rising and walking toward her. "My wife, well, she's expectin' our first young'un, and I want to be there when it's birthed. We live near St. Louie. I had finished up a cattle drive an' was headin' home when some bastard—'Scuse me, ma'am, when some bastard—" He smiled sheepishly and shrugged. "Guess I cain't think of no other word, ma'am, just like I cain't seem to call you nothin' but ma'am, ma'am."

"What did the bastard do to you, Mr. Osborne?"

"He shot my horse, ma'am, and stole the saddlebag with my pay."

"I'm so very sorry, Mr. Osborne."

"Roy, ma'am. Mostly I'm called Roy, sometimes plain ol' Osborne, never mister."

"I'm so sorry, Roy."

"Ain't your fault, Miss Jenny."

"There! You did not call me ma'am this time. That is a good start."

"A good start for what, ma'am?"

Angelique pictured the banknotes *Monsieur* Barnum had thrust into her hand, despite her insistence that she had not written Jenny's ode. "Suppose I gave you two hundred dollars, Mr. Osborne. Could you buy two horses, saddles, blankets . . . maybe some food?"

He shook his head. "I don't take money—"

"From a girl. Yes, I know. But would you consider taking money from a girl who offered you honest employment?"

"No, ma'am."

Angelique felt tears blur her eyes. Crossing her fingers behind her back, she said, "Mr. Osborne . . . Roy, I need you to help me find my husband. He's somewhere in Missouri, and he needs me very badly. I have a map, and if you help me, I'll let you keep both horses."

She followed his gaze and saw that he was looking at several large trunks, stacked in the corner of the dressing room. "The trunks stay here. I shall take one gown, one pair of shoes, one pair of gloves and one bonnet."

He scratched his head. "Don't you have to sing, Miss Jenny? The gent outside said—"

"My supporting baritone, Giovanni Belletti, and my London arranger and conductor, Julius Benedict, will continue the tour until I can rejoin them."

The grin he gave Angelique made him almost handsome. "Seems you're in a big hurry too, ma'am. Already got me a saddle and bedroll, but if you grab up them flowers and that yella' bird, we'll find us some horses."

"One moment, Mr. Osborne . . . Roy. I promise this will not take long." Angelique walked to where Jenny had been writing her letter to *Monsieur* Barnum and fetched a piece of clean stationery, a pen, and an inkpot. She dipped the pen in the ink and quickly wrote:

My dear Miss Lind,

It has come to my attention that my fiancé is nearby. Therefore, I must leave your employ and join him. He needs me more than you do. I am taking one gown, one pair of shoes, one pair of gloves, and one bonnet. Please give the remainder of my clothes to a poorhouse. Thank you for all your kindnesses. I shall treasure the angel on a chain that you gave me for Christmas and carry it with me always.

I know that, in the dead of night, you sometimes doubt your God-given gift, but please remember what Mr. William Shakespeare said: "Be not afraid of greatness: some are born great, some achieve greatness, and some have greatness thrust upon them."

Au revoir,
Angel Aumont

When she had finished writing her good-bye letter and snatched her bonnet from a nearby hat rack, she said, "Sorry to keep you waiting, Roy, but I'm ready now. May we please leave for St. Louis as soon as possible?"

Roy Osborne walked forward. Tilting her chin with his callused finger, he said, "Do you ride, Miss Jenny?"

Non, she thought.

"Yes," she said.

CHAPTER TWENTY-SIX:
TIMOTHY PROPOSITIONS THE OWNER
OF ROSIE'S

The piano inside Rosie's Watering Hole and Betting House was on Timothy's right. The bar's scarred wood seemed to wend its way left, toward a hazy horizon. The distant haze was actually a large cloud of smoke from several evil-smelling cigars.

Timothy's elbows rested on the bar's surface as he sipped his warm beer and studied the woman behind the bar.

Holy shite! She wore trousers of *serge de Nîmes*. He had never seen a woman in trousers before. Knickers, yes. Trousers, no. Over her trousers, halfway to her knees, she wore a gray-brown wool shirt, belted at the waist, with gussets under the arms, which allowed her plenty of room for movement. The shirt was nicely fringed at the collar and along the bottom, with a double row of fringe at the cuffs. Timothy had the impression the fringes were a self-indulgence, her one concession to vanity. On another woman the shirt might have looked outlandish, but it suited this woman, even enhanced her femininity. She wore black leather Cossack boots, and she had tried to tame her dark, curly hair by braiding it in two plaits, both as thick as a man's wrist. Her left plait fell to just below her breast. *Lucky breast,* thought Timothy.

The freckles looked Irish. Her slanted eyes, tightly-coiled hair, and chiseled cheekbones looked Indian; worthy of note, because Timothy, during his wanderings, had learned that the Indians who had lived here before the discovery of gold had left the area, or been massacred *en masse,* and he had the feeling that even a few drops of Indian blood would have prohibited her, or for that matter disallowed *any* Indian, from entering a saloon or gambling establishment.

She must be one hell of a barkeep!

Timothy turned to the man sitting on the stool to his left. Obviously a miner, his eyes possessed an eternal squint. One eye was half shut, as though he had begun to blink, or wink, and quit halfway. His face, weathered by the sun, was the color of the tea Timothy's right old cow, Hortense, had brewed every afternoon and then served with French pastries and what she liked to call "finger sandwiches." Beneath a mangy coonskin cap, lines crisscrossed the miner's brow. A long, gray beard was tucked inside his red flannel shirt. Timothy was fascinated to see the man's beard emerge four buttonholes down from his neck, where a missing button and a balloon belly caused a gap.

"Pardon me," Timothy said to the miner, "but is that Rosie behind the bar?"

"Ain't nothin' to pardon you fer, and that ain't Rosie. That there's Peggy."

Timothy stuck out his right hand. "Name's Timothy. Do you know where I can find Rosie?"

The miner gave Timothy's hand a quick shake. "Name's Charlie. Ain't no Rosie. That there's Peggy."

"Yes, so you said. I'm looking for Rosie, the owner of this gambling house. I have a proposition—"

"Ain't no Rosie, and Peggy owns this here gamblin' house."

"Oh, I see. Did Peggy buy it from Rosie?"

Charlie stared at Timothy, then waggled his right hand as if he'd been stung by a pesky insect and its stinger was still embedded in his palm. "Ain't no Rosie," he said for the fourth time. "Peggy's a widder woman. Her husband was George Rose. He died at that table over there, holdin' four aces and a king o' hearts, shot in the back of the head. Never caught the varmint what done it. Folks say he hightailed it outa' Coloma and made tracks to another gold field. Peggy was behind the bar when Mr. Rose was shot. She could have sold Rosie's. Plenty would have bought it. She made her mind up to keep it. Taught herself shootin' till she was the fastest draw in Coloma. No one messes with Peggy Rose. She's already kilt one man and wounded two others that tried to bushwhack her, but I'd wager all I own, which ain't much, that the wounded fellers wish they'd been kilt."

"Really! Why?"

" 'Cause they lost their dangly bits."

"Their dangly bits," Timothy echoed.

"Where you from, stranger? Their twiddle-diddles." Charlie gestured toward his lap.

"Oh. *Oh!*" Timothy winced.

As if she had heard Charlie and Timothy talking about her, Peggy Rose approached.

Timothy was usually on the dot when it came to a woman's age, but his mind struggled to count up the years for this gal. Twenty-seven, perhaps thirty, was his guess. Up close her hair was not dark but black—vestment black. Her mouth was as dark as a bruise, and her deep-blue eyes seemed to be coming toward Timothy without her getting any closer.

In short, her face gave away precisely nothing, and, for some reason he couldn't fathom, it made him worry that she knew something he didn't.

He almost laughed aloud at the fanciful notion.

Mr. Clutterbuck would say Peggy's expression had diabolical archness written all over it, but Timothy disagreed. He felt her expression had a desirability, a shrewd wisdom, as if she'd seen the worst the world could dish out and was still tough enough to eat it.

He felt a stirring between his legs. When was the last time

he'd made love to a woman?

Had it really been Annie Laurie, up in the Clutterbuck hayloft?

Yes, it had, for no woman had tempted him since then.

Until now.

Ah jaysus, me pissflaps are burnin' with desire, he thought as he moved closer to the bar, hoping he could shield his swollen "flute" from Peggy's deep-blue eyes.

"Mister," she said, staring into his eyes, "if you are not planning to order another drink, there are others waiting to be seated."

Her voice had the trace of an Irish lilt, although if Timothy had not been Irish himself, he might have missed it.

"I have no objection if you want to stand behind the players, hanging 'round till someone leaves a table," she continued, "but the barstools are for my drinkers."

He noted the emphasis she put on the word "my," and his admiration for her grew. So, unfortunately, did his desire. He tried for a stone-face but couldn't be sure he achieved it.

"I'd very much like to have a few minutes of your time," he said, motioning toward the corner where the piano crouched in all its glory. "You won't regret it."

"I won't?"

"I give you my word, Mrs. Rose."

"Peggy, if you please. And you are?"

"Timothy Kelley, and I have a proposition for you."

"Never you mind, Timothy. I've had enough propositions to last a lifetime, and I have not the slightest interest in a lover or a husband, even if you were as rich as Midas."

"Not that kind of proposition. A business proposition. And King Midas died of starvation, thanks to his 'golden touch.' " As she arched one eyebrow in surprise, or perhaps admiration, Timothy silently blessed Mr. Clutterbuck for his frequent lapses into Greek mythology. "Every time King Midas touched a piece of food, it turned to gold."

"In a version told by the writer Nathaniel Hawthorne," Peggy said, "King Midas didn't die of starvation. Instead, he found that when he touched his daughter, *she* turned to gold. He hated the gift he had yearned for, so he prayed to Dionysus and begged to be freed from the 'golden touch.' Dionysus said okay, fine, and told King Midas to git. Dionysus said for Midas to wash in the river Pactolus. Midas washed in the Pactolus, and, when he touched the waters, the power flowed from his hands into the river, and the river sands turned into gold."

"Just like the American River here in Coloma," Timothy said earnestly, then grinned. "Somebody once told me that the gods live in a cloud palace above Mount Olympus, the highest mountain in Greece. They like to look down to watch what people are doing, and, from time to time they choose to interfere. I wonder if Dionysus looked down upon California. I wonder if John Sutter had the Midas touch. I wonder—Why are you shaking your head?"

"Because it wasn't Sutter who had the Midas touch. It was James Marshall, a foreman working for Mr. Sutter. He found shiny metal in the tailrace of a lumber mill he was building for Sutter on the American River. Marshall brought the shiny metal to Sutter, and the two of them privately tested it. After the tests showed that it was gold, Sutter wanted to keep the news quiet, because he feared what would happen to his plans for an agricultural empire if there were a mass search for gold. However, rumors soon started to spread and were confirmed by a man named Samuel Brannan, who set up a store to sell supplies to the miners, because he knew they'd soon be flooding in. After his store was built, Brannan ran through the streets of San Francisco and shouted, 'Gold! Gold! Gold from the American River' . . . and how come you know so much about Greek mythology?"

"How come *you* know so much?"

"I asked you first."

"A gent I worked for liked to natter on and on about the various gods. Greek *and* Roman. Men and women. I think he liked the Roman goddess, Diana, best. I liked her, too. She could control and talk to wild animals."

"You like animals?"

"Very much," he said with an emphatic nod. "Mr. Clutter— The gent I worked for also talked about Pig-somebody. And of course Midas. What about you?"

"My late husband liked to natter on and on about the various gods," she said with a smile. "Most folks think a barkeep 'don't know nothing' and I like to keep them thinking that way."

"Why?"

"I hear things."

"What kinds of things?"

"Never you mind. Things that might prove useful some day, that's all. Like San Francisco. I hear it's a cow town, with muddy streets in the summer, mud holes in the winter. Also, lots and lots of gambling houses and brothels; fleas, rats, dirt, and noise. However, some day . . ." She clamped her mouth shut.

"What about my business proposition, Peggy? That might prove useful now, rather than some day."

"All right, Timothy. You win. There's a small office in the back where I'll listen to your proposition, but only because you like animals. I do, too." She looked toward the end of the bar, near the cigar smokers, and beckoned toward the young man with the handlebar mustache.

"Aidan, please see if anyone needs another drink," she called. "I'll be gone for a short while." She turned to Timothy. "Aidan is my late husband's nephew, a good lad when he isn't itching to find himself some gold."

"Has he ever found any?"

"Not one speck, but he'll keep looking. If you drop a dream, it breaks."

Timothy grinned. "May God give you a rainbow for every storm."

"If you look down, you'll never see a rainbow."

"I knew you were Irish!"

Together they said, "May you get to heaven a half hour before the devil knows you're dead" and burst out laughing.

"You are Indian as well?" he asked.

"My mother was Kumeyaay. I never met her. She died giving me life."

Timothy heard the hurt in her voice and knew better than to question her further.

Peggy's "small office" was not a figure of speech. There was barely enough room for a chair, a wooden desk with three decks of cards on top, a small wooden file cabinet, and a crude, hand-built wooden bookshelf set against the wall. On its cluttered shelves, Timothy could discern a few novels and what looked like several religious volumes—

Yes, that's what they were. He could make out *Practical Discourses on the Perfections and Wonderful Works of God* and what looked like a Jewish religious tome called *The Ten Commandments*.

He longed to add his Alexandre Dumas book to the shelves. During his travels he had read *The Count of Monte Cristo* more than once, but, for some reason he didn't entirely understand, he was reluctant to discard the book. He thought maybe it had something to do with a longing to see—and talk to—Mr. Clutterbuck again, which was, of course, absurd.

Somehow Peggy's office also managed to contain a cot with a colorful woven blanket tossed haphazardly across its bottom half. Eyeing the cot, Timothy said, "Do you sleep here?"

"No. Don't fancy sharing the privy with gamblers and drinkers. I have a small house a few miles from Coloma. And a big dog for protection. His name is Rochester, and he'd bite you as soon as look at you."

"The only Rochester I've ever heard of is in a book called *Jane Eyre.*"

She arched an eyebrow. "Charlotte Brontë. You continue to surprise me. What's your proposition, Timothy?"

"I'd like to run a private game. I'm an honest dealer, and I know how to make a profit."

"Prove it," she said, settling herself in the chair behind the desk. Reaching for a deck of cards, she shuffled it with one hand.

"You charge five percent for the house, correct?"

"That's right, when there's a private game."

"Five percent doesn't sound like much," he said, looking for another chair, finding none, gingerly sitting on the edge of the cot, "until you add the figures. Let's assume each player starts with a hundred dollars. The usual game has eight players, so the total amount at the start is eight hundred dollars. Let's also assume each player receives the number of good, bad, and indifferent hands probability says he can expect in the long run. That means the dealer collects three hundred and sixty dollars, leaving only four hundred and forty in the game. Each player has paid forty-five dollars out of his original hundred, and your five percent has grown to forty-five percent."

"Very good, Timothy. I'm impressed."

"Wait. It gets better," he said, rising from the hard cot, keeping in check the urge to rub his backside. "Suppose the game lasts several hours? If, by that time, six players have gone broke, leaving two, they will have two hundred dollars between them. The dealer has taken a charge of six hundred out of the original eight, or seventy-five percent of the total amount the players brought into the game."

Still shuffling, she looked thoughtful. "I have two dealers for private games," she finally said. "Miguel and Danielle."

"You let gals deal?" he asked, surprised.

"Why shouldn't I? Do you have something against a woman dealing cards?"

Her voice had turned brusque, hard-edged. "No, ma'am," Timothy replied. "None at all."

"Women often gamble at Rosie's, too. They seem to lose more cheerfully than men. I'll tell you what, Timothy. If either one of my dealers leaves my employ, I'll hire you to take his or her place."

"I appreciate the offer, Peggy, but I need a position now, or I'll have to move on to another town." Timothy desperately tried not to sound desperate.

"I'm sorry, but that's the best I can offer. I cannot sack any of my dealers without cause."

"I can sing," he blurted.

She stopped shuffling. "You can sing? And why would that interest me?"

"You have a piano. Do you play?"

"No. The piano is my daughter's. She's back east, finishing up her schooling. She wants to be a schoolteacher," Peggy added, her voice prideful.

"I'll sing for gratuities and that there cot to sleep on."

She looked at the cot, then back at Timothy, a doubtful expression on her freckled face.

"When I sing, the angels turn green with envy," he added and flushed at the self-puffery.

"Prove it," she said with another smile.

Once they had returned to the bar, she waved both hands at a black man who was trying to sweep up cigar ashes as soon as they hit the floor. "Jefferson, play the piano for this gent, if you please."

Timothy's mind raced. "The Galway Piper"? "Eileen Arun"? "The Banks of Roses"? He mentally discarded several other songs until he hit upon what he knew would be the right choice. That is, if he had any chance at all of making an impression on Peggy Rose.

He waited until the elderly, bald-headed Negro was seated at the piano. "Jefferson," he said, "do you know an Irish tune called 'Peggy Bawn'?"

"No, sir, but I can follow along."

Timothy winked at Peggy and then faced the crowded room.

"Day being come and breakfast o'er," he sang,
"To the parlour I was ta'en;
The gudeman kindly asked me
If I'd marry his daughter Jane?
Five hundred marks I'll give her,
Beside a piece of lan',
But scarcely had he spoken the word,
Than I thought of Peggy Bawn.

'Your offer, sir, is very good,
And I thank you,' said I,
'But I cannot be your son-in-law,
And I'll tell you the reason why:
My bus'ness calleth me in haste,
I am the king's servant bound,
And I must gang awa' this day,
Straight to Edinburgh town.'

Oh! *Peggy* Bawn, thou art my own,
Thy heart lies in my breast,

And though we at a distance are,
Yet I love thee still the best."

Within a month, Timothy dealt from his own poker table. He had made friends with Peggy's dog, Rochester. He had watched a man toss a floppy-eared puppy—inside a sack, knotted with a rope at the top—into the American River. He had fished the puppy out and named it Jane Eyre, and he had moved from the office cot into Peggy's house and bed.

Chapter Twenty-Seven:
Blowdowns Hurt the Circus

"If you ride like that again," Sean said to Maureen O'Connor, "I'll cancel your next performance. And the one after that. And the one after—"

"If the wind picks up, you'll have to call off the whole bloody show," she interrupted, her willowy body as tense as a tightly drawn bullwhip, her chin slanted skyward, her beautiful blue eyes bright with anger. As the wind whipped her dark-red hair around her neck like a noose, she pointed toward the circus tent, a short distance away.

"Ah, heebie, hebby, hobby, hole, golong," chanted the Rope Caller, boss of the guying-out crew. His men worked their way systematically around the tent, taking up slack in the canvas, but they were nearly bent over double, fighting the frequent gusts of air, and almost all of them had lost their caps.

Sean swallowed a sigh. For the third day in a row, blustery weather threatened his circus, and the result could be a blowdown. Damned windstorms were unpredictable monsters. His rope caller was usually adept at reading warnings in the sky, always ready to drive an extra stake line, guy down the Big Top, or move in a barricade of wagons to break the wind's force. Sean would rely on the man's advice today, even though yesterday he had suggested that "the boss" cancel the show and the storm had not even arrived.

Sean's attention was drawn to the horizon, where billows of smoke had begun to rise from a barn. Even as he watched, tongues of flame licked upward. Shouting figures ran toward the burning building. If the capricious winds shifted, burning bits of debris might blow in the direction of his circus. He would have to issue orders not to open for business until the barn fire was extinguished. Horses had to be hitched to wagons. The crew had to be prepared to tear the tent down quickly if catastrophe struck.

"You're shaking like a leaf, *asthore*," he said, bringing his attention back to his lovely equestrian. "Come inside the silver wagon and rest a while."

"Why do you keep calling me 'as-thor-ee'? You've even used the name for my act."

"It's an Irish word for treasure. Come inside the silver wagon. Please?"

She looked toward the Big Top again, shrugged her slender shoulders, and allowed him to lead her to the silver wagon—the wagon where he counted and stored all proceeds from the shows and, more often than not collapsed, exhausted, and slept like a bear upon a sturdy, red-cushioned sofa.

Once inside, she folded her body atop the red sofa. Beneath the rolled-up sleeves of her shirt, her arms were dotted with gooseflesh. Sean opened a desk drawer, removed a bottle, and poured, filling a water glass. "Drink this, Maureen."

"You know I don't drink, Sean. Even if I did, I would never guzzle before a show."

"I don't want you to guzzle. I want you to relax. And unless the winds die down and the barn's fire is put out quickly, there's no chance we'll open."

She accepted the glass from his outstretched hand. Sean watched her swallow. As the fiery liquid burned its way down her throat, it brought tears to her eyes.

"This is awful," she gasped. "How can you tolerate the taste?"

"It's an acquired taste, like caviar. Have you ever eaten caviar?"

"The quick lunch wagon serves it every day," she quipped, leaning back against a cushion. "Where did you taste caviar?"

"At a party given by a New York showman named P. T. Barnum. Slow down, *asthore*. You don't have to consume it all at once."

"How can you tolerate the taste?" she asked again.

"Flavor is not always the reason a person drinks. It's the effect afterwards."

"What effect? I don't feel a thing."

"Have another wee sip. I said sip, Maureen, not guzzle."

"But if I sip, I don't like it. When I drink fast, it's much better. See? All gone. May I have some more?" She accepted another portion and gulped it down. "More?"

Sean sat next to her on the sofa. "When did you last eat?"

"This morning, I think. It's so hot in here. Isn't it hot in here?" She gave him her empty glass and tugged her shirt free from her skirt's waistband, then her shoulders, then her arms and wrists. She bent over, giving Sean a quick glimpse of her breasts, hidden behind her loose chemise, and let her shirt fall from her fingertips. Straightening, she said, "More, please."

Quirking an eyebrow, he poured and handed her the glass. "Is that enough? No? I'll give you all you want, but if you should get corned and spew it up, don't be blaming me."

She stood, lost her sense of balance, wobbled, and then, with an effort, regained her equilibrium. "All my problems seem blurry now," she said, her voice dreamy.

"Ah, my beautiful equestrian," he said, "you're corned."

"Not true. A lady is never corned."

"I've known several corned ladies."

"Did you meet them at the party you mentioned? The party given by that Bar-min fella'?"

"Barnum, not Bar-min, and no." Sean recalled Sportsmen's Hall. "I've been with Mr. Barnum when he's indulged in a beer or two, but at heart he's a teetotaler and likes to give speeches on the evils of liquor. Drinking is forbidden in his American Museum—he has a very successful museum in New York City— and visitors to its lecture room are treated to performances of *The Drunkard,* a cautionary play about dipsomania."

Staggering up and down the wagon, on the verge of falling, Maureen seemed to discover the empty water glass, still clutched in her hand. For a moment she looked puzzled. Then she carefully placed the glass on the floor, next to her shirt. "Why aren't you guzzling, Sean?"

"I must remain sober."

"Why?"

"Liquor may make your problems blurry, *asthore,* but it also makes you ardent."

Maureen stretched, her arms above her head, her breasts pushing against her oft-washed, oft-mended chemise. Sean swallowed a sigh.

"That's why I didn't sip or guzzle," he continued, "for then I would surely kiss you, and we would never stop with one kiss."

"You don't want me," she whispered.

"I want you to tell me why whiskey makes your problems shadowy," he said, trying to sound like a friend, not a ringmaster or seducer of women, or, even worse, a tyrant. "I know very little about you, Maureen, and therefore cannot help you solve any of your problems, especially if I don't know what they are or where they come from or—"

"Too many words." She placed her hands over her ears. "Maureen this, Maureen that, friends laughing, bottles and bottles of wine. Please, Aaron, too many words. Dizzy."

Aaron? Who the hell was Aaron? The missing husband? Before Sean could ask, she took one deep breath, then another, and slumped forward.

As he caught her and carried her toward the wagon she shared with her son, his hand brushed against her chemise. He felt her breasts, young and firm, and he grinned, thinking how she was too bemused to acknowledge the accidental caress. Poor lass. Tomorrow morning her head would feel like a balloon about to burst.

He was about to burst through his trousers. It had taken every ounce of willpower he possessed to keep from responding to her "you don't want me."

Yes, he wanted her. And he didn't want her. He had given his heart and soul to Angelique, and, even though she had betrayed him, he could not betray her.

Which didn't make a lick of sense.

What did make sense was dousing himself in a nearby river until his ardor cooled.

He pictured his mother, Molly, and wondered how long it had taken for his father to bury Molly in his mind as well as the ground.

CHAPTER TWENTY-EIGHT:
MAUREEN PERFORMS

By the next evening the windstorm had become an occasional breeze, and the charred barn was the only unpleasant image to mar a perfect landscape. The setting sun shaded distant hills, creating a vista filled with pink, blue, and violet streamers—silk handkerchiefs drawn from a master magician's vest pocket.

Although low from lack of rain, a nearby river had enough water for bathing. There was even an adequate amount to spray the grounds so that slippers, boots, and hooves wouldn't raise squalls of dust.

Outside the circus tent, an Opener leaned against the Red Wagon, his hand resting on the ticket window's sill. A sign over the window read: CHILDREN HALF PRICE. Soon the Opener would talk the crowd into buying tickets by loudly ballyhooing the acts. One vendor, a Bugman, stopped to converse, holding his basket of chameleons.

Sean glanced around the cook top's corner, toward the backyard, where a bright banner line proclaimed: CONGRESS OF FREAKS. Black Jack the Giant stood on a bally box, facing a small crowd of men and a few women. "Come one, come all!" he shouted. "Watch Duncan, the strongest man in the world, heftin' up Donald and Christie, the fattest twins in the universe. Watch Cuckoo the Bird Girl swaller some sharp *worms*. Did I say worms? I meant *swords*. I ain't promisin' nothin', but mebbe, just mebbe, you'll see a princess with three titties."

They didn't have a princess with three breasts, Sean thought

191

with a grin. They didn't even have a princess. But then Jack wasn't "promisin' nothin'."

Two hours later Sean stood inside the tent, by the center pole. White cuffs hung from the sleeves of his gray linen jacket. He wore a batwing collar and a black cravat, and his necktie's knot sported a diamond stickpin as big as an acorn—a gift from Jenny Lind. The spectator benches were more than half filled, thank goodness, although Sean longed for the day when they'd be full to overflowing. He needed another big act—a bigger act than Maureen's—to attract a bigger audience. Once again he wished he could use Brian, now eight, as a cat tamer. But if he pressed Maureen for permission, he had no doubt whatsoever she'd leave straightaway . . . and take Brian with her. Sean had grown exceedingly fond of the boy, the son he'd never have, at least not with Angelique.

Last but not least he needed the elephant Barnum had promised. A farmer from Somers, New York, had a brother who was a sea captain. While in London, the brother would buy an African elephant at auction for as little as twenty dollars and then sell the animal to Barnum for a thousand dollars. With a bit of Irish luck, by the time the Sean Kelley Circus reached Missouri, Barnum would have delivered Sean's elephant.

Sean planned to name it Goliath.

Right now his star performer was Maureen O'Connor, who had insisted she ride despite his misgivings. Clearing his throat, he announced her act.

It began with six riders dressed as Cossacks, who stood on top of their galloping horses and raced around the ring. From their midst, as if by magic, emerged Maureen. Clothed in tights, leotard, and short ruffled skirt, she sat sideways on her chestnut mare, Derry. Maureen's legs were crossed one over the other while the fingers of her right hand clasped the mare's mane. Then, rising to her toes, still atop Derry's back, she performed a series of dazzling stunts.

With perfect precision, a Cossack's gray Arabian appeared next to Maureen's mare. On the stallion's hindquarters, behind the Cossack, stood a Russian lass named Anastasiya. Next to the Arabian galloped a riderless black.

Sean saw Maureen count "One, two, three," while her fellow equestrians did the same.

Maureen leaped high in the air and somersaulted, alighting on the gray stallion's haunches. Anastasiya somersaulted at the same time, landing atop Derry, while the nimble Cossack cartwheeled onto the black horse. The audience cheered as all three performers reversed their routine.

A smile creased the corners of Maureen's lips as she nudged Derry from the ring, riding the mare away from the bright lanterns, through the performers' entrance. Sean let out the breath he didn't know he'd been holding. Derry was highly strung and sometimes difficult to control, but she had been a perfect lady today and would receive a special treat in her feedbag.

The five other Cossacks joined their fellow Cossack and Anastasiya, as Maureen collected her props for her final stunts.

The musicians executed a drum roll.

Once again Sean stood by the center pole. "Ladies and gentlemen and children of all ages," he announced. "Presenting a performance the likes of which you have never seen before. Our star equestrian, *Acushla*, will dazzle you with her daring and bemuse you with her beauty. We need complete silence. Not one muffled oath, not one misplaced sigh, not one whispered confession, not even a lover's kiss."

The band played "La Savane."

Maureen slapped Derry lightly on the haunch, and the chestnut, mane and tail flowing, pranced into the ring. Maureen followed on foot, bowed to the audience, and removed her cape.

She now wore a white evening gown with a small bustle and Chinese-style slits up both sides. Her arms were covered by elbow-length kid gloves, and in her left hand she carried an ostrich-feathered fan. Seizing Derry's mane, she flipped onto the mare's back.

A clown entered the ring, stuck the ostrich-feathered fan in his hat brim, handed Maureen a gun, and retreated, all the time expressing exaggerated gestures of fearful concern.

Maureen fired at a target, releasing a flock of pigeons. They flew straight toward her, alighting on her outstretched arms. At her command, Derry halted and knelt in the center of the ring. A spotted pony trotted around the ring, harnessed to a cart with a cage labeled "Hotel des Pigeons." The birds flew into the cage, and the pony withdrew, while the clown returned to retrieve the gun.

Maureen dismounted to thunderous applause.

Sean shouted, "Ladies and gentlemen and children of all ages, *Acushla,* the *treasure* of the Sean Kelley Circus, will now attempt a daring and difficult feat. Atop a galloping horse she will leap through a circle of fire. Again, I must ask—no, beg—for silence."

The slits in Maureen's long gown allowed her to land astraddle and rise to her feet. Sean watched her quickly adjust her balance to Derry's stride.

Another clown entered the ring and secured a hoop onto an iron block.

Sean held his breath again. Maureen's stunt depended on split-second timing.

The audience hushed.

The music's tempo increased.

Derry quickened her pace from a controlled canter to a gallop.

The clown struck a wooden match on the heel of his boot

and lit the hoop.

"Now!" Maureen screamed, and Derry leaped gracefully through the air and cleared the fire.

Sean exhaled and applauded with the audience, all of whom were shouting, "Bravo!"

Someone tossed a flowered nosegay into the ring. Derry shied and kicked out with her hind hooves. Maureen's legs became tangled in her long skirt.

Oh, my God! No! The clown who'd lit the hoop of fire had left the ring, and Sean didn't have time to run into the ring and catch Maureen when she fell. Barring a miracle, there was no way she'd stay atop Derry's back.

The crowd screamed as Maureen landed on _her_ back.

The clowns who were part of Maureen's equestrian act raced into the ring, joining Sean, who knelt by Maureen. The clowns carried a stretcher. With Sean, they carefully lifted Maureen's broken body and put it on the stretcher. She moaned, which meant she was alive. As Sean thanked God, he felt tears of relief run down his face.

He also thanked God that Brian was in the menagerie tent, helping Coben, the lion tamer, get the cats ready for their act. Thus, he had missed his mum's fall.

As the clowns carried Maureen into the silver wagon, Black Jack swiftly entered the tent and raced to the center pole. In a loud ringmaster's voice he said that "Acushla" was dazed but she'd be fine. Then, as the audience quieted down, he announced the next act, starring Panama, the trapeze artist.

Meanwhile, Sean sent Anastasiya and a Cossack, both on individual horses, to a nearby town. He prayed they would find a doctor there. Anastasiya would give the doctor her horse, since every minute counted, and it took time to hitch a horse to a wagon. The Cossack would lead the doctor to the circus grounds.

Inside the silver wagon, Sean covered Maureen's body with a blanket and knelt by the sofa. He didn't bother to ask where she hurt. He was fairly certain she'd broken her back, or her neck, and possibly one of her legs. Rising, he filled a glass with the last of yesterday's whiskey, which she gratefully accepted. "I've sent Anastasiya for a doctor," he said.

"You need to know," she replied, her voice full of pain but strangely calm.

"Know what, darlin'?"

"The reason why yesterday's drinking made my problems shadowy."

"No, *acushla,* not if you don't want to tell me."

"But I do want to tell you. After that, I need you to fetch Brian."

"Please, Maureen, save your breath until the doctor—"

"Sean, are you daft? No doctor can sew me back together. Have you ever heard of Humpty Dumpty?"

"I don't think—"

"It's a riddle. 'Humpty Dumpty sat on a wall. Humpty Dumpty had a great fall. All the king's horses and all the king's men. Couldn't put Humpty Dumpty together again.' "

"The answer to the riddle is an egg?"

" 'Humpty Dumpty lay in a beck,' " she continued. " 'With all his sinews around his neck. Forty doctors and forty wrights. Couldn't put Humpty Dumpty to rights.' " She tried to shake her head but could not manage it. "You are correct, Sean. The answer to the riddle is an egg . . . and Maureen O'Connor."

"Please, darlin', please hang on. Please don't give up. The doctor should be here any minute and—"

"I'm sorry, Sean. I'm not an egg, but I sincerely doubt any doctor can put me to rights. And now, you must hear my confession."

"I'm no priest!"

"It's not that kind of confession."

Maureen told Sean how she had met a wealthy rancher named Aaron Fox and believed she was wed with words spoken by Fox's friend, who wore a borrowed frock coat and clerical collar. She should have known when Aaron's friends laughed and laughed, during and after the ceremony, but she was so much in love and a wee bit the worse for wine. Eventually, she discovered Aaron's duplicity. However, it was too late, for she had already conceived his son. She wasn't sure, but she thought Aaron Fox lived "somewhere out west, perhaps Colorado."

"The Irish can only love once," Sean murmured, stroking her perspiration-soaked hair away from her hot forehead.

"Sean, promise me . . ."

"Anything, darlin'."

"Promise you'll raise Brian the same way you'd raise your own son."

Since Sean was already devoted to the boy and considered him a member of the family, it was an easy vow to make, and it seemed to ease Maureen's pain as well as her mind.

"Please find Brian," she said, "and allow him to come into the silver wagon alone. Will you do that for me?"

"Of course, my *acushla.*"

Sean found Brian in the menagerie tent. Like a shot from a cannon, he raced toward the silver wagon. When he emerged a short while later, his upper body was bare, and he carried a bloody shirt. He said, "My mama's in heaven. She coughed up lots of blood, and when I tried to stop the blood with my shirt, she said to let her be. She said that's what people dying of con . . . consumption did. They coughed up blood, and then they died."

Consumption? Sean couldn't quite hide his startled reaction, but the lad was looking up at the sky. A person wasted away for months if she had consumption. Maureen had lied about her twisted, broken body, hidden from sight by a blanket, because she didn't want Brian to associate the circus with her death. Sean had promised to look after Brian, and Sean and his circus were one and the same, peas in a pod.

What was she thinking? Brian would learn the truth from the other performers by this evening, if not sooner, unless Sean and Black Jack could convince everyone, including the crew, to keep her fall from Derry a secret—leastwise until after her burial.

Sean sighed. Later, when he was well and truly alone, he would grieve for Maureen—so young, so beautiful, her star-bright light extinguished so tragically—but right now he wondered if he might put Brian in the ring with two or three cats.

He could see the posters. The lad would make a splendid figure—

No! He had to get that image out of his head. Like most, if not all circus performers, he was superstitious, and he was more than certain if he used Brian in center ring, Maureen O'Connor would haunt him for the rest of his life.

On the other hand, if he couldn't find a star attraction by the time he reached Missouri, he'd have to give up the ghost!

Sean looked down at Brian. The lad's lips quivered. He was trying very hard not to cry. Sean led him to the cook tent, where there were benches. Once they were both seated, he said, "Brian, have you ever heard the expression 'I have seen the elephant'?"

"No, sir."

"It means overcoming the tough breaks and hardships in your life. There's a story circus folk like to tell. It's about a farmer who heard the circus was coming to town. The circus had an elephant, and he had never seen an elephant. So he hitched his horse to a cart and headed to town. He planned to sell his produce and see the elephant. On the road he encountered the elephant. Unfortunately his horse had never seen an elephant, either. The horse spooked, upset the farmer's cart, and ran off, destroying every bit of the farmer's produce. Even so, the farmer said, 'I don't care, for I have seen the elephant.' "

Sean stared into Brian's eyes, shiny with unshed tears, and saw that the boy was listening intently. "Do you understand the moral . . . the lesson of the story, Brian?"

"I think so, sir. Inside the silver wagon my mama told me about my father. Some day when I'm older, no matter how long it takes, no matter what I have to do, no matter how many tough breaks I have to overcome, I will find him. And then, from the tip of his trunk to the end of his tail, I will have seen the elephant."

CHAPTER TWENTY-NINE:
MAD DOG VIEWS THE NEW CORPSE

Once again, Mad Dog Connolly was flummoxed.

Thomas had found a naked male corpse at the bottom of one of Alistaire McCoy's two carriages, inside the carriage house. With an eagerness that could be described as gleeful, Thomas had led Mad Dog straight to the dead body.

The man's head had been bashed in. Mad Dog also noted that the carcass had been wrapped in a horse blanket, and, although the dead man's feet had been securely enclosed within the confines of the blanket, his head and shoulders had not, and he'd stained the carriage floor almost beyond repair with copious amounts of red, now brown, blood. The brown blood meant that the man had been dead for quite a while.

That's an underestimation, you eejit!

Obviously, the dead man was Henry, the coachman who, according to the upstairs maid Gertrude, had "done a moonlight flit."

In Mad Dog's opinion, the carriage house looked more like a cart shed. It was a small building, an open-fronted, single-story structure with the roof supported by regularly spaced pillars. It housed one agitated horse, who reared up at the sight of Mad Dog and Thomas. Mad Dog glanced here and there for a weapon, in all probability a hammer of some sort, but didn't see anything amiss; nothing that could be used to bash someone's head in. The carriage house (*or cart shed*) was, in truth, as neat as a pin. Except for the bloody corpse, of course.

Congratulating Thomas on his find, Mad Dog compared the discovery of the corpse to a dig for buried treasure, then silently chastised himself for the absurd analogy, even though Thomas nodded more than once and looked pleased as punch.

At least, thought Mad Dog, he hadn't compared Thomas's "astute observation" to a needle in a haystack.

Instructing Thomas not to touch anything, and not to smoke inside the carriage house, Mad Dog said he'd send someone for the dead wagon, and he'd return to the carriage house as soon as he could. Whereupon, he raced back to the Tapestry Room—

Where his orderly, efficient chess lineup of servants had disbanded.

He had left his favorite copper, Samuel, sometimes called "Bull" (*behind his back*), more often than not called Samson, to guard the door. Over six feet tall and heavily muscled, Samson possessed bulging, watery-blue eyes, a bloated face, and a swaggering gait. Within his strong hands, he held a struggling Nella, who stopped thrashing about when he saw Mad Dog.

"No one's left the room, sir," Samson said, "except for the housekeeper, in order to fetch some salts, but she's back now. This one here was tryin' to leave."

"Let me go, sir," Nella pleaded, staring up into Mad Dog's face. "I ain't done nothin'."

Mad Dog shot an accusatory glare in the housekeeper's direction. She had claimed Nella did not speak English. She was unquestionably wide of the mark, for the lanky, ill-clothed man not only spoke English, but he had a British accent that was not unlike the obvious inflection of the missing niece's housemaid, Gertrude. You could almost swear Nella and Gertrude were members of the same family, first cousins perhaps, or brother and sister.

Mad Dog shifted his gaze to Gertrude, who was now slumped over in a chair, pinned there by the butler as the housekeeper waved smelling salts under her nose.

Choking from the pungent salts, she jerked her head up and down a few times and opened her eyes. She looked around wildly, then screamed, "Why did you kill Henry? Once we managed to escape from Mrs. McCoy, we were going to be wed. Why, Allen?" Then she clamped a hand over her mouth.

Between her fingers she said, "I didn't mean that, about killing Henry. I'm sure, if you . . . if you killed him, you had a good reason, Allen . . . uh, Nella . . . oh, God . . ." She hastily pulled up her skirts, bent her head between her legs, and commenced to vomit.

"Not in the Tapestry Room," hissed the housekeeper. "Gertie, stop it this very minute! Oh, very well, if you really must. Someone fetch a chamber pot to hold under her chin. And a mop and pail."

No one moved. The flock of servants looked down at the floor and shuffled their feet in a weird dance. The underbutler, the flunky, and the valet stared at Gertie's legs, above her stockings, as if they'd never seen a girl's bare thighs before. The flunky licked his lips.

The upstairs maid, Mary, gave a piercing laugh. "Ain't so high and mighty no more, are we, Gert the flirt? The mistress will whip you to a bloody pulp when she sees her Tapestry Room floor."

"Mrs. McCoy is dead, you dog's bollocks!" Gertie wiped her mouth on her sleeve. "The dead don't give a shite 'bout a room's bleedin' floor!"

"Maybe she ain't dead, Dirty Gertie. Maybe it's some kind of trick, and who the bloody hell is Allen?"

"Bugger off, Mary." Looking directly at Nella, Gertie began to sob. "I'm so . . . so . . . very . . . very . . . sorry, Allen."

"That's okay, Gertie. You couldn't help it, and the bobby standin' over there looks like he already knows it was me wot done the brickbat inside the carriage house. Stop crying."

Jaysus! Mad Dog thwacked his forehead with the palm of his hand. *Allen is Nella spelled backwards.*

He walked over to the sobbing girl. "Young lady," he said, not unkindly. "Who is Allen, and what is he to you?"

"He . . . he's my . . . my brother," she sobbed. "He finally had . . . had enough in his nest egg to . . . to come to America."

"And?" Mad Dog encouraged.

"My name is Allen Starling, and I'm the most excellent trapeze artist in all of London and Paris," the newly christened Allen interjected, his voice prideful. Stripping the self-importance from his voice, he said, "My sister sent me a letter. In it she said that Angelique, Mrs. McCoy's niece, was unhappy, her aunt an evil woman. I borrowed enough money to add to my nest egg and booked a passage to America. I planned to ask Angelique to marry me. I appeared with her at the Cirque in Paris, France. I've loved her for a long, long time. I didn't know she was in love with another man."

The anguish on the young man's face was tangible. Poor bugger.

"I found my sister beaten to a bloody pulp," Allen Starling continued. "Show 'im, Gertie."

The girl issued forth a last sob. Clutching the arms of the chair, she hopped it sideways, away from the pile of vomit. Then she leaned over, took off her shoes, rolled down and discarded her woolen stockings, and showed Mad Dog her feet.

His breath caught in his throat as he noted the angry welts on both of her soles. He couldn't imagine how she had even walked to the Tapestry Room.

"Show 'im your back, Gertie."

"Not in front of all these people, Allen."

"I'll hide you."

The young man shed Samson's loose grip and stepped in

front of his sister, shielding the front of her body from curious eyes as she pulled her gown from her shoulders and let the bodice fall to her waist.

Mad Dog walked around, behind the chair. This time he couldn't prevent the intake of breath that rose in his throat and escaped through his open mouth as he stared at the swollen flesh and bloody gashes on her back and shoulders.

He thought of many things to say, but could only gasp out, "Mrs. McCoy used a whip and a cat 'o nine tales on your back, a cane on your feet?"

"Yes, sir."

"Why would she do that? What did *you* do?"

"I would not tell her where *Petite Ange* was or where she'd gone."

"Petite Ange?"

"Angelique. Her niece. After Mrs. McCoy beat me, she was downright skeered, afraid I might die, so she had Mrs. Morgan put cold cloths and salve on my back and feet."

"If I had not tended to Gertie's back, or if I tittle-tattled to the master when he returned," Grace Morgan said, "I would've been sacked. Per'aps beaten as well. Do you understand, sir?"

"No, I do not. You could have reported Mrs. McCoy to the authorities. Beating Gertie like she did would be considered attempted murder."

"And then what? The mistress would be hauled away, taken into custody by you or a different copper"—she gestured with her thumb toward Samson—"and Mrs. McCoy would be at liberty just as soon as the master returned. I'd lose my housekeeper position, and I disbelieve I could find another arrangement, once she'd finished gabbing 'bout me to her friends."

Mad Dog studied Allen, who stood alone, unshackled by Samson's hands, yet had made no move to flee from the room. "Why did you kill Henry, Mr. Starling?"

"As I said before, I came here to see Angelique, hoping I could convince her to run away with me. Mr. McCoy wouldn't hire me. He said he was pleased with the servants he had, and when I learned Angelique wasn't allowed to leave the house, I knew I had to get inside, at the very least join the servants for meals. Mr. McCoy left on a business trip and—"

"And when Henry appeared to have vanished into thin air, thanks to you, you convinced Mrs. McCoy to hire you as her coachman."

The young man nodded. "But it was an accident, sir. Inside the carriage house, I mean. The coachman . . . Henry . . . came at me, and I fought back."

"What did you use on Henry's head, Mr. Starling?" Mad Dog asked amidst the loud cronks from the gaggle of servants.

"A horseshoe."

"A horseshoe," Mad Dog echoed.

"It hung above the carriage house entrance, on pegs, still does. I felt bad about that, still do. I didn't know then, when the coachman attacked, that my sister was inside her room, too sick to move about. She had a fever from the whipping, you see. I managed to sneak inside her room. Gertie was so happy to see me, she cried. She said she hoped to work for a man named Barnum, as a trapeze artist, and that Angelique had gone to stay with Mr. Barnum's wife at a place called Iranistan. I asked if she'd ever been there, and she said yes. She said Henry had driven her there when she delivered letters to a man named Sean, the man Angelique loved. I wanted to cry when I heard Angelique loved someone else, but I told Gertie that the coachman had done a moonlight flit and we . . . Gertie and I . . . would leave together for Mrs. Barnum's as soon as her back healed a bit more and she could move without fainting and—"

"Why did you kill Mrs. McCoy?"

Allen Starling shook his head so vigorously, Mad Dog thought

205

the boy's neck would give a loud snap and detach itself from the rest of his body.

"I did not kill Mrs. McCoy," Starling said. "I swear to God and all that's holy, I had no hand in the death of Angelique's aunt. How did she die, sir? I don't own a knife or a gun. I have no cane or whip. So unless she was killed with a horseshoe, someone else butchered her."

Throughout his career Mad Dog had questioned a sufficient amount of felons to be able to determine the young trapeze artist was telling the truth.

As he turned his back on the servants so they'd be unable to read the bemused expression on his face, Mad Dog had one single, solitary thought.

If Allen Starling didn't kill Mrs. Bernadette Browning-Hale McCoy, who did?

CHAPTER THIRTY:
ANGELIQUE PLAYS EQUILIBRIST

Watching circus equestrians, Angelique had always thought that riding a horse would be easy as pie. She should have known better, especially since she had never baked a pie. In truth, she had never cooked anything at all.

Circuses had cook tops and cook tents.

Uncle Alistaire and Auntie Bernadette employed a cook.

Roy Osborne couldn't cook, either. If she'd had any money left from the horses and gear, Angelique would have handed it over for a nice hot cup of tea. Roy's coffee tasted like gooey mud, and his hardtack tasted like—Well, to be perfectly honest, she had never tasted anything that tasted like hardtack. It was salt-less. It was bread. It was hard. And when it came time to describe it to Sean, that would be all she could say.

She and Roy were getting closer to the *X* on Sean's map, even if she *had* delayed their journey by falling off her damnfool horse so many times she had lost count.

And *she* rode the seventy-five dollar horse.

Angelique heard the echo of Sean's voice: *Should our wee lasses fall from their horses, 'tis not such a lengthy journey to the ground.*

She heard her reply: *I would rather count the stars.*

Tonight there were a multitude of stars overhead, and a full moon provided enough "lamp light" for a rope to be strung between two trees. Coiled across Roy's saddle was a rope, only he called it a lasso.

"Want more coffee, Miss Jenny?"

"No, thank you." Angelique wrinkled her nose at the thought. "But I would like to borrow your lasso, *s'il vous plaît.*"

"Is that Swede talk, see-vu-play?" Roy nodded toward the canary, which, for some reason Angelique couldn't fathom, he had insisted they take along on their journey. "The gent with the blooms said you was a Swedish bird, Miss Jenny. Knew a Swede once. Big yella-haired fella', same color hair as that there bird. Nice feller. Why do you want my lasso, Miss Jenny?"

"I thought I might string it up between those two trees and walk on it. If the rope is tight enough, I can do back flips. If it's really guyed out—, I mean stretched—I can try a forward somersault, which has never before been done by a woman."

Roy removed his hat, scratched his scalp, tossed the remains of his coffee into the fire, listened to the hiss, and put his hat back on. "Okay," he said.

Once they had strung Roy's lasso as tightly as humanly possible, he hoisted her up onto the rope. Immediately, Angelique clung to the nearest tree. Damn and blast! Too many months had passed since she had played the equilibrist.

Then she felt the magic.

Her bare feet practically skimmed the rough rope as she danced to the middle. Her gown was a hindrance, but she had removed every petticoat, leaving only her chemise and drawers beneath the gown. Dare she remove the gown? No. She trusted Roy, but knew him well enough to know his cheeks would turn bright crimson, and he wouldn't watch. She wanted him to watch her perform. She wanted the canary and the night critters that inhabited the woods to watch: the owls and possums. She wanted the fish in the stream to watch. She wanted God to watch.

This is what she had been born to do.

CHAPTER THIRTY-ONE:
MARKED CARDS

Standing behind the bar, Timothy watched Peggy watch her nephew, Aidan, converse with both miners and women as he poured and served drinks. Tall and good-looking, with a cheerful, devil-may-care disposition, Aidan attracted women the same way flames enticed moths.

Peggy leaned against the counter that held the money drawer. She negligibly shuffled a deck of cards as she looked up at Timothy and said, "I heard you invited several guests to join your poker game tonight."

"You heard right." Timothy stood next to her. He had been lazily mesmerized by her shuffling, but now he quirked an eyebrow and looked into her dark-blue eyes. "Is there some kind of setback I don't know about? Surely there are enough cards to go around."

"There's no setback, darling. It's just that tonight you'll deal a private game for high stakes."

"How high?"

"No limit."

Startled, Timothy tried to keep his face unresponsive but, instead, felt his eyes widen. "What's our cut?"

"The usual five percent. You'll deal while Danielle sits in for the house."

"Let Danielle deal. I'm the better player. Especially in a serious game for high stakes. Danielle uses her obvious assets to distract, but an earnest player won't be bamboozled." He cocked his head. "Okay, Peggy. Tell me why I can't play for the house."

"Because the host asked that you deal."

"Who's the host?"

"Don Antonio Dominguez de Estudillo."

"The wealthy rancher?"

"Correct, although 'wealthy' is an understatement," she said with a grin that merged her freckles. "His herd of palominos is the finest in all of California. Did you know that, after his wife died, he asked me to marry him?"

"Don Antonio Dominguez de Estudillo asked you to marry him?"

"Yes," she said, looking like a cat who had just lapped up a bowl of cream. Despite her trousers, Peggy had the heart—and self-worth—of a woman who knows damned well she's pretty.

"I'm mighty glad you said no, sweetheart, but I imagine I'm not exactly Don Antonio's favorite dealer."

Hard as he tried, Timothy hadn't been able to keep his *affaire* with Peggy a secret, and—with a decisive shrug—she had decided they needn't bother. The only person who could be affected was her daughter, Ruby Rose, who was finishing up her education back east. Ruby planned to start a school in San Francisco, where, she insisted, they needed a school more than Coloma did.

Peggy had once said she'd birthed Ruby at age sixteen, having wed George Rose at fifteen. Ruby's birth had been long and difficult, Peggy had almost died, and she'd been told her chances of having another child were next to none.

When Timothy heard that, he was vastly relieved. It meant he didn't have to pull out before spilling his seed. He had told Peggy about Molly, more than once, but he sat on the fence when it came to Hortense, whom he guessed had divorced him by now. Surely her proper British dad and mum had paved the way. What was the use of even mentioning her name?

"It occurs to me that I'm not Don Antonio Dominguez de Estudillo's favorite resident of Coloma, either," Timothy said, "since I was fortunate enough to win the prize he desired."

"*Au contraire,* darling. He's bringing along his eldest son, Esteban Estudillo y Estudillo. Don Antonio says he wants the boy to learn how to play cards by watching a high-stakes poker game, and he wants our best dealer. I told him that was you and he had no objection. In fact, he insisted you deal."

"Boy? How old is the son?"

"Fifteen, I believe."

"Jesus!"

"I'd let Him play, too," Peggy said with a wink and a smile, "assuming He carried an adequate amount of silver, bronze, and brass coins in the belt of His tunic. During the time of Jesus Christ, Jews used common metals . . . probably minted at Caesarea . . . rather than gold." She glanced around the room, chock-a-block with gamblers, many shaking the gold dust from their crude leather pouches. "Those Jews were smart."

One afternoon, after he and Peggy had urgently made love on the cot in her office, Timothy said, "Why don't poker players indulge in private games without a dealer? That's what I did in Paris."

"They can, of course, but they're afraid of getting cheated."

"Have you ever cheated, Peg 'o my heart?"

She rose from the cot, donned her clothes, walked over to the desk, sat on the chair, and pulled a new deck of cards from a middle drawer.

"Choose a card, darling," she said as she fanned the deck.

He drew one out and shielded it with his hand.

"Queen of hearts," she said.

"Yes. How did you know?"

"The cards are marked."

"But it was a new deck. I saw you break the seal."

Reaching into the drawer again, Peggy pulled out four more sealed decks. "One of these decks is marked," she said. "Let's see if you can find it."

Timothy examined the cards one by one, an arduous task. After thirty minutes, he couldn't spot the marked deck. "All right, Peggy, I give up."

"I'll confess. I lied when I said one deck is marked."

"Damn you, Peggy Rose! What a cruel trick! I can't believe you'd play—"

"As a matter of fact, all of the decks are marked."

"I don't believe it."

With a wicked grin, Peggy read each card from the back. When she had finished, Timothy said, "I've never cheated in any of my games."

"And never will. That's why we charge the five percent." She grinned again. "Would you like to learn these cards?"

"Yes. But first I want to finish lunch and eat dessert. I'm still hungry. In truth, I'm starving."

He walked around the desk, pulled her from her chair, then tugged her trousers and a pair of frilly drawers down to her ankles. Sinking to his knees, he snaked his arms around her generous body, grasped her bare buttocks with both hands, and drew her closer.

His tongue made lazy circles around her belly button.

"The cot," she gasped.

"Soon," he said, tickling her belly with his thick head of hair as he moved lower and lower and—

"Ohmygod," she cried, quivering from head to toe. "Don't stop, my love!"

It was the first time she'd used the word "love."

CHAPTER THIRTY-TWO:
TIMOTHY PLAYS POKER

Fuming, Timothy watched Danielle lose big pots. Her bluffs were useless, and she stayed in the game when she should have folded. Danielle was usually a far better poker player, but she spent too much time flirting with Don Antonio Dominguez de Estudillo.

At long last the game halted so that the players could refresh themselves with the food and drink Peggy had provided.

Don Antonio approached Timothy. In a reserved yet arrogant voice, he said, "This is my son, Esteban, *mi orgullo y alegría*. Esteban, this is Señor Kelley, the best card player in all of California."

Mi orgullo y alegría. My pride and joy. Timothy swallowed a smile as he wondered if he should shake Esteban's hand or genuflect.

The boy, who couldn't have been much more than five feet, three inches tall, forcefully thrust out his hand, but his handshake was merely a quick brush of his fingers against Timothy's, as if he were afraid of getting his hand dirty. He wore black trousers, a white linen shirt with a stand-up collar, a four-in-hand necktie with the pointed ends sticking out to form "wings," a fitted frock coat, and a black waistcoat. His clothes were expertly tailored to his size, each piece an exact—and expensive—replica of the clothing his father wore.

"*Papá*, I want to play cards with him," the boy said, pointing rudely at Timothy.

"You are here to watch, not to play," Don Antonio replied.

"What objection do you have to me playing a few hands while you eat and drink, *Papá*? That's the best way to learn."

"Let the little tyke play, sen-yore Estu-dillo," a player said around the fat cigar that bloated his lips. His upper lip was very nearly hidden by a generous mustache that had caught crumbs from the little cakes Peggy served.

"*Gracias, señor*," Esteban said to the cigar-chewing man, but Timothy could detect a murderous glint in the lad's eyes, which were as dark as burnt bread. Evidently, he didn't like being called a little tyke and would just as soon run a knife through any guest who dared to call him little. Or tyke.

"Do you know poker rules?" asked another player, who was dabbing at his mouth with a linen napkin.

"I think so," Esteban said. "I've watched the *vaqueros* on my father's ranch."

"If you gentlemen all agree," said Peggy, "I'll let Timothy and Don Antonio's son, Esteban, play for half an hour. There will be no house percentage since they share the deal."

The others had no objection. Instead, they gave the boy indulgent looks and smiles.

"*Gracias, Señora* Rose," said Esteban, sliding onto the chair his father had occupied.

"We can cut for first deal," Timothy said, swallowing a sigh as he sat back down in his dealer's chair. He didn't want to . . . what was the miners' favorite expression? Take candy from a baby? Shoot fish in a barrel?

He and Esteban made their cuts, with Esteban winning the first deal.

It took about ninety seconds to play out a hand, and after ten minutes it became obvious Esteban had done more than just *watch* his father's *vaqueros*.

"Does this win?" he'd ask, smugly showing his three of a kind to Timothy's two pair.

He was having an extraordinary run of luck, Timothy mused, unless the ranch hands had taught the lad more than the fact that a full house beats a flush.

Timothy felt his shoulders tense up as he realized Esteban was cheating. No doubt about it. He was palming the cards. Palming could be learned by almost anyone, but doing it well required talent and assiduous practice. The boy was doing it well, palming cards and placing his hand on his arm in a natural curved position, or resting his hand, fingers together, on the table.

Before Timothy could expose him, Esteban lost a small pot and tossed the cards toward Timothy, who played the odds, winning the next three hands. Finally, he lost.

This time Esteban seemed to be dealing honestly, but he was still winning, and Timothy couldn't detect his cheating method. Peggy would probably tell him later.

Why didn't she expose the *tricheur*? Was she afraid of offending the boy's wealthy father? After all, Don Antonio had asked Peggy to be his wife, and Timothy could tell the rancher hadn't changed his mind. He had greeted Peggy with *"La hermosa rosa"* and a kiss on the wrist. Furthermore, he'd been casting ardent glances toward her all evening. Timothy knew enough Spanish to translate *la hermosa rosa* into "the beautiful rose," and he tried to shake off the sharp stabs of jealousy that invaded his head.

"This is too easy, and I'm bored," Esteban said. "Let's finish the game with one hand." Grinning complacently, he pushed all his money toward the middle of the table.

Timothy reciprocated, then added a thousand dollars.

"But I don't have any more money," Esteban said.

This time Timothy grinned. "If you can't match my thousand, you forfeit."

"But I'm sure I can win. I'm the better player. *Papá*, would you give me more money?"

"No. You risked your entire stake and must now assume the consequences."

The other players had drawn close to the table. Some were still smiling indulgently, some making *tsk-tsk* sounds.

Esteban's face had turned tomato red. Looking around the room, he said, "Would anyone care to buy my palomino stallion? He's worth much more than a thousand dollars."

"*¿Estás loco?*" Don Antonio roared. "You cannot do that."

"The stallion is mine, *Papá*, a birthday present. You have no right to tell me what I can or cannot do with my own horse."

"I'll buy your stallion for a thousand dollars," said the man who chewed a cigar. Shifting his gaze to Don Antonio, he added, "If your boy wins, I'll sell the horse back to him for two thousand dollars."

"If you lose, Esteban," Don Antonio said, "you'll walk home!"

"I have no intention of losing, *Papá*. Luck is on my side. Shall we proceed?"

I have to do something, Timothy thought desperately. But he couldn't figure out how the boy was cheating. The shuffle. It had to be in the shuffle.

He pictured Esteban riffling the cards, and all at once it became clear. How simple. Of course. Esteban simply put the cards he wanted on the bottom of the deck. Then, during the shuffle, he pulled one from the bottom and one from the top.

But it's too late to expose him. He's already shuffled, and I've made the cut. If I insist he show the cards, he'll say it's unintentional, and who would dare refute the son of Don Antonio Dominguez de Estudillo?

"I believe a wager of this magnitude calls for new cards," said a familiar voice. "Please excuse me for interrupting, but I just arrived and was told by the man pouring drinks that my good friend Paddy was inside this room."

"You are mistaken," said Peggy, unsuccessfully attempting to hide her annoyance. "There is no 'Paddy' here."

"I believe you mean Timothy, not Paddy," Timothy said, his voice as hard as granite. "Isn't that right, Mr. Clutterbuck?"

What the bloody hell are you doing here, Mr. Clutterbuck?

"Timothy Kelley," Mr. Clutterbuck said with a smile. "Of course. And my name is Buck. Jim Buck."

Before Timothy could utter another word, Peggy said, "Mr. Buck is correct. A wager of this magnitude calls for new cards."

"But I want to use these cards." Esteban gestured toward the deck he had just shuffled. "They've been lucky." His mouth twisted in a snarl. "They've been so lucky that your *best card player in all of California* is a fucking loser."

"Esteban, watch your mouth," Don Antonio said. With an effort obvious to everybody in the room, he managed to keep his temper under control.

"Our rules state that a losing player can request a new deck at any time," Peggy said, as she pulled a sealed deck from her trouser pocket. "Would you like new cards, Timothy?"

"Yes, please."

"I don't care what the fucking rules say!" Esteban screamed, sounding like the fifteen-year-old he was.

"Let's get this over with," said a furious Don Antonio. He reached out, accepted the new deck from Peggy, broke the seal, and handed the cards to Esteban.

Immediately, Timothy recognized the markings on the back. It was one of the five decks Peggy had teased him with the afternoon they had shared "dessert" inside her office.

By the time Esteban finished dealing, Timothy saw that the incensed boy held two pair—aces and sevens—while Timothy's hand included two tens and two deuces.

Hesitating, trying to look indecisive, Timothy pulled one card from his hand and placed it, face down, on the table, trusting Esteban would believe he hoped to complete an inside straight. Upon receiving the new card, Timothy scowled, then assumed his usual stone face.

Esteban discarded a queen.

Timothy watched Esteban clutch the next card and knew from its markings that it was another queen.

"Are you ready to resume the betting?" Timothy asked.

"But we've finished," Esteban snarled. "I've matched your stake."

"You said you were bored. You said I was a loser. You said you were the better player."

"I *am* the better player. Besides, you're bluffing."

"In that case, call my bluff." Timothy withdrew a gold cigarette case from his vest pocket. "I bought this in Sonora. It's worth a thousand dollars, and I have the receipt to prove it, although you're welcome to have it appraised in Colona, should you win the pot. If I've misled you, I'll pay you double." He pushed the cigarette case toward the middle of the table. "I'll bet this against a colt from your father's herd."

"Papá?"

"Yes, yes, just get this over with."

Esteban fanned out his cards. "Two pair, ace high," he said triumphantly. "Now show me your straight."

"I don't have a straight."

"I knew it!" Esteban reached for the money and the gold cigarette case.

"But I do have a full house, tens and deuces."

"What? You cheated. You must have. I saw the look on your face when I dealt your last card."

"That, my boy, is what's called a bluff." Timothy stood up and stretched. "Thank you for your patience, gentlemen. Danielle may deal now. I'd like to be reunited with my old friend,

Mr. Clut—uh, Jim Buck. Is that satisfactory?" Timothy asked Don Antonio.

"Of course. But I'm afraid I must withdraw from the game. My son has had an accident and must return home immediately. I'll have your colt delivered as soon as I can arrange it."

An accident? Timothy turned his gaze on the lad, who still sat in his chair. Esteban's face was once again tomato red as he held his hands over his lap, frantically trying to hide the wetness that stained and darkened his trousers.

Don Antonio withdrew a money clip from his coat pocket and counted out three thousand dollars, which he handed to the cigar-chomping man. "This should cover the cost of my son's stallion," he said. Then, facing Esteban, he added, "We will be leaving for home now, *mi hijo*. I believe you've learned enough for one day."

Mi hijo. My child. Not *mi orgullo y alegría*—my pride and joy. It was a gentle slap in the face. Timothy almost felt sorry for the lad.

Almost.

CHAPTER THIRTY-THREE:
A PROPOSITION

Outside, in front of Rosie's, was a covered wagon filled with various goods and produce. Sitting primly atop the wagon seat was Annie Laurie Cloncannon, attracting stares from every man who passed her way. One miner tripped over his own feet and sprawled in the dirt. Dusting himself off, still staring at Annie Laurie, he smiled sheepishly.

She held a bonnet in her hands, while her cherry-red curls tumbled down her back, to her waist. She wore a gown of white lace and satin with the neckline off her shoulders, indifferently, or perhaps on purpose, showing off her obvious assets. A shawl, large enough to cover her obvious assets, had been casually tossed on the wagon's seat. Her face looked more mature than when Timothy had last seen it, but in a good way.

The newly-named Jim Buck introduced her as his fiancée.

"You divorced Mrs. Clutterbuck?" Timothy managed, despite the feeling that his mouth still hung down past his chin at the sight of Annie Laurie.

"Don't talk rubbish, Paddy. Sorry. I meant Timothy. Why would I divorce Caroline? She will keep the home fires burning at Buckingham Manor, where I'll return one day, if only to secure more funds and retrieve my statue of Diana. Turning to Peggy, he said, "Do you mind if I set up a tent in front of your establishment and sell my paraphernalia to the miners? I'll let you have first choice of the food and the clothing, and I'll pay you a percentage of all sales. I can set the tent up tomorrow morning. Meanwhile, I'll move my wagon to a new neck of the woods."

"A new neck of the woods," she echoed with a smile. "My house happens to be surrounded by trees and shrubs, Mr. Buck, so you can set your wagon there. That will give me a chance to select my goods ahead of time."

Later, situated inside Peggy's house, drinking brandy in front of the living room's stone fireplace, Mr. Clutterbuck, who insisted on being called Buck without the Mister, looked at Timothy and said, "I have a proposition for you."

Timothy caught Peggy's gaze as both recalled their first meeting, and, as one, they broke into gales of laughter.

"I said something funny?" Buck gave Timothy a tentative grin.

"Yes, sir. No, sir," he replied. "What's your proposition?"

"I plan to build a gambling house and restaurant in San Francisco. People like to call San Francisco a cow town, but I believe it will soon become a thriving city. To that end, I've purchased three lots."

"What does your gambling house and restaurant have to do with me?"

"I'd like you to be my partner in this venture. You're smart to a fault, and I know for a fact you watched Cook prepare and serve large dinners at Buckingham Manor. If it pleases you, I'll call our restaurant 'Diamond Tim's Agora.' Agora is Greek for a gathering place."

"Why Diamond?"

"It sounds more . . . what's the French word for high class?"

"*Haute société.*"

"Right. *Haute société.* Don't you agree, Mrs. Rose?"

"Peggy, if you please," she said, sounding dazed.

"Whoa, wait," Timothy said. "I appreciate the offer, Mr. Clutterbuck . . . Buck, but I don't have enough money to invest." As he spoke, Timothy pictured the food, the plates, the cutlery at the formal dinner that had ultimately led to his good fortune. He stifled an urge to lick his lips.

"You'll have more than enough to pay me back in a year or two, assuming you agree to run my restaurant." He turned to Peggy. "And I'd like you to run my gambling house. We can call it 'The Rose and the Buck,' or a different name if you prefer."

Hands on hips, Peggy said, "Pardon me for asking, Jim Buck, but what do you know about me, and how on earth did you find Timothy?"

"I'll answer your last question first. Timothy's fame has traveled beyond Colona, and I happened to come across his name."

Timothy jerked his chin up. "What are you talking about? What fame? My gambling?"

"No, your singing. At Rosie's. A reporter who visited the gold fields wrote it up in San Francisco's *Alta California,* and I imagine you are well aware that I read newspapers." He scowled, then chuckled.

"And what do you know about me?" Peggy said.

"I know that you've made a success of Rosie's. I know that your daughter intends to open a school in San Francisco, and, by the way, I'll be happy to finance that venture if you agree to run my establishment."

Blackmail, thought Timothy, still astonished that his singing had made the pages of the *Alta California.*

"The school will be for everyone," Peggy said. "Girls as well as boys, colored and white, rich and—"

"That might be a problem. I'm not sure I approve of a school for girls. But even if I don't invest in your daughter's school, you'll soon have more than enough money to bankroll the enterprise yourself."

Timothy had to admit that *Buck* was a clever bastard to keep baiting Peggy with Ruby.

"The man I saw earlier inside Rosie's . . . the man pouring drinks . . . is he a relative?" Buck asked Peggy.

"I think you already know he is," she said with a smile. "That's how you found out about Ruby. The man pouring drinks is my nephew, Aidan."

"Can he run Rosie's without you?"

"Yes, I believe he can."

"Well, there you go. You and Timothy can visit Rosie's every so often to keep an eye on things. It's not a difficult journey from San Francisco, and you can deliver goods for the miners, which I'll provide."

Timothy finished off his brandy. "You said three lots, sir . . ." *Stop calling him sir, you eejit!* "What plans do you have for the third lot?"

"A dress shop to be run by Annie Laurie, assuming I can secure dress materials, hats, and other womanly gewgaws from the ships that dock there. She has impeccable taste in clothing."

Timothy turned his gaze on Annie Laurie. Her lace and satin gown proved the worth of Mr. Clutterbuck . . . Buck's statement. She gazed back at him, her eyes colder than the hinges of hell, and he realized she hadn't forgiven him for the words he'd tossed in her lap at their last meeting. He couldn't really blame her. He'd have to apologize. Profusely.

He suddenly realized how much he'd changed. Perhaps it was his relationship with Peggy, knowing full well she'd shoot his "twiddle-diddles" if he crossed her. Briefly, he grinned at the notion, then once again silently vowed to track down his daughter Charlotte and, somehow, transport her to California. Was Sean still in Paris?

Facing Peggy, he said, "What do you think?"

"You've always wanted to own a restaurant. You've mentioned it more than a dozen times. It's a dream come true."

"No, sweetheart, what do you think about moving to San

Francisco? I won't join Buck if you stay here."

"Jim, let's go outside," said Annie Laurie. "The sky is clear, and, if you do not mind, I'd like to look at the stars."

It was the first time she had joined in the conversation. Timothy heard the Irish lilt in her voice, still very strong.

After the door clicked shut, Timothy said, "Jim Buck is correct. If we move to San Francisco, we can leave every once in a while to check up on Aidan. Perhaps Jim Buck will take an interest in Aidan's mine and Aidan can hire some partners to help pan it. Meanwhile, we can find a house in San Francisco big enough for the two of us and the dogs—"

"We?"

"Yes, we." Timothy pulled a small box from his pocket and handed it to Peggy. "Open it," he said.

Nestled inside the box, on a piece of velvet, was a diamond ring.

"The diamond from your stickpin!" Peggy exclaimed. "I wondered why you weren't wearing it, and why you didn't offer it during the last hand of your poker game with that child, Esteban. *Gold* cigarette case, my arse." She snorted.

"The stickpin no longer exists, my darling. I brought it to a jeweler, who turned it into a diamond ring." Timothy fell to one knee. "Peggy Rose, will you marry me?"

He was prepared to hold his breath. Instead, almost immediately she said, "I suppose I must."

"Why must you?"

"Because I'm going to have a baby."

"You are? But you said . . . I thought . . ."

"You thought what?"

"That I was too old," he replied quickly. "How do you know?"

Rather than answer his fool-headed question, her eyes probed his. "Are you displeased, Timothy?"

"No, my love," he replied and found to his relief that he was

224

thrilled at the notion.

"If it's a girl," Peggy said softly, "we'll name her Molly."

CHAPTER THIRTY-FOUR:
BRIAN IS CAST INTO THE LIONS' DEN

Every fly, flea, and mosquito had joined their circus parade, yet stinkbugs and hellish heat didn't seem to bother the people who watched from the red-brick sidewalk.

Sunlight hit ground-floor windows, casting a reflection of backward letters across the red brick. Sean pulled a handkerchief from his pocket and dabbed at the sweat that dripped from his forehead into his eyes. The salty perspiration stung, and everything looked blurry, especially the sidewalk children who jumped up and down, wavering like the stripes in Brian O'Connor's fluttering flag.

Brian waved an American flag that was half as big as he was. He also had to contend with his performing pig. The *petit pourceau* rode inside a wooden cart whose wheels kept bouncing over cobblestones. Every bounce produced an angry oink. The pig wore a diaper with its curly tail stuck through a cut-out hole. Brian called the pig's diapers "piggy knickers."

Although the cart was a short distance away, Sean thought he could smell rancid bacon. He didn't like the pig, and the pig didn't like him. The small piggy did, however, like Brian, who had a way with all animals. A farmer had traded the pig for tickets to the show. For his whole family. Thirty-three cousins, nieces, nephews, aunts, uncles, and children.

Children of all ages, Sean had thought wryly.

It turned out to be a terrible trade, even though Brian had trained the malodorous porker to perform a number of stunts.

It rolled a vinegar barrel by trotting hind-legged against it and rode the hooped sides as the barrel rotated. It answered questions with guttural grunts and spelled P-I-G and C-O-R-N by nudging letter cards with its snout. It even worked a teeterboard and wove a figure eight between Brian's legs as Brian sang "A Sequence to the Three Little Pigs" by Alfred Scott Gatty.

"This old lady sow was so vain," Brian would sing at the top of his lungs, "she wished to look young like a girl, so this silly old pig grew a regular prig, and put her old tail into a curl. Said Piggy, I have to grow fat, yet I must not be ugly, you see. 'Tis a rule of good taste to be thin in the waist, so I'll pinch and still learn to say wee. So I'll pinch and still learn to say wee! She ate and grew fat, but she pinched and she pinched, till her eyes started out of her head. Yet you know she was vain, so she stifled the pain, but her nose grew enormously red!"

Named Whiggy, after the Whigs party that successfully ran Millard Fillmore for president, the pig's disposition was so mean, Sean was tempted to butcher the fat-bellied porker and serve it to his performers. Fried pork would taste mighty fine between slabs of thick bread.

Whiggy was also aptly named because he had a thatch of hair that looked like a wig, falling over his forehead toward his piggy eyes and piggy snout. In one town a lithographer had made posters of Brian and Whiggy, and Sean thought those posters had a lot to do with today's parade crowd. So, at least for now, Whiggy was safe from the butcher's knife and frying pan.

Brian still begged to perform with the cats, pestering Sean at every opportunity, and, despite his fear of Maureen's ghost haunting his circus, Sean knew he was weakening.

Just like Whiggy the Piggy, the cats loved the boy.

With a heavy sigh, Sean made up his mind. Tonight he'd allow Brian to work with the cats. He planned to give two performances before he moved on to Missouri. He had no time to print up posters, but the people who watched today's performance would tell other people, and tomorrow the show would be well attended by the curious, and by fools who, watching Rome's gladiators perform in the ring, would have cheered for the lions.

He looked up at the cloudy sky. *Forgive me, Maureen. I promised to treat Brian as if he were my own son, but I didn't give you my word that I'd keep him out of the cat cage.*

Musicians sat on folding chairs. They had just finished playing for the equestrians and clowns. Only the drummer would play for the cat act, a drumroll after Sean's introduction.

Watching his eight-year-old cat tamer tuck his shirt more securely into his breeches and his pant legs into his boots, Sean was already regretting the impulse he'd had during the parade, even though Brian had been overjoyed and had sworn he'd be very, very careful, and Sean had felt a small measure of relief when the elderly cat tamer, Coben, said the boy was "more than ready to perform."

"Will you have Coben direct the cats through the chute?" Brian now asked.

"No," Sean replied. "Coben left for town, to drink as much shandy-gaff as he can afford."

"Shandy-gaff?"

"A mixture of ale and gin."

"Do you drink shandy-gaff, Sean?"

"No. I drink whiskey. In Paris I 'smothered the parrot.' Smothering the parrot means drinking a spirit called absinthe. Absinthe is *la fée verte* . . . green fairy green . . . like a parrot."

"I think I'll drink that spirit when I grow up."

"Yes, well . . ." Sean cleared his throat. "Black Jack and I will direct the cats, Brian. Meanwhile, all of our clowns will be stationed outside the ring."

"Why?"

"If the cats give you any trouble, the clowns will distract the audience while you make your escape."

"There won't be any trouble, Sean. I've known some of these cats since they were cubs. I've fed and watered them." Brian wrinkled his nose. "I've even cleaned their cages."

"It's different inside the ring, lad."

"I've watched Coben and learned his every move. I'm not scared."

"You should be scared."

"Well, I'm not."

"Tigers are the most cunning, Brian. Lions give warning, since they have a slow way of turning before they strike."

There was a burst of applause, which meant the clowns had finished their act. The clowns could always be relied on to put the audience in a happy mood, and Sean was happy to see they had followed his orders and stood near the cat cage. "Where's Whiggy?" he asked Brian.

"Asleep in his baby buggy."

"Good. Keep your piggy away from the cat cage. I don't want the cats to catch his scent."

"Okay." The boy cocked his head. "What's wrong, Sean?"

"Nothing, Brian, nothing at all." He couldn't tell the lad he kept seeing Maureen everywhere he looked, her expression enraged, her dark-blue eyes accusatory.

Shaking off his jimjams, Sean began his introduction. "Ladies and gentlemen and children of all ages. Our cat tamer is not a small adult, nor is he a midget. He is eight years old. He is the one and only eight-year-old to perform in the ring with lions and tigers."

Eight going on eighteen, Sean thought as he heard a satisfying gasp from the audience.

"Our lions and tigers appear together," Sean continued. "It is very dangerous, so we need complete silence. If anybody has to cough, do it now."

There were several hacking gags, followed by laughter. Finally, the crowd hushed.

"Presenting Brian O'Connor, the fearless cat tamer," Sean concluded, waving his cane at the cage before he nodded at the clowns, dropped his cane, grabbed an iron bar, and joined Black Jack.

Brian strutted into the ring, where he waited patiently, coiling and uncoiling his whip. A few people applauded but were hushed by others.

The chute's wooden panel entrance opened. The first tawny lion appeared, followed by another. Beatrice and Bottom. All the cats were named for Shakespearian characters.

Six tigers entered the cage. Sean could see Brian's fingers tighten around his whipstock and hickory club until his knuckles turned white. Good. The lad had enough sense to be scared, but he was smart enough to confine his fear to his hands. His expression was blissful. The audience had caught his enthusiasm and were smiling along with him.

Brian snapped his whip and the beasts settled. So far, so good.

Not so good. One of the tigers was slinking toward the boy, its ears flattened, its tail swishing softly. Romeo. Sweet, lovable Romeo, whose lips were now curled in a nasty snarl. Brian snapped his whip again. Romeo's ears twitched forward. His muzzle seemed to expand in a tiger smile as he climbed up onto his pedestal. Sean could almost hear him purr.

Brian gave Sean a triumphant look.

"Don't lose eye contact!" Sean shouted.

"Huh?" With a quick jerk of his head, Brian returned his gaze to the cats.

Too late! Romeo had jumped down from his pedestal and

was chasing his tail, exciting the lions. Sean watched the old lion-tiger jungle hatred flare. Sure enough, Bottom sprang from his high pedestal, landing within inches of Romeo. They both locked together, struggling fiercely for tooth and claw advantage.

While Sean rattled the cage with his iron bar, a signal for the cats to retreat through their chute, Black Jack ran to open the cage door—and found it stuck.

Brian brandished his club at the flailing cats, then gave Bottom a generous clout on the top of his head. The lion let go of the tiger's neck, and Romeo scampered through the chute.

Bottom turned, glared, and growled at Brian.

Survival fought bravery. Survival won. Dropping his whip and club, Brian ran toward the exit, where Jack was throwing his whole body against the stuck door. Meanwhile, Sean ran to the baby buggy, scooped up Whiggy, and pressed the squealing porker against the bars of the cage.

Bottom skidded to a halt and swiped at the pig with his paw.

"Sean, no!" Brian yelled, as the stuck door finally gave way and he stumbled through the opening, then shut the door behind him. "Don't give Bottom my pig!"

"Are you daft, boy?" Sweat streamed down Sean's face, mingling with his tears, as he walked, rubber-legged, toward Brian. Whiggy continued to oink indignantly until he was safe in Brian's arms. "Your blasted piggy is far too fat to fit through the bars of the cage. But if it was a choice between you and your piggy—"

"You didn't have to make that choice."

"And never will again!"

The cats were still agitated but settling in their separate cages, inside the menagerie tent, where Coben had returned, pished as a fart, an equally drunk lady clinging to his arm.

"Her dress was open, and she kept saying she wanted to 'pet

the kitties,' " Brian had confided to Sean. "Coben kept petting *her*. When he saw me, he told me to leave. Do you think he'll let her pet the cats?"

"I doubt he'll let her pet even one cat."

"Will he remember to feed the cats?"

"I'm sure he'll remember to feed them, Brian, but just in case, you and I can check it out later."

Sean leaned back against the planked table and stretched his legs. He and Brian sat on their usual bench near the cook top.

"I'll be more careful next time," Brian said.

"There won't be a next time."

"Until I'm bigger?"

"Yes." *And older!*

"How big?"

Sean spied Bobby Duncan, the Strongman. Bobby's muscles made up in width what he lacked in height. "As big as Duncan," Sean replied.

"That's not awfully big." Brian cocked his head, a mannerism Sean found endearing. "I'll start working on it."

"Tell you what, lad. When Mr. Barnum delivers my elephant, Goliath, I'll let you train it, like you did with Whiggy, and I'll let you ride it in the parade and perform in the ring."

"How is Mr. Barnum toting your elephant?"

"By water."

"On a *boat*?"

"Not the kind of boat I think you mean, the kind with sails. Mr. Barnum will travel by horseback in the north and by river barges in the south. Or if Mr. Barnum is lucky, he can catch a showboat."

"Showboat," Brian echoed, his voice a question.

"A showboat is a floating theater, lad, a special riverboat designed to carry passengers rather than cargo. It has a paddle-wheel. That's a wheel in which a number of paddles are set around the outside edge of the wheel. Performers live on the boat. Mr. Barnum told me that the first showboat was actually a keelboat, bought by a man named Noah Ludlow, who called it Noah's Ark."

"But wouldn't a showboat sink with an elephant on board?"

Sean shook his head. "There's a showboat called the *Spaulding and Rogers Floating Circus Palace*. It has a menagerie as well as three thousand-four hundred seats on two decks. Nine hundred of those seats are for colored people."

Looking toward his tent, Sean heaved a deep sigh. "One thing for sure. Spaulding and Rogers never have to worry about blow-downs."

"Did you see the showboat, Sean? Did you see the show?"

Sean thought he could reach out and touch the boy's excite-ment. "No, lad," he replied. "Black Jack and I walked to the dock, planning to buy tickets for the Floating Circus Palace's next performance, but we didn't like the separate seats for colored folk, so we never went on board." Anticipating the boy's next question, Sean said, "The boat was big enough for an elephant. Maybe even two elephants."

"I would have sat in the seats for the colored folk."

"Why?"

"Because Black Jack is my best friend."

"He's my best friend, too." Sean crossed his legs, still shaky from Brian's near-death experience inside the cat cage. "I'm hoping Mr. Barnum will dock his barge at roughly the same time we reach Missouri, assuming the luck of the Irish prevails."

If it didn't, Sean mused, he'd have to sell his menagerie and equipment to Dan Rice, or some other *entrepreneur*, and return to Brooklyn. Dan Rice might buy Whiggy. Hadn't Barnum said Dan Rice used pigs in his show?

Sean was fairly certain P.T. would employ all of the Kid Show "freaks" for his Hall of Living Curiosities, perhaps other performers, as well, for his Saturday afternoon museum acts.

The only bright side to losing his dream and returning to New York was that Angelique would be long gone, living a life of ease in South Carolina.

CHAPTER THIRTY-FIVE:
THE MURDERER CONFESSES

Mad Dog felt exhaustion envelop his body like a heavy cloak, but he had one more trick up his sleeve.

Directing all the servants, with the exception of Allen and Gertrude Starling, to stand in a straight line, he retrieved the tasseled pillow with its bible verse and handprint—the pillow that he had discovered in the Billiards Room and, earlier, had furtively placed against a Tapestry Room window pane, hidden behind one of the velvet drapes.

Allen Starling once again stood next to Samson, and Mad Dog started with him. Ordering the trapeze artist to place his hand on the pillow's handprint, Mad Dog was both disappointed and elated to see that the young man's hand was too big to fit the handprint. Elated because his conviction that Starling had told the truth about killing Mrs. Bernadette Browning-Hale McCoy had panned out.

Next, the butler placed his hand on the pillow, then the valet, then Mrs. Morgan and the upstairs maid, Mary. One by one the servants extended a hand and placed it against the pillow. Mad Dog couldn't help picturing his wife Katie telling their five children the story of Cinderella. Not the version he'd heard from the upstairs maid, Mary, where birds pecked out the sisters' eyes, but a less violent tale, written by Charles Perrault, where mice were turned into horses, a pumpkin became a coach, and all the ladies of the land tried on a golden slipper, left behind at some kind of ball. Mad Dog loved to eavesdrop when Katie told that story.

The trying on of the golden slipper was reminiscent of the servants placing their hands on the pillow. Except, of course, the "reward" for the servant was prison or hanging, rather than marriage to a prince. Mad Dog had mixed feelings about hangings, which often led to a cruel death as the prisoner was strangled by the rope. He was familiar with the Constitution and had read it several times. The eighth amendment said: "Excessive bail shall not be required, nor excessive fines imposed, nor cruel and unusual punishments inflicted." In his opinion, hanging was cruel.

He patiently held out the tasseled pillow for all of the servants, one after another. The closest fit was the hand of the scullery maid, another Mary. She burst into tears and kept repeating, "I ain't done nothin', I ain't kilt the mistress," until Mad Dog assured her, again and again, that she wasn't in any kind of trouble.

That left Gertrude Starling, whose stockings and bodice were back in place. Still seated on her chair, she looked bewildered, as if her body was in the Tapestry Room but her head was in a far-away place, a forest filled with fairy godmothers, perhaps. Or maybe she saw herself flying through the air, her trapeze tied to the arc of a rainbow—*and aren't I being the fanciful one?* Mad Dog hid a self-deprecating grin behind a cough.

Gertrude Starling's hand was a perfect fit.

Mad Dog told Samson to truss Allen Starling and wait in the entranceway, then ordered the rest of the servants to leave the room. Grace Morgan said she had to stay "to take care of Gertie, should she swoon again." Mad Dog said no, and with a markedly disdainful show of dragging her feet, Mrs. Morgan departed with the other reluctant menials.

Mad Dog made an effort to modulate his voice as he said, "Gertrude . . . Gertie, why did you kill Mrs. Browning-Hale

McCoy? Why did you kill your mistress?"

The girl's eyes sparked, no longer unfocused, no longer confused. "She weren't no mistress of mine. I served *Petite Ange.*"

"That doesn't answer my question."

"Mrs. McCoy said she'd examine me again before nightfall. That was the word she used, examine. She didn't say 'whip you,' but that's what she meant. I knew if I had another whipping I'd die. I couldn't wait for Allen or Henry to collect me. My back and feet were hurting something fierce, so bad I swear I don't remember putting my circus togs and dressing gown inside the marriage quilt I got from *Petite Ange.* I sewed the gown from petticoat material *Petite Ange* gave me the very same night she found the man she loved at Mrs. Barnum's gala."

"Go on."

"I made it down the main staircase, then saw that Mrs. Mc-Coy was in the billiards room. The door was open. When Mrs. Morgan tended to my back, she said Mrs. McCoy had ordered them smelly little fish for tea, but I didn't think she'd be puttin' on the feedbag in the billiards room. She were laughin' loud-like, as if she'd drowned a dog, and tossin' some of them smelly fish to her cats. She saw me through the open doorway, grabbed me, and dragged me inside the room by my hair."

"And that's where you fought with her."

"I don't remember fightin' with her, but I must have, because the next thing I remember, clear-like, she was on the floor, and I was pressin' a pillow as hard as I could 'cross her mouth. I held the pillow on her face till she weren't breathin' no more, and then I put the pink dressing gown on her. It weren't easy. Have you ever tried to put a dressing gown on a dead body?"

"Not that I can recall. Why did you put the dressing gown on Mrs. McCoy?"

The girl shrugged. "It seemed proper, her being dead and all.

For the burial, I mean. I'd want to be buried in a pretty dressing gown."

That didn't make much sense, but Mad Dog merely said, "And then you returned to your room."

"Yes, sir."

"That wasn't a question. How did you return to your room?"

"I don't rightly know. I suppose I went back up the stairs, crawled you might say. I couldn't leave by the front door."

"Why not?"

"Servants ain't allowed to leave that way."

"But . . . but you . . . never mind. Why did you put the stuffed canary's talons in Mrs. McCoy's hair?"

"Did I? Well then, I don't know."

"Did you think the cats would go after the bird and scratch Mrs. McCoy's face?"

"Maybe I did, sir. I don't remember."

"*Maybe* you remembered the story Mrs. McCoy's niece told you, the story about the birds pecking—"

"What difference does it make? The law can kill me back; I don't care. I'd do it all over again, rather than get whipped again."

"Listen to me carefully, girl. I'll take you to a doctor who'll care for the wounds on your back and feet and make sure they don't get infected, but I've a feeling the law won't 'kill you back.' In my opinion, Miss Starling, you acted in self defense, and I'll say so if there's a trial."

"That's good of you, sir." She wrung her hands. "Will my brother hang?"

"A lawyer might claim your brother killed Henry in self-defense, but there's the little matter of the horseshoe. It didn't get down off the carriage house by itself. There, there, don't cry. Please don't cry, Miss Starling . . . Gertie. You'll make yourself sick again."

Mad Dog felt helpless, unable to do anything except wrap the weeping girl's fingers around the handkerchief he drew from deep within his trouser pocket. However, his pity, as well as his exhaustion, faded away when he realized he'd solved two murders in one day.

He had never solved *one* murder in one day before. Neither had anyone else he knew. He was no C. Auguste Dupin, the unnamed narrator of Edgar Allan Poe's stories, who appeared to read the mind of his companion. But he, Malachi Daniel Connolly, had definitely used what Poe called "ratiocination"— reasoning that was exact, valid, and rational.

Despite Gertrude Starling's unstoppable tears, he couldn't stop grinning.

He needed to supervise the transfer of the coachman's corpse to the dead wagon. Then he had planned to ride home, drink a couple of glasses of Old Crow, and go straight to bed.

Now he had a different plan in mind. His twin girls were two and a half, and Katie had been hinting about having another baby.

If she agreed, they could start making a baby tonight.

CHAPTER THIRTY-SIX:
SEAN GETS THREE SURPRISES

Although it was the crack of dawn, every member of the Sean Kelley circus was busy getting ready for this afternoon's performance.

Sean had made a bargain with a Missouri farmer to use his field. However, this would be the circus troupe's last performance. He had only enough money from his last show to purchase food for sale: Cracker Jack, brick-shaped popcorn balls, hard candy, lollypops, roasted peanuts and lemonade. The money he made from those sales would go toward meat for the cats.

A crew would ordinarily travel ahead to order vegetables from greengrocers, beef from butchers, baked goods from bakeries, and hay and grain for the horses and the goat. Sean had never stinted on food for his performers before, but this time he had no choice.

The hay and grain were a necessity, but his performers and crew would have to eat eggs, purchased from the same farmer who had allowed Sean to use his field. Sean had also bargained for chickens, and he could already smell them cooking, along with potatoes in their skins.

He was down to his last few dollars, and unless he could draw a crowd . . .

"Look what's coming, Sean." Black Jack extended his arm and pointed.

Sean thought Jack looked like the Ghost of Christmas Yet-to-

Come, in a story by a man named Charles Dickens, one of the
many books Sean collected and treasured. He had inherited his
love of reading from his father.

Shading his eyes with his forearm, he followed Jack's finger-
compass. In the distance were two figures on horseback. As they
drew nigh, he could see that the smaller figure, a lass, held the
reins with one hand and carried something in her other hand.

A birdcage?

He couldn't quite make out the girl's features and yet his
heart began to beat like a circus musician's drumroll. Trying to
ignore the uneven *thump-thump-thump*, he staggered backward
until he felt the silver wagon's slats against his spine.

Was he brainsick? The girl who rode the dappled horse wore
a floppy bonnet, a tattered gown, slippers tied to her feet with
vines, and dirty gloves. She looked like his small angel, except,
if he remembered rightly, Angelique had never learned how to
ride.

In one of her letters, in response to his second vow that their
wee daughters would be equestrians, she had written: "Someone
else will have to teach our daughters how to ride, for I will
never ride a horse. Should I fall from my rope, the net beneath
will catch me, and I will bounce. If I fell to the ground, I would
not bounce. In truth, *Monsieur* Paon, I would rather walk *cinq
cent milles* than ride a horse."

She'd rather walk five hundred miles than ride a horse, so
that couldn't be Angelique.

A capricious breeze lifted the girl's bonnet from her head. As
it spun toward the ground, she made a futile attempt to catch
it. Sean shut his eyes, then opened them again, but the lass,
closer now, still looked like Angelique. The same robust breasts
and shoulders. The same honey-colored hair, falling down her
back to her waist. And he would wager the elephant Barnum
had not yet delivered that her eyes were gray-green.

Maybe he *could* wager his elephant. Shifting his gaze, Sean saw a large, dark shape advance, eclipsing the rising sun. Even though the large, dark shape was a wee bit farther away than the girl and her companion, the ground shook.

Once again, Sean focused on the two horseback riders. He had expected Barnum to deliver an elephant, or at least prayed it would arrive soon, but what would Angelique Aumont, niece of a Connecticut society matron, be doing in the middle of a Missouri farmer's field? Perhaps her companion was her husband, Matthew Gray. Perhaps, unable to sell their plow-elephant, they had decided to visit the Sean Kelley Circus and ask for a bid.

The idea was so ludicrous, Sean laughed. Even if true, Matthew Gray, wealthy beyond measure, would have used a carriage to transport his young wife. He wouldn't want her beautiful buttocks bruised.

Furthermore, the girl's companion didn't look like a rich plantation owner. Clothed in buckskin, his long legs straddled an animal that could only be described as a nag.

Or crow bait.

Maybe the two figures on horseback were figments of Sean's imagination, the result of yet another long, lonely night with a book and his whiskey bottle.

Except, if this scene was a mere figment of his imagination, why had Black Jack pointed? Why had his circus troupe joined him at the silver wagon? Why were they all staring across the farmer's field?

A few watched the lass and her companion, but most watched the humped blob that shaded the sun, and the troupe's joyous expressions confirmed what Sean had already deduced.

P. T. Barnum was, at long last, delivering the elephant he had promised.

P. T. Barnum rode a white horse and led a pack mule.

Next to P. T. Barnum, a child rode atop a small brown horse.

Duncan the Strong Man; Morgan the Skeleton Man; Miss Conway, the Albino Vampire; Donald and Christie, the "fattest twins in the universe;" Charlene Johnson, the Bearded Lady; and, of course, Black Jack, all grinned from ear to ear.

The clowns smiled through their painted frowns.

The Cossacks, Anastasiya, Panama, and Cuckoo the Bird Girl had made a circle by joining hands, and they were now dancing a wild jig.

Quite a few roustabouts had tears running down their weathered cheeks.

Only the goat expressed dismay—by bleating indignantly. Fearless Bianca could jump through hoops while riding around the ring on the back of a horse, but it seemed the sight and smell of elephant was not her cup of tea. Sean had to laugh at the image of his goat sitting on her haunches, delicately sipping from a china teacup.

At this moment Sean would have laughed at Dearg-due, a female vampire who looked a lot like his Kid Show freak, Miss Conway. Dearg-due seduced men, then drained them of their blood.

"Why do you laugh like a hyena?" asked a familiar voice. Angelique's voice.

"I pictured Dearg-due, a female vampire who looks exactly like one of my Kid Show performers," Sean replied truthfully, then once again wondered if he was dreaming. He might as well keep talking, or else he'd wake up, and he didn't want to wake up.

"According to Irish legend, a woman who was known for her beauty fell in love with a local peasant. Her father didn't like that idea at all, so he forced her into an arranged marriage with a rich man who treated her badly." Sean paused, peering at Angelique's face for some kind of reaction. If she replaced *father* with *auntie* and *peasant* with *circus owner*—

All he saw was confusion.

"Eventually," Sean continued, "she committed suicide. One night she rose from her grave to seek revenge on her father and her husband by sucking their blood until they dropped dead. It is said that once a year she rises from her grave and uses her beauty to lure men to their deaths."

"And why do you tell me this story?"

Because I'm dreaming and don't want to wake up. "What do you have in that cage?" he countered. Which wasn't at all what he wanted to say, especially if he was still dreaming. But it was the first thing that came to mind since he couldn't tell if she sported a wedding band beneath her dirt-encrusted glove.

"Cage? Oh, birdcage. A canary. It sings as sweetly as Jenny Lind but has a much better disposition."

"You sound very American, lass."

"And you sound flummoxed, *Monsieur* Kelley."

"Odd way to greet your husband, Miss Jenny," Roy muttered, climbing down from his horse, retrieving the birdcage from Angelique's outstretched fingers, then heading, reins and birdcage in hand, toward the roustabouts.

"Husband?" Sean quirked an eyebrow.

"An *honest* ploy, *Monsieur* Kelley. It is a long story. Briefly, I pretended to be Jenny Lind because my cowboy escort thought I was Jenny Lind. He never asked me to sing, thank heaven. He was kind enough to help me find you and your *cirque*. I do not think I would have made it here, had he not led the way."

"And did you change your name and nationality, lass?"

"*Non,* I am still French and proud of it. I shall be *Mademoiselle* Paonne or *Mademoiselle Petite Ange,* if that is your desire, but if you do not help me off this blasted horse, I shall be *Mademoiselle* Sore Derrière."

"As long as you are *Mademoiselle,* I care not."

"Ah," she said.

"Do you mean 'ah, the circus owner has lost his wits' or 'ah, Sean Kelley is a bumptious noodlehead'?"

"You thought me wed to that pompous *imbécile*, Monsieur Gray, and I cannot fault you for that. It is the very reason I embarked on my journey of the heart. Because you are my heart, Sean, and without a heart, one cannot live."

He wanted to laugh like a happy fountain in a cave. He wanted to soar through the air on cobwebby wings. He wanted to sing like his father, Timothy, although he knew he couldn't carry a tune in a bucket. He wanted to dance a Bohemian polka with Bottom the lion, or step-kick a *jeté assemblé* with Whiggy the Piggy. He settled for a grin that stretched from ear to ear.

Angelique smiled at his besotted expression. "I can dismount on my own," she said, "but I crave your touch, so will you please help me down?"

As he reached up, she brought her right leg over the saddle horn. A lion roared, and the horse shied, and Angelique pitched forward. She landed on top of Sean, and they both went down together, all in a heap.

Sean held onto her shoulders and rolled them over, away from the horse's hooves, until she was on the bottom and he was on top.

"Ooof," she said. "I think you weigh more than an elephant."

"Perhaps a wee baby elephant," he teased, pressing his palms against the ground and lifting his weight from her body. Then, he simply could not help himself. Her face was so close to his. Slowly, deliberately, he traced her mouth with the tip of his tongue until he felt the soft, moist, inner edges of her lips yield.

As he reluctantly ended the kiss, he could see that an adorable blush stained her cheeks. He could also see that her gray-green eyes were focused on something to the left of his shoulder. Turning his head, Sean followed her gaze.

A woman had hunkered down near them. She had brittle, rust-colored hair and wore enough paint to challenge the clowns. Her breasts were bulldozed forward, aided by a tight corset. Above her stood Black Jack, who must have looked, to Angelique, like an ebony giant.

"The roustabouts are wanting you, Sean," the painted woman said. "And your friend might have to pee," she added with mock politeness.

"Thank you, Panama." Sean rose to his feet and helped Angelique rise. "Do you have need of the dunny, Angelique?"

"Non," she replied with another blush. "And it is a long time since I've heard a *toilette* called a dunny. Oh, how I've missed the circus," she added in a whisper.

"Angelique, this is Panama, our trapeze artist, and my friend, Jack. And this," Sean said as Brian approached with Whiggy in his arms, "is my son, Brian."

"Your son?" Angelique bent forward to scratch Whiggy behind his ears. The pig gave an ecstatic oink. "How do you do, *Monsieur* Brian Kelley?"

"Brian O'Connor, ma'am."

"Oh, I'm sorry. How do you do, *Monsieur* Brian O'Connor?"

Sean mouthed "later" when Angelique gave him a puzzled glance.

"And what is the name of your pig?" she asked Brian, rather than asking the question that Sean knew burned her tongue: *Why does Sean call you his son?*

"My pig's name is Whiggy," Brian replied. "He likes you and he don't . . . doesn't usually like people."

Of course the pig liked Angelique, Sean thought with another grin. So did Brian, whose cheeks were flushed and whose face wore an expression of blissful awe. Sean had a feeling Black Jack would soon lose his standing as Brian's best friend.

Turning to Jack, Sean said, "Please help the roustabouts

secure our elephant. There will also be a man with the face of a bulldog. His name is Barnum. Tell him to make himself at home. The child on the brown horse, as well."

"That ain't no child, Sean."

"What do you mean?"

"Look," said Jack, assuming his Christmas-Yet-to-Come stance again.

Sean followed Jack's finger. *Jaysus!* Was that . . . could that possibly be . . . Tom Thumb?

CHAPTER THIRTY-SEVEN: TOM THUMB

Thunderstruck, Sean watched P. T. Barnum and Tom Thumb draw nigh.

Tom Thumb, Barnum explained, had made the trip out west as a favor to him, as long as he promised to leave for New York no later than the day after tomorrow. Tom Thumb had begun growing and now stood at two feet, five inches tall. Tom felt he'd soon grow even taller.

The performers and crew crowded around him, almost crushing him. Pushing them back, Jack swung Tom up onto his shoulders and headed toward the cook top. The others followed.

"They look like a circus parade," Sean said.

Barnum laughed. "Speaking of parades, have you had yours yet?"

"Yes, when we arrived, yesterday afternoon."

"Then I suggest you hitch a horse to a circus wagon. Have one of your performers, or one of your clowns, ride through town and ballyhoo General Tom Thumb, who will appear at the Sean Kelley Circus today and tomorrow. I have posters." He gestured toward his pack mule. "The posters don't have a date, but they do have a picture of Tom Thumb and the name of your circus. If I'm right, and I'm sure I am, you'll have to beat the crowds off with a stick."

"That's incredibly generous of Tom Thumb," Angelique said.

"Rubbish. He owes me a favor. More than one."

"I'll prepare two wagons," said Sean, taking Angelique by the

248

hand, afraid he might lose her if he didn't. "I need to send somebody to town to pick up a dress for my girl here. The dress she has on is beyond repair. I need material for a costume, too, should she choose to perform."

Sean looked at Angelique, who nodded. "We had an expert seamstress," Sean continued, "but she wed the lithographer who made posters of Brian and his pig. Can you beat that? In less than a day they fell in love."

"It didn't take us an entire day to fall in love," Angelique chastised with a soft laugh, "and I know the very best seamstress. My friend Gertie. Perhaps she can join us and—"

"I have a message for you, from Charity," Barnum interrupted. "Please give Angelique and me a few minutes alone, Sean."

"Take all the time you need. As long as you don't try and talk her into going back to New York with you." It was a tease, and Sean expected Barnum to laugh. He didn't crack a smile.

Suffering from the jimjams, Sean walked away, then made an abrupt about-face. The two figures were out of earshot, but not out of sight, and he watched Angelique stagger and clutch Barnum's arm for support. Thoroughly alarmed, Sean ran toward her. As he got closer, he could see that, under the trail dust, her face was very white.

"What is it? What happened?" he called.

"Auntie Bernadette is dead. *Monsieur* Barnum did not tell me the last time I saw him because . . . well, because he's a 'cowardly custard.' "

Sean swallowed his relief. "Angelique, I'm so sorry. You have every right to mourn, even though she was an evil woman who—"

"I'm not mourning, Sean. I won't even pretend I care. It's just that my friend Gertie killed her and might be tried by the law and hanged."

"I do not believe that will be the case," Barnum said, his face red from Angelique's "cowardly custard" remark. "Charity insists it was self-defense, and the police chief tends to agree. The truth is, Gertrude Starling was beaten to a bloody pulp by Bernadette."

"Because she wouldn't tell Auntie Bernadette where I was. It is all my fault."

"Nonsense. It's Bernadette's fault. Gertie is staying with Charity and me until her wounds heal. Charity is treating her like a fifth daughter. If Gertie is found innocent, and I give you my word I'll spend as much money as necessary to prove it, she'll perform at the museum. Or, if she prefers, I'll send her to you."

Gently grasping Angelique by the elbow, Sean led her toward the silver wagon.

Entering, he told her about the promise he had made to Maureen and why Brian was now his son.

"Then he's my son, too," she said. "Sean, the trapeze artist who asked if I needed to use the dunny stared at me with daggers in her eyes."

"You have nothing to fear from Panama, darlin'."

"I did not say I feared her."

"I swear by all that's holy that I have not slept with, nor even kissed another lass since the first time I saw you dance across a rope."

"A rope! Sean, I have performed the forward somersault!"

"And where, may I ask, would you be doin' a forward?"

"In the woods. On my way to you. My cowboy, Roy, and I guyed-out his lasso between two trees. Why do you look at me like that?"

"When I hired my last rope walker, I asked why he could not somersault forward as well as backward, and he said somersaulting forward reverses natural reflexes, and the arms are no help because they get in the way."

"I wrap my arms about my chest so they will not catch between my legs."

"Nevertheless, it's too dangerous."

"Nevertheless, I shall perform it."

"May we discuss this later, darlin'?"

Just like their first meeting, his eyes undressed her, discarding her tattered gown, her petticoats, her chemise and her flannel drawers.

"It is not somersaults I have on my mind," he said.

"Have you *changed* your mind, Sean? The night of Charity Barnum's dinner party you insisted we must be wed first."

"*Your cowboy* believes I am your husband, 'Miss Jenny.' "

"I told you; that was an honest ploy."

Sean laughed, then cradled her chin with his hand. "You have been my wife since the day we met, Angelique, for after that I could not imagine myself wed to anyone but you. We do not need a man in a frock coat and clerical collar to say the words that will bind us." He kissed the long lashes that shaded her cheeks. "Though hundreds of miles apart, we were still bound to one another." He traced the graceful arc of her neck with his thumb until he reached her gown's bodice buttons. "There must be a preacher in this town, and I give you my word we shall have a legal ceremony, but for now, may we love God and be merry?"

Angelique replied by helping him remove her clothing, then his.

Oh, what a glorious sight, she thought, gazing immodestly at Sean's nakedness. Jenny Lind's voice might be God-given, but Sean's body was, too, and Angelique knew that, if she ever composed another ode, her own ode, she would not dwell on nightingales.

Roy Osborne liked to share his knowledge of critters and birds. He had told her that the nightingale's song was trilled by the male. So she would play the male nightingale with Sean because she wanted to sing.

After their passion had been spent, she covered her face with her hands and began to sob.

"What's wrong?" Sean asked. "Did I hurt you? Are you all right? Angelique, answer me!"

"Jenny Lind once said she could never forget the seriousness of life. Therefore, she preferred sorrow to joy."

"And that is why you are weeping, you daft colleen?"

"My tears are tears of joy, Sean. And I have shed a few for Jenny."

CHAPTER THIRTY-EIGHT:
ANGELIQUE PERFORMS

Angelique stood on Roy Osborne's guyed-out lasso, only this time the rope had been strung tightly between the tops of two circus wagons.

All of the performers watched, along with members of the crew.

So did P. T. Barnum.

The "giant" by the name of Jack stood nearby. Sean had told him to catch her, should she fall.

She didn't intend to fall.

Once he had accepted what he called her daft notion, once he knew he couldn't change her mind, Sean had said he'd play ringmaster.

"Ladies and gentlemen," he began. "The Sean Kelley Circus proudly presents *Petite Ange,* the first female equilibrist to perform a forward somersault. Picture tossing an egg into the air. Imagine stretching a piece of sewing thread out in front of you, then trying to catch the rotating egg. What happens if you miss?"

Barnum, who had been sitting on the ground, jumped to his feet. So did Tom Thumb.

"I know what you're thinking," Sean continued. "You are thinking *Petite Ange* has eyes to see where she'll land while an egg does not. But her legs will come between her eyes and the rope, permitting no optical help with her landing. The forward somersault requires the utmost in bodily coordination, muscular precision, and faultless technique and has never been successfully completed by a woman." Angelique saw him take a deep breath and swallow hard. "Presenting Sean Kelley's small angel . . . *Petite Ange!*"

Angelique leaped toward the sky. At the same time, she lowered her head. Wrapping her arms about her chest, she felt her body rotate. All she could see were her knees. Her golden hair whipped around her throat as she landed slantwise and teetered on the rope's edge. Then, with the greatest effort of her young life, she restored her balance.

The circus performers and crew applauded wildly.

Barnum looked dazed.

Sean helped her down from the rope and gave her a kiss, the best applause of all.

CHAPTER THIRTY-NINE:
ANOTHER PROPOSAL

Sean had "traded" a sturdy stock horse for Roy Osborne's nag and insisted Roy keep Angelique's seventy-five-dollar horse to tote his gifts.

The gifts were for his wife, Isabelle, whom he called Izzy. During a night when there were no trees close enough to guy out his lasso, Roy had talked about "his Izzy."

Her father was a pig farmer. She was one of eight children, the only girl. Her mother died when she was twelve, and Izzy was convinced her mother preferred to live in heaven, where there weren't any floors to be scrubbed, clothes to be washed, privies to be cleaned, meals to be cooked, pigs to be fed, and, most of all, babies to be born. Izzy took over the chores. A year later her father remarried, and Izzy was delighted that there'd be someone to help her. But, instead, her stepmother treated her like a slave, adding even more tasks to Izzy's daily list. She was living in her father's house at the moment, Roy said. He had hoped to earn enough money on the cattle drive to buy a small ranch, his dream, but now he'd have to leave the baby and Izzy with her father and work another cattle drive.

Angelique had been appalled and said so.

"Some things are meant to be, Miss Jenny," Roy had said. "It just takes a few tries to git there. We dream to give ourselves hope."

Angelique had cornered *Monsieur* Barnum and told him Roy's story.

As Roy made ready to leave, *Monsieur* Barnum handed him a bank draft . . . "to buy a small ranch." Also, a sufficient amount of banknotes to purchase food, after Angelique had attempted to describe hardtack.

At first Roy protested, but nobody could gainsay P. T. Barnum, especially when he insisted that Roy deserved every cent for "delivering a valuable cargo."

"Thank you for keeping her safe," *Monsieur* Barnum said, sincerely.

"Nothin' to thank me fer, sir. If we'd been attacked by wolves or coyotes, she'd have them eatin' out of her hand in no time."

Women performers had contributed evening gowns in so many garish colors, Angelique wondered if Izzy would wear them anywhere but in the privacy of her own bedroom. Or maybe, after the baby was born, she'd don one or two gowns and strut in front of her blasted stepmother. The gowns were wrapped in a quilt that boasted a circus motif.

Roy made two requests. He wanted the yellow canary. He said it would be for his new son or daughter, "so he or she will never be alone without no singing," and some elephant dung, so he could prove to everybody that he'd truly seen the "big gray critter."

When the last of Roy's trail dust had disappeared, Sean excused himself to help Brian feed the cats, and *Monsieur* Barnum turned to Angelique.

"Jenny Lind has severed all ties with me," he said, his voice brusque. "Turns out she was uncomfortable with my marketing of the tour. She plans to continue under her own management."

"I'm sorry, sir. I had a feeling—"

"I want you to finish Jenny's tour, and by the time we return to New York, newspapers will be singing your praises."

"Are you teasing me?"

"Not at all. You are the only woman in the world who can do

a forward somersault, and you look like poetry in motion when you perform. Therefore, I'll offer you the same terms I offered Jenny. One hundred and fifty thousand dollars, payable in advance."

"What about Sean?" she asked, stunned.

"You shall be my protégé," Barnum replied, "but Sean will be your manager."

"His circus—"

"Can be run by someone else until the tour is finished. If Sean wants to direct the Sean Kelley Circus himself, which you and I know he might prefer, I'll give him my most popular American Museum exhibits. In fact, I'll promise him anything he wants, except Tom Thumb."

"May I have time to think about your offer?"

"Of course."

"I have a question. What has become of Auntie Bernadette's cats? I doubt my uncle wants to keep them."

Monsieur Barnum told her the cats now dwelt in a comfortable enclosure at the American Museum. Despite the capture of Gertrude Starling, the sign above the enclosure read KILLER CATS and spectators could purchase vials of "Killer Cat Fish Oil."

Later, in the privacy of their wagon, Angelique told Sean about Barnum's offer.

"Do you want to accept, lass?"

"Aside from the money, a great deal of money, you could choose the museum attractions that would increase your business tenfold. And I'd return to our *cirque* a star."

"Did Barnum happen to mention when you would return?"

"He said two or three years. He wants me to perform in London, for the queen."

"Then say yes, Angelique."

"Would you travel with me?"

"Of course. You are my heart," he said, repeating the words she had uttered earlier, "and without a heart, one cannot live."

"But one cannot live without a dream, and your circus is your dream."

He shook his head. "You are my dream."

"Non."

"There you go again, saying no to me. *You* are my dream, Angelique, and I shall follow you to New York or London or—"

"I meant I shall tell *Monsieur* Barnum *non*. Not because of hearts and dreams, but because of our time spent this afternoon inside the silver wagon." She felt her cheeks bake.

"We can make love in London, Angelique. We can even make love in Buckingham Palace." He grinned. "After you perform for the queen."

"But I cannot perform the forward somersault when my belly is filled with your son."

"My daughter. And what makes you think you are with child, you daft colleen?"

"If we did not make a baby this afternoon, we might tonight. Or tomorrow. Or the day after tomorrow."

"You would give up the money, Angelique? The fame?"

"I give up nothing, Sean. All I want is you. And now, would you please hush so that we can love God and be merry?"

Epilogue

Sean retrieved the letter he had been using as a bookmark. Holding the piece of paper up to the light from the silver wagon's window, he read the letter for the third time.

My dear boy,
I hope this letter finds you well. I hope this letter finds you.

Have you read a book called *The Count of Monte Cristo*? The count said, "Life is a storm, my young friend. You will bask in the sunlight one moment, be shattered on the rocks the next. What makes you a man is what you do when that storm comes." I have faced the storm, Sean, and now bask in the sunlight. I hope you have done the same. I met a man who worked for you. He left your traveling circus to pan for gold in California. He remarked on how much you and I looked alike. When he discovered we had the same last name, he knew we were father and son. I am living in San Francisco. In the not too distant future there will be a railroad to California. The signing of the Gadsden Purchase is a good start. Maybe we can meet up some day. I would like that very much.

Your father,
Timothy Kelley

Sean remembered his last conversation with little Charlotte, when she had told him Angelique had gone to America, and he had said, " 'Tis a podgy place, America."

Perhaps, he thought, *America wasn't such a podgy place after all.*

AUTHOR'S POSTSCRIPT

The first bar (countertop) was allegedly invented in 1855 by Isambard Kingdom Brunel as a more efficient way of serving patrons at the Great Western Hotel in London, but the term "bar" was already in use long before that time. It represented any oblong object including countertops, railings, bars of metals, etc. In old courtrooms, the separation between lawmakers, lawyers, and judges and the common people was called a bar. I used a bar, rather than countertop, for Rosie's Watering Hole.

The "learned pig" was a pig taught to respond to commands in such a way that it appeared to be able to answer questions by picking up cards in its mouth. By choosing the correct cards, it answered math problems and spelled out words. The pig caused a sensation in London during the 1780s. The original learned pig was followed by newly trained pigs. They became a feature of fairs and other public attractions in Europe and America during the 19th century. Nicholas Hoare, an illusionist, exhibited "Toby the sapient pig" in London, and around 1817 Toby published an autobiography: *The life and adventures of Toby, the sapient pig: with his opinions on men and manners. Written by himself.*

"Toby" became a standard name for a learned pig, but I preferred "Whiggy."

No animals were hurt in the writing of this book.

ABOUT THE AUTHOR

Mary Ellen Dennis is the bestselling author of *The Landlord's Black-Eyed Daughter*, chosen by Booklist as one of the 101 best romance novels of the last ten years. When she was very young, Mary Ellen developed a love for Alfred Noyes's poem *The Highwayman* and the Angélique series by Sergeanne Golon. Mary Ellen's fifth grade teacher was gobsmacked to hear her rambunctious student state that someday she'd write novels inspired by her favorite poem and favorite series. It has taken years to achieve her goal, but Mary Ellen says, "If you drop a dream, it breaks" (a saying coined by her alter ego, author Denise Dietz). Mary Ellen lives on Vancouver Island with her husband, novelist Gordon Aalborg, and her chocolate Lab, Magic.

The employees of Five Star Publishing hope you have enjoyed this book.

Our Five Star novels explore little-known chapters from America's history, stories told from unique perspectives that will entertain a broad range of readers.

Other Five Star books are available at your local library, bookstore, all major book distributors, and directly from Five Star/Gale.

Connect with Five Star Publishing

Visit us on Facebook:
    https://www.facebook.com/FiveStarCengage

Email:
    FiveStar@cengage.com

For information about titles and placing orders:
    (800) 223-1244
    gale.orders@cengage.com

To share your comments, write to us:
    Five Star Publishing
    Attn: Publisher
    10 Water St., Suite 310
    Waterville, ME 04901